'So, you're bo̶̶̶̶̶̶ ̶̶̶̶̶̶sts, or submissives, or what?' Juliet asked, sounding slightly embarrassed.

'Probably a bit of both,' Alice said. 'Those are Overworld terms. In Underland being a girling includes all of that and also being a slave, a pleasure toy, a working animal . . .'

'Ughh! How can you do that? It means you don't have any choice, any freedom.'

'I'm free if I'm honestly being who I am,' Alice replied.

'You really like pain?'

'As part of being dominated or foreplay, it can be fantastically exciting. Sex is much more intense here.'

'I saw you come a few times in the garden when Ruddle was stimulating fruiting,' Suzanne said to Juliet. 'And what about when the insects took your nectar? Don't pretend that didn't feel good.'

'But I couldn't help myself!' Juliet exclaimed defensively.

'Exactly. You were just following your instincts. Well it's the same for us, for all the girlings down here as far as I know. I just want to be with my master and please him. If it doesn't hurt anybody else, who are you to judge?'

By the same author:

THE OBEDIENT ALICE

ALICE IN CHAINS

Adriana Arden

This book is a work of fiction.
In real life, make sure you practise safe, sane and consensual sex.

First published in 2004 by
Nexus
Thames Wharf Studios
Rainville Road
London W6 9HA

www.nexus-books.co.uk

Typeset by TW Typesetting, Plymouth, Devon

Printed and bound by
Clays Ltd, St Ives PLC

ISBN 0 352 33908 X

You'll notice that we have introduced a set of symbols onto our book jackets, so that you can tell at a glance what fetishes each of our brand new novels contains. Here's the key – enjoy!

cp (traditional)

cp (modern)

spanking

restraint/bondage

rope bondage/hojojutsu

latex/rubber/leather/enclosure

fem dom

willing captivity

medical

period setting

uniforms

sex rituals

One

Alice Brown sat naked and miserable on the side of her bed.

What could she do? Who could she ask for help?

She stood up and, for what seemed the tenth time that morning, examined herself critically in the full-length mirror on the back of her wardrobe door. Most eighteen-year-old girls would have been pleased with what was reflected in the glass. So was Alice up to a point.

Her face, when not creased with worry as now, was pretty and nicely proportioned; capped by a golden bob of collar-length hair, its fringe brushing her brow. Her eyes, when not red-rimmed from crying, were normally clear and bright. Her body, so recently matured into young-womanhood, combined pleasing curves with suppleness. Full breasts stood out from her slender chest, their pneumatic resilience imparting a slight convexity to the creamy flesh of their upper slopes. Though sadly crinkled and cold now, they were normally crowned by a pair of perky pink nipples. Alice's waist was slim, her stomach flat, her hips a little on the narrow side, which however only served to accentuate the rotundity of her buttocks, the curve of her strong thighs and firm calves.

In all it was a body of which to be proud, except for one bizarre feature.

Once more Alice's hand crept reluctantly down to the delta of her pubes. Where there should have been a triangle of fluffy honey-blonde hair, there was instead a growth of fine golden feathers.

They were downy soft, tiny at the top but growing slightly larger with each layer, pointing downwards and closely following the pouting curve of her pubic mound and dividing neatly about her cleft. At least she could pee without wetting them. The feathers tapered off between her legs just short of her anus.

As Alice turned slightly to look in the mirror sideways the sunlight caught the feathers, making them sparkle with warm golden highlights that played over her inner thighs. On a bird such growth would have looked remarkable, even beautiful. On her it was a nightmare.

She had tried pulling them out with tweezers, but the pain had been horrible. Feathers, as she had discovered to her cost, had much thicker roots than hair. In any case she could not go through life literally plucking herself! She ran her fingers through the hair on her head. Underneath there were more tiny feathers sprouting from her scalp. At the moment they were concealed, but what if they kept on growing until they spread all over her?

With a groan Alice sank back onto her bed and buried her face in her hands. What a mess! Even the timing was terrible. She was sitting her A levels in ten days. Right now she should be revising, not driving herself insane about growing pubic feathers! And she would not be able to conceal the fact much longer. Her parents were already worried about her behaviour. They had even asked her the big question: was she pregnant? If only it was that simple!

Alice knew they loved her and only wanted what was best for her, but how could she explain this? If she secretly went to a doctor what could he do for her? Send her to a vet? In any case, he would want to know how had it happened, and that was something so impossibly crazy that he would never believe it. Her parents were not the most imaginative people and to accept what had happened to her they would need a whole lot of imagination. They would either think she was mad, or if she convinced them it was true, they would completely freak out. But then who would believe her story? Alice had endlessly rehearsed the words, even though she knew she could never speak them aloud . . .

'Dad, Mum, it's like this . . .

'A few weeks ago when I was coming back from school through Shifley Woods, I met a White Rabbit just like the one from *Alice in Wonderland*, except that he said the place was called Underland now and it wasn't for children. He had a watch that opened what he called a "transdimensional portal" in a rabbit hole, and I followed him through.

'Well, he wasn't kidding about it being adults only, because they call girls from our world "girlings" and use them as sex slaves. And they made me one, which wasn't so bad, actually. You see I found out I'm a bit, well, turned on by bondage and also quite masochistic and bisexual and OK about doing it with animals, at least the talking ones they have down there, who are really just like people . . . only not.

'Anyway, a lot of very weird things happened and I ended up getting the Queen of Hearts – who's even crazier than in the book – thinking I was part of a revolution to overthrow her. She ordered my head cut off, but I managed to get away by taking a potion that turned me into a bird. That was actually pretty wonderful, the flying bit anyway, but the problem was I didn't take all the antidote. So when I got back here I found I've got these feathers growing on me and I'm very frightened and please help me . . .'

Of course, long before that her father would have that baffled disapproving expression on his face and her

3

mother would be looking sad and despairing, because they would think she was telling some kind of freaky story just to shock them and show up the generation gap. And if she ever did convince them it was all true (how could she ever flash her pubes at her father?) there would be shouting and tears and the whole package that went with them.

Eventually she knew they would support her, because they did love her and she loved them, but then what? They would try medical specialists and keep going up the ladder. And what if the government found out and she ended up in some secret laboratory being interrogated about whether Underland posed a threat to national security?

The only person she could think of who might accept her story and not totally gross out was Simon Gately, her sort of half-boyfriend who was a bit nerdish and deeply into science fiction and fantasy stuff. But even if she convinced him her story was true and he'd said, 'That's just amazing!' seventeen times, what could he do? He wasn't going to be able to mix up an antidote in the school chemistry lab, or make a duplicate of the White Rabbit's dimension-twisting watch like some teen genius in a comic book.

The ultimate bottom line remained where it always had been. She was on her own.

Alice shivered, wiped her eyes and blew her nose, pulled on her clothes so that the sight of her feathered pubes would not depress her further, and tried to think rationally.

There was only one place she had any chance of getting a cure and that was back in Underland. Any Underlander who knew the right mix of local ingredients could probably put her right in five minutes. There was something about the laws of nature there that meant you could do wild things to bodies with the help of a few special herbs and mushrooms. But she had lost

4

the White Rabbit's watch, which had reopened the portal returning her through time and space to a point only seconds after she had left, back in Underland. Unless the Rabbit had found it and came calling locally again she couldn't travel that way. Alice had taken several walks through Shifley Woods in the last few days just in case, but there was no sign of him.

There remained just one other slim chance.

She had met several girling slaves in her travels through Underland. Most had been transported there by the Rabbit or some other procurer, presumably using similar means. But two of them, Keli and Barbara, had made the trip accidentally. What had they said to her? Keli had been hiding from a man she thought was going to rape her and had fallen asleep desperately wishing she was somewhere else. Barbara had been half stoned when she read the Alice story and also wanted to get away from a dead-end existence.

But simply going to sleep wishing you were somewhere else could not be all there was to it, or else Underland would be full of Overworlders.

Was there a pattern she could make sense of? Well, they were both young women in a similar state of mind experiencing heightened emotions. Perhaps being alone or somehow isolated from others at the time was also significant. But dare she experiment with drugs, assuming she could get any, while in her condition? And though she was feeling pretty miserable, she was not in fear of her life. No, there had to be a better way.

Once again she took the book off her shelf that had been the cause of both the most amazing adventure she had ever had and her current dilemma. Idly she flipped through the pages, looking at the incredible world brought to life by those meticulous and often eerily grotesque line drawings. Before her eyes passed the likenesses of people and creatures whose near doubles she had met in the most intimate, degrading

5

or wonderful circumstances (occasionally all three). And there was her namesake gingerly stepping through the looking glass. If only it was as simple as that . . .

The breath caught in Alice's throat.

Slowly she turned to look at her wardrobe mirror and then back at the illustration, feeling a tiny flicker of hope. Why not? Why couldn't she just step through the mirror?

Of course she knew, or at least, in view of her recent experience, she was fairly certain, that the real Alice the story was based upon had never actually entered Wonderland by such means. But nevertheless the image of her doing so had captured the imaginations of millions of people for over a century. In their dreams perhaps they even believed it could be done. Indeed it was the power of that belief that may have created Underland in the beginning and was even modifying it to this day. And Alice had the advantage of knowing that Wonderland, or at least its contemporary and rather perverted equivalent Underland, really existed. It was there, somewhere in another world hiding just around some multidimensional corner. She also knew it was possible to reach it without any special mechanical aids if only the circumstances were right. Did the answer lie in the plane of a mirror where it seemed two worlds touched? She sprang to her feet and ran over to her mirror reaching out in desperate need, only to snatch her hand back at the last moment.

No, she must do this properly. Nothing must distract her from believing, when the moment came, that there was something more there than a silvered pane of glass. She peered at it closely, noting the dust and careless fingermarks on the mirror. That wouldn't do.

She ran downstairs, thankful that her parents were out, found a cloth and spray can of glass polish, rushed back up to her room and gave her mirror the most intense clean and shine it had ever had. By the time she had finished she was breathing heavily and the mirror looked perfect.

What else did you need when setting out on a journey? A destination! As she was going to be her own pilot and means of transport, so to speak, she had to know exactly where she wanted to end up. It might be just one step away, but it had to be the right step.

She grabbed the book and sprawled face down across her bed with it wedged between her elbows, covering her ears so that no external sounds intruded. Then she read the story line by line more intensely than she had ever done before, fixing it in her mind. As she did so she tried to recall the unique quality of Underland. The freshness of the air and the improbable greens of the woods, the pearly bright but sunless sky and the dim twilight that was the closest it ever came to night; immersing herself in the smell and touch of Underland, letting it fill every corner of her mind.

She reached the last page as though in a dream.

Calmly she got up from her bed and walked towards the wardrobe mirror. All she had to do was reach out and let her fingers slip through into Underland.

From downstairs came the sound of a key turning in the latch, then her mother's voice calling out, 'Hello, Alice, it's only me.'

No, not now! Alice wailed in silent rage, and in her frustration she beat her clenched fists against the mirror.

And met no resistance.

Her arms sunk into the mirror as though it was no more substantial than a soap bubble.

Without a moment's hesitation, Alice stepped through the looking glass.

Alice stood in a perfectly reversed simulacrum of her own bedroom hardly daring to breathe. She was filled with a dizzy sense both of elation and disorientation. Everything was exactly reproduced down to the smallest detail.

No, not quite. The image in the wardrobe mirror she had just stepped through was now misty and somehow distant, and she could see no sign of her own reflection. Also the daylight coming through this bedroom window was muted and green-tinted. Where the roofs of houses across the road should have been visible there was only an indistinct blur. She was reaching out to pull the net curtains aside when she realised there was no time to indulge her curiosity. What if her mother came in looking for her and saw Alice walking about on the other side of the mirror? She ran to the door, wondering if her whole house was duplicated in reverse as well, and pulled it cautiously open. But there was no landing outside.

Alice stepped onto lush green grass and shut the door behind her.

The mirror copy of her bedroom door was embedded in the side of a towering oak, giving the disconcerting impression that it had been there for a few hundred years while the tree had grown round it. The oak was one of a few dozen ringing an open glade, illuminated by a pearly bright but sunless sky. Though she had never seen this exact spot before she had no doubt she was in Underland. Nowhere else could you find nature so unspoiled, with sweet air, multicoloured flowers carelessly dappling the ground, flitting butterflies and, yes, little clumps of improbably perfect red-and-white spotted toadstools nesting between the tree roots. It was too good to be true, yet at the same time somehow more intense and alive than the world she had just left.

Alice looked back at her door thoughtfully. The Underland end of the portal through which she had chased the White Rabbit had terminated in a hollow under a similarly massive oak tree. Was that significant, somehow? She dismissed the detail from her mind. What mattered was that she had made it! Now she had a chance to . . .

Suddenly a shiver ran like an electric current through her. Somebody has walked over my grave, Alice thought in alarm, suddenly appreciating the old saying more keenly than ever before. She glanced quickly about her, overwhelmed by the uncomfortable sensation that she was not alone. But she saw only the perfect woodland and the feeling gradually faded. A delayed reaction to her interdimensional hop? she wondered. Well, she couldn't stand here all day. She had a cure to find.

A track had been worn in the grass close to her tree, as though by regular use. It was as good a way to go as any other so she set off along it.

But she had hardly gone twenty paces when the background buzz of insects suddenly grew louder. An angrier buzzing came to her ears, like the whir of miniature outboard motors, and a pair of huge dragon-flies shot past her.

As she turned to watch the bizarre creatures go with a smile, she heard a woman's voice cry out: 'I see you, spies!'

With a crack of displaced air, a spear of red light lashed out through the trees and one of the dragonflies exploded into a shower of smoking fragments. By reflex Alice threw herself off the path into a carpet of tangled ivy as another form raced along the path. But this was no insect.

It was a very tall woman in a red dress and billowing cloak. She sped past Alice, sparing her the briefest of glances as she did so, running at tremendous speed. Running? No, she was flying!

She was bent sharply forward with arms spread wide, her legs making long lazy gliding strides, her red slippers delicately pointing as she skimmed over the ground without quite touching it, as though the air itself gave her support and traction. In her right hand she held a rod-like device which she pointed ahead of her. Another bolt of fire flashed from the rod. 'You can't escape me!' the woman cried, and was gone.

For some moments Alice lay on the ground, too stunned to move. What had that all been about? Who was the woman in red?

A crack and bang echoed through the trees, followed by a triumphant: 'Now I'm rid of you!'

An image from the book came back to Alice of a figure half flying, half running in a very similar way to that she had just seen. Of course, it was the local version of the Red Queen. That would fit if she had arrived in a twisted version of the Looking Glass scenario, though as she knew to her cost she could not take the book as a firm guide. As the White Rabbit had warned her at the start of her first adventure, Underland was a mad place, and people and places changed here in strange ways. What was the Red Queen doing zapping insects, and when did she get a laser gun, or whatever it was, built into her sceptre?

Alice was just climbing to her feet when there was a flicker of red through the greenery and the Queen was striding back along the path and dropping out of the air onto the ground. Her eyes were narrowed and her face was a mask of suspicion as she looked Alice up and down.

'What have we here?' she said as though half to herself. 'A native child? No, a girling. How fortunate. I was seeking a girling. But not one so strangely dressed, or even dressed at all.' She circled round Alice. 'Another spy, perhaps?' She sniffed. 'But you do not smell like one of her creatures. Who are you, girling, and where are you from?'

But Alice was temporarily speechless, not only from surprise but because the Queen was far more beautiful than the original illustrations had portrayed her. Like all the human inhabitants of Underland, the Queen was very tall, though perfectly proportioned, and seemingly built to a slightly larger than normal scale. The top of Alice's head would not reach her shoulders. This alone would make her imposing, but it was her eyes that caught the attention. They were large, clear and dark-lashed, not brown but true feral red. Intense, passionate and dangerous, they complemented the perfect firm full scarlet bow of her lips. Her nose was strong and slightly aquiline and her cheeks high, reinforcing the impression of an imperious and commanding nature. A slender neck was emphasised by a pompadour of upswept hair, on top of which was perched a red filigree crown. The long gold-embroidered crimson silk dress she wore under her cloak moulded itself about the curves of her slender body and small but prominent bust. The dress was ankle-length but slashed up the front. As the Queen moved it parted to reveal a slice of creamy smooth thigh.

As the sceptre jabbed at her chest Alice recovered herself and said quickly, 'My name is Alice Brown and I'm from Wellstone.'

'And I am Her Royal Highness Magenta Alizarine Fuchsine Carnelian, Queen of Stauntonia,' the Queen replied grandly. 'I see no collar on you so I claim you as my own.' She smiled for the first time: a calculating, hungry, masterful smile. 'Now remove those ridiculous clothes. It is not right a slave should be dressed in front of her mistress.'

There, she's said the 'S' word already, Alice thought. Hardly five minutes in Underland and already she was the property of another! It must set some sort of crazy record. At least last time she had resisted a little longer. But she was not the same innocent as she had been. The Queen's eyes were boring into her: imperious and expectant. Alice's heart gave a little leap as a sickening sense of inevitability crept over her. How stupid to think she could avoid the fate Underland held in store for anybody of her sort. It just took a little courage to make the transition . . .

Heart pounding, her insides turning to jelly, Alice pulled her T-shirt over her head, then unclipped her bra and dropped it to the ground. Her full pale breasts hung bare and free, her nipples standing up proudly, as though welcoming their release. Taking a deep breath she unbuttoned her jeans, hooked her thumbs through the waistband of her panties and slipped both down to her ankles. She sat down and tugged off her trainers and socks, then shed her jeans and pants.

Slowly she stood straight again, so the Queen could see both her golden pubic down and pale trembling buttocks. A lingering instinctive reflex told Alice she should try to cover herself, but she ignored it and let her arms hang passively by her sides. She must abandon coyness and shame now.

'Spread your legs,' the Queen commanded.

Alice obeyed, splaying her legs wide and automatically clasping her interlaced fingers behind her neck to show off her breasts to best advantage. It was a display posture she had learned under the tutelage of the Mad Hatter and March Hare, known in Underland as Topper and Lepus: girling brokers and trainers.

The Queen walked round her, looking Alice's naked body up and down with almost clinical intensity.

'Bend forward. Display your rear aspect.'

Alice bent over, her legs still splayed, raising her bottom high and resting her palms on the grass, acutely conscious of the open air caressing her exposed groin. Looking back up through her legs she saw the Queen's gaze lingering on the open cleft of her buttocks, the dark pit of her anus, the golden-feathered mound of her lovemouth split by the impudent crinkled tongue of her inner lips.

A growing thrill of dark pleasure coursed through Alice as memories of her slave training flooded back. She had felt like this before. Would she once more straddle that narrow dangerous divide between helpless outrage and perverse delight? Oh God, she was getting excited! Now she was lubricating. The Queen would see the exudation on her vagina and know her for what she was: a submissive, a natural slave and a plaything for any with the force of will to use her. And the Queen had just such a will, of that Alice was certain. She would be putty in her hands.

'Stand straight,' the Queen said and Alice obeyed, trembling now with nervous excitement. Suddenly it was important that the Queen approved of her.

The trefoil head of the sceptre brushed over her pubic feathers and idly ran along her cleft. Alice groaned as it teased her. The Queen withdrew the sceptre and brought the tip, glistening with Alice's secretions, up to her nose. She sniffed thoughtfully, then smiled.

'I smell passion which is good. And your looks are most pleasing. But these feathers. I have not seen the like on a girling before. Are they natural to you?'

'Well, it's a long story, Your Majesty, I . . .'

'You will address me as "Mistress",' the Queen said sharply. 'You are slave to my person above all else.'

Alice shivered at the words. 'Yes, Mistress. Well, there was a potion I took when I was in Underland before and the effects haven't quite gone away. I came back to find a cure.'

'Back to Underland?' the Queen frowned. 'Where is this "Wellstone"? Is it not in the Boardland or over the far hills? That is where girlings usually come from.'

'Wellstone isn't in Underland, Mistress. It's in the Overworld.'

The Queen's frown deepened. 'I have heard tales of this "Overworld" compared with which perfect nonsense would seem as sensible as a dictionary.' She moved a step closer, looming menacingly over Alice, her red eyes almost seeming to glow. 'Are you lying to me, girling?'

Alice gulped. 'No, it's real, Mistress,' she said, her voice breaking into a shameful squeak. It was hard to concentrate with those magnificent eyes shining upon her. 'There's a doorway. It's just along the path . . .'

'Very well then,' the Queen said. She reached out and her slim strong fingers tipped by long red nails closed about a handful of Alice's golden bob of hair at the back of her neck. 'Show me this doorway to Overworld and perhaps I will believe you are not in league with those insect spies!'

As Alice walked back along the path, her head held stiffly in the Queen's grasp, fearful thoughts ran through her mind. What happens if the door won't open, or is gone? She realised she had no idea how long the portal between worlds she had apparently opened would last. If it had vanished could she return via another mirror somewhere else?

But the door in the oak tree was as she had left it and opened without any resistance. The Queen, pushing Alice ahead of her, ducked her head under the door-frame and they stepped into the reversed version of Alice's room. Alice glanced anxiously at her mirror but there was no sign of life on the other side.

The Queen, seeming even larger within the confines of the room and making it appear drab and cramped by comparison, was looking round her curiously. 'Is this the Overworld? Very strange.'

'It's sort of a transition point between here and there, Mistress,' Alice explained. 'It's actually a copy of my bedroom. That's the real one, which is in the Overworld through there.' She pointed at the mirror.

The Queen stepped over to examine it, running her fingers over the glass. Suddenly she withdrew them as though the contact was painful. 'Yes, I can feel its otherness. So the Overworld really exists. But how did you breach the dividing barrier?'

'I just kind of imagined there was a way between my world and this, Mistress.'

The Queen looked at Alice with growing interest, as though assessing her for some purpose only she knew. 'Was it as simple as that? An exercise of will alone?'

'More or less, Mistress,' Alice admitted. 'Of course it helped that I already knew Underland existed.'

The Queen looked at her intensely, her red eyes seeming to lance right through Alice. 'And you returned to Underland to find a cure for this odd affliction of yours?'

'Yes, Mistress.'

'And how badly do you want it?'

'Very badly, Mistress.'

'What will you do to get it?'

Alice gulped, feeling herself being manoeuvred in some way while being helpless to prevent it. 'Anything, Mistress.'

'Then take me into your world!'

Alice blinked. 'S . . . sorry, Mistress?'

'Take me into your world, then bring me back. Show me it can be done. I command you!'

Those red eyes had her in their spell. Hers was not to question, just to obey. Dumbly Alice nodded and, having no real idea what she was doing, took the Queen's hand and walked up to the mirror. I know it's possible, she told herself. She thought of her world, her bedroom. It was not a reflection before her but another place. Taking a deep breath she stepped through the mirror . . . and the Queen stepped through after her.

She was back home. It was as easy as that!

Even as she felt a dizzy sense of elation course through her, a little voice inside her said, You've no idea what she wants you to do for her. She can't be as powerful here as in Underland. Now's your chance to get away!

But the Queen's hand was closed firmly about hers, strong and cool. Somehow Alice could not even muster the will to make an effort to prise apart those slender red-tipped fingers and tear herself away. Besides, did she really want to escape whatever fate held in store for her back in the world of slaves and submission?

There was a faint murmur of voices from downstairs and a whiff of freshly brewed coffee. Her mother must have a visitor. Please don't come upstairs because there's no way I could explain what's going on right now! Alice thought.

The Queen was sniffing the air and wrinkling her nose. 'Your world has a foul smell compared to which a dungheap would seem as fragrant as a rose garden . . . what was that?'

A pantechnicon had driven past on the road outside and the rumble of its engine had penetrated the room as its blocky shadow passed across the curtains.

'Just a lorry. A mechanical device for carrying people and goods about, Mistress,' Alice explained. 'Like a cart but without horses.'

'How do you live in such a place? It is no wonder you choose to return to Underland.' An edge of alarm entered the Queen's voice. 'You have proved yourself, girl. Now take me back!'

In a dream, Alice turned and stepped back through into Underland with the Queen at her heels.

On the other side the Queen sighed in relief, breathing deeply and looking exultant. She smiled at Alice, who felt a thrill of delight in the warmth she saw behind it.

'I had need of a girling, but I never expected to find one with your ability,' the Queen said. 'Serve me well and you will have your cure. That I promise.'

'Thank you, Mistress',

'Now we go to my pavilion. Come!'

And she strode back outside into the green Underland wood, with Alice trotting helplessly after her like a faithful dog.

Two

As Alice followed obediently after her new mistress she silently strove to come to terms with the strange and sudden turn of events. She was a slave again. Well, she knew more or less what that entailed; pain and pleasure. But it was vital that she did not let herself surrender completely to its intoxicating combination. She had to hold a little of herself back or else she might lose track of her own objectives and never return home. Nevertheless, she would do whatever it took to find a cure, both for her own and her parents' peace of mind.

Her parents! Presumably when her mother found the house empty she would think Alice had gone out to see a friend or something. But if she did not return that night . . . oh no! They knew she had been worried about something and would think . . . well, any number of unpleasant things. She would put them through even more anguish! But there was nothing she could do about it now. She would just have to hope it worked out in the end. Meanwhile she had to concentrate on getting herself through the next hours or days, however long it took.

I'm the Queen's slave now, she told herself. So I'd better act like one!

Yes, she was just a girling doing what came naturally. It was surprisingly easy to push her other life into the background. She felt herself slipping into a submissive

17

state of mind where, paradoxically, she was free to live without mundane worries and only obedience mattered. Underland had always seemed more real than her own grey world. Had she been born in the wrong set of dimensions, or was this the only way to get here?

The Red Queen's pavilion was a red-and-white-striped tent with a high conical roof and round walls, reminding Alice vaguely of the tents medieval knights lived in while camped about a jousting tournament. It nestled in a small dark clearing in the woods and was half smothered by a mass of ivy, which coiled about the guy ropes and across the roof like thick shaggy ropes. Was it intended as some sort of camouflage, or had the tent simply been there a long time?

More strands of ivy twined about a ring of a dozen statues that circled the glade. They were life-sized, carved in white stone and portrayed either men in armour carrying swords and maces, or else in long robes wielding ornate staffs. They were not mounted on plinths but rested directly on the ground, where the encroaching ivy made it appear as though the earth was trying to reclaim them. As Alice followed the Queen into the tent she noticed they were finished to a minute level of detailing.

The interior of the tent was carpeted with a scattering of thick rugs while its sides were hung about with tapestries depicting marching armies and battle scenes. A thick pile of silks and furs served as a bed. There were a couple of large brassbound wooden trunks and a single ornate chair. On a low table was set a huge golden platter piled with bread, fruits and slices of meat, and a matching golden pitcher and pair of goblets. Placed against the tent side was an odd device formed of curving strips of wood bolted together to form a broad U-shaped frame, standing a little higher than Alice's head. Its base was mounted on a thick spindle rising

18

from a solid stand, and pairs of cuffs dangled on chains hanging from heavy hooks which ringed the tops of the frame posts. Beside it was a rack holding a selection of chains, shackles and various corrective instruments, all of which Alice eyed anxiously.

But the focus of the interior seemed to be a chess-board inlaid on its own table, the squares made of red and white ivory divided by thin bands of gold. Taken pieces, also in red and white ivory and beautifully carved, were lined up on opposing sides of the board. Apparently the game was nearing a finish because there were very few pieces left in play.

'You cannot be my slave without a collar,' her new mistress said briskly. She sorted through the items on the rack until she found a plain steel collar with a single large securing ring. 'There,' she said with satisfaction, 'solid and practical. Come here, girl, and lift your hair out of the way.'

Alice did as she was told and the Queen closed the collar about her neck with a click of some hidden spring. It fitted snugly, not too tight but nonetheless heavy and bringing with it a sense of confinement. Its metal hardness enclosing the soft flesh of her throat contrasted with the exposure of the rest of her body.

'Beautiful,' the Queen said, admiring the collar as though it was an expensive necklace. 'Now onto the frame, girl. I want to examine you properly.'

With a little shiver of perverse anticipation, Alice stood on the base of the frame between the arms of the 'U'. The Queen buckled thick broad cuffs about her wrists and adjusted the chain links over the hooks so that Alice's arms were raised and outstretched. Then she took down the second pair of cuffs and secured them about Alice's ankles. With easy strength she lifted and bent Alice's legs up and out and hooked their trailing chains beside those securing her wrists. From the rack the Queen then selected a plain length of chain which she threaded through the ring on the front of Alice's collar. Drawing on the ends of the chain until they were taut, she hooked them over the frame tops, doubling Alice over a little more but also supporting her neck and head and relieving a little of the strain on her arms. Alice was now slung in mid-air between the arms of the frame dangling from her wrists, ankles and neck, with her head raised a little higher than her bottom. She could feel the tendons at the back of her knees standing out under the tension, but most of all she was conscious of how completely her enforced posture exposed her groin, thrusting out her mound of Venus and opening the crinkled star of her anus.

The Queen took a step back and admired this blatant display. 'What a pretty creature you are. It's been so long since I've had a girling to play with. I acquired a few during the last game, I recall.' She frowned. 'How long ago was that? No matter . . .'

She began to undress, untying her cloak and tossing it aside, then unbuttoning her dress. With a whisper of silk it slipped down to the ground and she was naked except for her slippers and filigree crown.

The Queen was pale and perfectly formed, her skin the lightest shade of pink. Her legs were long and slender and seemed to go on for ever. Her waist was trim, her navel deep and her breasts, perfectly rounded and small only in comparison to her size, carried cherry-like upstanding nipples. Between her thighs burned a close, tight pubic bush as fiery as the hair on her head.

Alice stared at her, helplessly aroused. The Queen smiled at Alice's own painfully swollen nipples. 'Do I excite you, girl?' she asked.

'You . . . you're very beautiful, Mistress.'

'Yes, I am,' the Queen said with sublime self-assurance.

She stepped onto the base of the U-frame so that she stood between Alice's stretched thighs. Alice felt the heat of the Queen's body and was aware of her own response in her loins. She was dripping with excitement and scenting the air with her intimate perfume. Weighed down with her troubles she had not had sex or even masturbated since she had returned from her first trip to Underland, which suddenly seemed an age ago.

The Queen gracefully knelt down to bring her face level with Alice's groin and examined her pubic mound.

'A novelty,' she commented as though half to herself, ruffling the soft feathers with her fingertips, 'but not unpleasant to the touch.' Watching Alice's face intently she teased her fingertips into her cleft, parting the tender pink folds of flesh and toying with the little bud concealed between them. Alice stifled a little moan as her clitoris pulsed harder under the expert manipulation and the liquid heat grew in her loins.

'You quicken nicely,' the Queen observed. 'Are you unchanged inside, I wonder?'

Two fingers slid up into Alice's vaginal passage, testing the elasticity of the ribbed sheath of hot flesh. Alice shuddered and tugged at her bonds; unable to quell the automatic uninhibited responses drilled into her, which were now inexorably reasserting themselves. No girling could resist such expert and confident handling, and she knew she was at heart a girling, with all the slavish sensuality that implied.

The Queen withdrew her fingers from the warm clinging embrace of Alice's passage and sniffed the exudation that glistened upon them. Then with an approving smile she licked her fingers clean, saying languidly: 'Such sweet oil.'

She reached between Alice's widespread thighs and pried them wider to expose her anus. Alice yelped as long red nails bit into her skin. The Queen examined the tightly crinkled bottom mouth, noting its nervous contractions.

'A neat little pucker, perhaps ripe for plugging. How well used is it?'

She ran a teasing fingernail round the fleshy wellhead which tightened and then opened under the intimate stimulation, as though in a welcoming pout. The inquisitive finger dipped again into Alice's slippery wet cleft to lubricate itself, then drove into her anus. Alice moaned as she felt the questing finger explore the smooth pliant duct of her rectum, but she was quite helpless to prevent the intimate examination. Nor could she stifle an instinctive clenching of her anal ring as the intruding finger was withdrawn, which made it seem as though she was trying to hold it inside her.

'A hot tight hole, but not inexperienced,' the Queen pronounced, standing up and wiping her finger clean on the inside of Alice's thigh. 'I'm sure much can be made of it.' Once again she stroked the delicate pubic cap of feathers. 'And this growth is the result of a potion you took?'

'Yes . . . Mistress,' Alice said, struggling to keep her voice level. 'I had to escape from Queen Redheart. She wanted to execute me . . .' Alice briefly related the events that had led to the dramatic conclusion of her first visit to Underland.

'A curious tale,' the Queen said when Alice had finished. 'I have heard of the excesses of the Redhearts. But then all the Cardians are rather coarse. They would play almost any game. So very common. And to think she would execute such a delightful creature as yourself.' She smiled. 'Why, I can think of a hundred better uses for you.'

She pressed even closer to Alice, her hips brushing the insides of Alice's thighs. Red pubic hair and golden feathers mingled. She ran her hands up Alice's body until she cupped her breasts. 'Will you submit to me?' she asked, kneading the hot, heavy, pliant mounds and pinching their rubber-hard nipples.

'Ahhh . . . yes, Mistress,' Alice gasped, unable to deny her new owner anything at that moment.

'Good,' the Queen said. 'I will hold you to that.'

She stroked her hands along the length of her sceptre, which now Alice realised she had not put down even while undressing. Before Alice's eyes it began to change shape, shortening and thickening. In moments the metamorphosis was complete and Alice gave a little gasp as she saw it had become a double-ended ribbed dildo with a golden ring of prongs about its middle section. Apart from their colour, the double shafts looked uncomfortably realistic, complete with veins down their sides and bulbous tips straining through rolled-back foreskins.

The Queen spread her legs apart and fed one end of the dildo into the red-lipped cleft of her auburn pubic mound. A dreamy expression came over her as the shaft vanished inside her until the middle ring of golden prongs was pressed into her furrow, leaving the rest jutting from between her thighs in an impudent upward curve. She stepped between Alice's thighs once more so that her captive could see the artificial erection in all its intimidating majesty.

'Would you like the other half of this inside you, girl?'

Alice thought it might split her in two. 'It may be a little big for me, Mistress.'

'We shall see. But first I must test your resolve. Through suffering I will bind you to me. I need to forge you to my purpose, little tool . . .'

From the rack she selected a rubber paddle blade with a wooden handle.

'I don't want to break that pretty skin, but I do want you to suffer,' she said as Alice's eyes widened in alarm. 'This should produce a satisfactory effect. Don't attempt to hold back your feelings,' she commanded Alice. 'The sobs and tears of a girling in torment are so attractive.'

Gazing at the anticipatory smile on the Queen's face, Alice realised the simple, frightening, wonderful truth.

The Queen was as mad and mercurial of temperament as any other Underlander, and Alice was her plaything.

The Queen squared up to Alice and swung the paddle. It connected with her taut buttocks with a meaty smack, causing Alice to jerk convulsively in her chains and give an anguished yelp.

'Was that painful?' the Queen asked.

'Yes, Mistress.'

'Extraordinary! Why, I've known pain compared to which that would be a lover's kiss. Now *this* is painful . . .'

And she swung the paddle with such force that the shockwave rippling through her flesh made Alice's breasts bounce spontaneously before the follow through set her body swinging like the gondola of a fairground ride. Alice shrieked at the top of her voice, then recovered her breath in a series of racking sobs as hot tears burned in her eyes and began to trickle down her cheeks.

'That's more like it,' her mistress said with approval, examining the broad scarlet band flaring across Alice's bottom cheeks. 'In fact I think the bloom of well-chastised flesh is quite my favourite colour,' she declared, raising her arm to deliver another blow.

Smack! Smack! Smack! The paddle beat against Alice's tender posterior from the left, the right, upwards and down.

Alice writhed from side to side and swung forwards and back between the supporting arms, bawling and sobbing as she did so, surrendering herself to the pain, feeling the Queen's pleasure in her display and drawing comfort from it. She knew what was to come. This was merely Underland foreplay.

Her whole bottom and the underside of her thighs felt as though they were ablaze now, and her anal ring tightened and relaxed in nervous pulsations. Though her pubic feathers might have taken a little of the sting out of the blows, her labial pouch still burned with the fire, its punishment for pouting so provocatively from between her thighs. Through the haze of pain she felt her nether mouth gaping wet and wide with excitement and her inner lips swelling perversely.

Then the searing blows stopped and she hung limp and dizzy in her chains. Her abused bottom pulsed with waves of heat and pinprick ripples. The Queen was bent over her, stroking her body, running her fingers into the open hollows of her armpits, scooping her heavy breasts together and kissing her nipples then her cleavage where sweat had run under their folds. Her red lips brushed across Alice's blushing cheeks, her tongue flicking over the salt trails that streaked them. Then those cherry lips were crushed against her own, the Queen's probing tongue forcing its way into Alice's mouth to curl and tease about her own, then sucking it out to nip between her white teeth. The Queen's hot sweet breath invaded her nostrils.

When the Queen raised her head, trailing little threads of saliva between Alice's lips and hers, there was a flush of pleasure on her cheeks. 'You screamed most prettily, Alice,' she said, her hungry eyes burning deep into Alice's own tear-bright orbs. 'Now you must beg.'

'B . . . beg for what . . . Mistress?' Alice gasped.

'You know what.'

Alice did know. Her eyes fixed on the huge dildo protruding grotesquely from the Queen's pubic delta; so frightening yet so desirable. 'Please . . . put it up me, Mistress. Screw me, fuck me! I don't care if it hurts. I'm empty. I want it. Shove it in hard. All the way . . . aahh . . . *aaaahh*!'

The Queen had cast aside the paddle, grasped Alice's bobbing hips and thrust the huge dildo up into her. Her cuntmouth stretched into an 'O' of surprise and almost choked on the monster as it forced its way inside her slick passage. Its fat head grated past her pliant inner rib walling. Her stomach bulged to accommodate the intruder, which now felt as warm as living flesh.

Alice cried out in delicious pain. It would burst her, split her poor suspended body in two! Then the bristling ring of prongs jabbed into her taut love lips and erect clitoris and pubic hair rubbed against her own downy growth and she realised she had taken her half of the dildo inside her. She and the Queen were coupled, their pubic lips kissing either side of the dildo's middle ring, their juices soaking between the prongs and dripping to the floor.

The Queen began to thrust with her hips, sucking out the shaft a little way and then pumping it back into Alice, watching the heavy fluid roll of her breasts, every helpless twitch and flutter of her slave's eyelids, the clenching of her teeth and the drool that escaped her lips. Alice felt the shaft pulsing inside her as though it was alive. But it was no longer smooth. Somehow it was changing shape. It was masturbating her clitoris from the inside, even as the prongs tormented it from without. Her loins were heavy with burning pleasure but she was too tightly plugged to let it out!

'Give yourself to me!' her mistress cried.

In panic and joy the orgasm exploded, saturating Alice's body and senses. It was a release without release and seemed to last for an eternity. Alice convulsed and screamed again and again, thighs straining, knees bending as she impaled herself on the Queen's dildo. Only when she was utterly spent did she finally hang limp as a rag from her bonds and let her consciousness slip away.

When Alice recovered her senses she found she was uncuffed and sprawled at the foot of the torture frame. The Queen, still naked, was standing over her. She nudged Alice with her toe.

'Onto your knees, girl!' she commanded, and Alice obeyed.

The Queen was holding her sceptre, now returned to its normal form. No, not quite, Alice realised. What had been a trefoil tip was now a slender golden figurine. Even as Alice stared in puzzlement the Queen pushed it closer for her to see.

'Does it remind you of anybody?' she asked.

Alice peered at the figurine. It was a young woman standing very straight, chains binding her ankles and circling her waist, securing her wrists behind her back. There was a collar round her neck. She gaped at the tiny ecstatic face.

'That's me!'

The Queen smiled. 'Yes, Alice, it's you. Shaped inside your body by the force of your pleasure. And now you have admitted it is so: here, if you've said a thing, that fixes it and you must live with the consequences.' As she spoke she reached out and plucked a single golden hair from Alice's head and deftly tied it about the figurine. 'And now the bond, forged in pain and pleasure, freely asserted, is sealed with a token. This is you and as I control it, so I control you.'

Alice sprang to her feet. The Queen had not said she should rise, but she knew without words it was what she desired. She stood ready, expectant, eager and utterly helpless to resist. The Queen's will was now her will. Her body and mind were now her tools. This was not slavery but almost total assimilation. A tiny insignificant part of her knew what was happening but could do nothing to prevent it.

'A little test,' the Queen said.

Like a robot, Alice marched out of the tent with the Queen behind her and began running round and round the small clearing just inside the circle of the statues. Knees lifting high, breasts bouncing, she made her circuits while the Queen watched in approval.

Suddenly Alice veered off into the trees. There was a large tangle of brambles in front of her and, screwing

27

her eyes shut, she threw herself into it, shrieking as the thorns pricked and cut and tore her skin. Rolling out the other side of the bush she scrambled to her feet and ran on, heedless of the stinging pain and raw red scrapes and blotches and the dozen broken thorns now lodged in her burning flesh.

Alice ran back into the camp and round the statues until she stopped before one depicting a warrior armed with a shield and mace. The carving was perfect in every detail, even down to the weave of the man's tunic and his eyelashes. He was crouching on one knee with his shield raised protectively, perhaps warding off a blow about to fall on him. His mace was held outwards as though frozen in mid swing.

Unhesitatingly Alice bent down and began licking the head of the mace, which was a large ball studded with small pyramidal spikes. That uncontrolled part of her shivered in anticipation, but it made no difference to her actions. Standing up she clawed apart her outer labia with her fingers and ground the soft pink inner flesh now exposed against the stone mace head. The studs jabbed her flesh, tormented her clitoris into renewed erection and scraped and teased the mouth of her vaginal passage. Whimpering with pain she clasped the shaft of the mace and rotated her hips, oscillating the slippery folds of her nether mouth about the spiked ball as though passionately kissing it.

This cruelly enforced masturbation rekindled her slavish capacity for sex, even though she had only spent herself so recently. The pain gradually melted into mounting lust and fiercer rubbing against the mace head despite, or perhaps because of, the pain. Is this my doing or hers? she wondered desperately. Then she cried out and convulsed, soaking the mace with orgasmic discharge.

Only then did she feel the Queen's will leave her and slumped like a puppet whose strings had been cut.

'Most satisfactory,' the Queen said. 'I think this proves my control is total. There is a stream over there. You may wash yourself and then return. If you attempt to run away I shall know it instantly through the sceptre. While you are close by you are under my absolute power at all times, do you understand?'

'Yes, Mistress,' Alice said weakly.

Alice sat in the stream washing off her scratches and picking thorns from her body. None had caused any serious damage and she knew the minor wounds would heal quickly enough, but her mind was still disturbed. She had never known such a sense of utter helplessness. Many times others had wielded complete control over her body physically and she had relished the sensation of being forced and broken through carefully applied pain and pleasure, of being dominated and finally submitting to their will. But it was her choice to do so, while this was mechanical joyless obedience. And why was it necessary at all?

As evening fell Alice attended the Queen, who lay sprawled naked on her bed of silks and furs. Alice was as attentive and subservient as she knew how, desperate to avoid another taste of control through the sceptre figurine, which the Queen toyed with as Alice served her with wine and a selection of fruits and bread from the platter. The vague idea of trying to snatch it from her hand passed through Alice's mind, but she could not summon up the courage. She knew how strong the Queen was and the penalty for failure would no doubt be hideously unpleasant. But would she ever put it down? As evening became night it appeared not. It was almost as though the sceptre was part of her, in the same way she still had her filigree crown on. Alice wondered if she would sleep in it.

The Queen began a little game with Alice. She took grapes from the fruit selection and tucked them into the furrow of her pubes and commanded Alice to dip for them. Soon the Queen was laughing at the sensation of Alice's burrowing tongue hooking the fruit out of the warm wet pocket of flesh.

She seemed more relaxed as time passed and the suspicious anger that had filled her when they had first met was now almost completely gone. Perhaps she had been lonely, Alice thought. There was no sign of anybody else sharing the tent. She had mentioned having other girlings in the past but there were none to be seen now. How long had she been camped out here in the woods?

'You are a pretty and sensuous creature,' the Queen declared, tousling Alice's hair and smiling at her face now wet with royal exudation. 'I hate to part with you but it must be done if we are to win through. Tomorrow I will send you on your mission. But afterwards . . . well, we shall see.'

'Mission, Mistress?' Alice asked hesitantly.

'The task I have prepared you for, girl. You shall learn all you need tomorrow. Now let me feel your tongue again . . .'

Alice slept between the Queen's splayed legs with her hands cuffed behind her back and her face buried in her mistress's sweet sticky mound of Venus. There was no doubt the woman had masterful power in abundance. If only she used it properly she could make Alice her devoted slave for life. But why go to the trouble of establishing such artificial control over her? And what was this mysterious mission?

The next morning the Queen led Alice a little way through the trees until they came to the edge of the wood. Alice caught her breath. Beyond was an incredible vista.

What she had taken to be a wood was in fact part of a great forest, which capped the summit of a high steep hillside. The hill was part of a continuous and unnaturally straight range that extended left and right as far as Alice could see. It overlooked a broad flat plain which at first glance resembled aerial pictures Alice had seen of sprawling crop fields in the plains of America, crossed by occasional roads and right-angled fences creating an unnatural checkerboard effect. But even those artificial landscapes had not been quite so precisely regimented. This land was partitioned into an array of perfectly regular squares all aligned in exact columns and rows and fading into the haze of the horizon. Of course, this was the beginning of the Looking Glass story. The plain was the setting for the living chess game Alice's namesake had played. She had read that story to fix the idea of Underland in her mind, so perhaps it was not surprising that she should have arrived here.

But the strange land was far larger than she had imagined, with many more than the sixty-four squares of a normal chessboard. And the longer she looked the more she noticed other details not mentioned in the original story. The divisions between the squares themselves appeared misty and unreal, as though not being quite in focus. Some squares gave the eye-watering impression of containing more land within the same external boundaries than their neighbours, or else they were much darker than those about them, suggesting they somehow enclosed blocks of twilight.

'This is the Boardland,' the Queen said. 'It is the great battle ground where my kind have fought countless wars over the years.' Her eyes grew bright as though recalling former glories. 'How we bestrode the land in those days! What strategies we employed, what titanic struggles were played out! We soared across the squares and the natives bowed before us. They respected our power, you see. They knew we fought by the code of the noblest of games.'

'You mean chess, Mistress?' Alice ventured.

31

'Of course I mean chess, girl!' the Queen snapped. 'What else is so pure, or offers such a challenge to the intellect? It is the supreme challenge of mind and valour.' She sighed. 'Alas, it is all gone now.'

Real battles played out on a battlefield-sized board according to the rules of chess, Alice thought. Well that made a kind of sense. Chess had developed as a symbolic version of warfare, and great military leaders in the past were supposed to have played it to hone their tactical skills in readiness for the real thing. In Underland it had simply been taken to a logical, if extreme, conclusion.

'What happened, Mistress?' she asked tentatively.

The Queen's face set. 'We impressed our rules and ourselves too strongly upon the land. As our games grew in scope the field of play was turned about to make the challenge greater, and we took our sides at each cardinal point. Our armies swept the Boardland from every direction. And, in time, it responded, one might say. At first the divisions between the battle squares were simple physical markers such as fences and ditches. With use they grew higher and wider, though this troubled us little as we could always leap across them. But gradually the very air began to resist us, so it took more effort to pass from one square to the next. Sometimes a weak point had to be sought before a move could be made. The pace of the game faltered. As it did so the squares began to change in nature, taking on different characters. Our beautiful regular battlefield degenerated into the patchwork you see down there.

'Yet the natives hardly seemed inconvenienced by the changes, passing as they would between the squares and spreading their settlements across the land. Eventually we fought to a stalemate and were forced to retreat beyond the edge of the Boardland while they flourished.' The Queen fell silent, as though in mourning for what she had lost.

What passed for reality in Underland was actually plastic and malleable and Alice knew it could, literally, be shaped by imagination and dreams if they were strong enough. Apparently the chesspeople lived by a set of rules, the established moves of the game, that governed their behaviour in battle. A knight could not move directly onto an adjacent square, but had to hop over it and then shift one square to the left or right, a bishop could only move along a diagonal on squares the same colour it started on, and so on. Even the Queen, the most powerful piece in the game, could not change direction during the course of any one move. To them, divisions between squares, no more than a line on a board or the junction of black and white, became impassable barriers in this reality if their permitted move did not allow them to cross it. Yes, there was a certain logic to that. And they had played their games across the Boardland from different directions, so at one time or another any division between any two squares could not be crossed within the rules. Somehow the land itself absorbed the concept of these boundaries and responded with a sort of positive feedback. The barriers became more substantial, at least to the chess-people. Was it trying to shut them out or merely amplifying their wishes, Alice wondered? And the barriers had extended upward. Presumably that was the cause of the hazy divisions between the squares she could see in front of her. Now what did that remind her of? Of course: force fields. That was a modern science fiction concept that had obviously filtered down here and found a new function to serve. Apparently the fields were selective if, according to the Queen, they did not significantly affect the locals. Presumably they were immune because they did not live by the rules of the game.

Alice felt pleased with herself at her rationalising, but she was still not sure exactly why the Queen was confiding in her, nor why the chesspeople had not taken the obvious course of action. She asked innocently, 'Why didn't you just return home when you could not play any more, Mistress?'

The Queen blinked and then glared at her in disbelief. 'What? Abandon the tournament? Capitulate? Leave victory to the Alabastrines? Never!'

Alice shivered under the force of her indignant wrath. 'Sorry, Mistress,' she said quickly. 'I didn't understand.'

With an effort the Queen appeared to contain her anger. 'No, I suppose I should not expect a simple creature like you to understand our ways. We of Stauntonia are a superior breed, one of the oldest peoples of Underland.'

Maybe so, but that has not stopped you being forced off the Boardland, Alice thought to herself. Aloud she said, 'What happened next, Mistress?'

The Queen grimaced, as though burdened by the memory. 'The game . . . changed. Something new appeared in the Boardland; a device of power. None know where it came from, only that it was called the "Crown of Auria". Its possession is now the only means to resolve the game. So we began one last crusade to win it for ourselves, as did the Alabastrines. But the barriers had become too strong and its location changed. We were reduced to gleaning information from the natives as to its whereabouts. But neither we nor our enemy could hunt it down before it moved again. The game drew on too long and the will to continue failed in some while others were scattered across the board following futile trails. We lost the respect of the natives and our power waned. There are few of us left playing now, but we cannot abandon this last game. It must end here!' The Queen considered Alice for a moment and shook her head. 'But what is the use? How can a mere girling comprehend such things?'

'But I do, Mistress,' Alice said, ignoring the slight on her intelligence. 'It must be due to the influence of my world on Underland. There are so many games played there now, not just board games but computer games and even computer chess, it's not surprising things change down here. This Crown of Auria sounds like a quest object from a fantasy role-playing game. Fantasy games and films are really huge at the moment, so that's probably where it came from. It fits right in with your needing something to end your war. But you'll probably have to go on one last quest to find it. That's how it works in the stories.'

The Queen was looking at her, if not with respect, at least with a slightly higher appraisal of her worth. 'I sensed some special quality about you. An adventurous nature unusual in a girling, yet also with some capacity for deeper thought. Now you have demonstrated unexpected understanding of the challenge that faces us.'

'Thank you, Mistress,' Alice said.

'I cannot enter the boardland without alerting my enemies, but you, a mere girling, can perhaps pass unnoticed. Look down at the Boardland. Do you see the field to the right of the one directly below us? Now count eight squares north from that.'

Alice counted. In the dim distance she came to a hazy dark square.

'That is where all clues say the Crown now lies, heavily guarded,' the Queen said. 'The square before it contains a large native town called "Brillig". Just to the north of that is a small wood. There you will meet with Sir Rubin, one of my most loyal warriors, who even now is making his way there from another part of the land. He will signal when you meet and you will then wait for me to join you. Together we will gain the Crown before the Alabastrines can counter my move.'

'Excuse me, Mistress, but I thought you could not move about the Boardland any more.'

A brief flicker of doubt passed across the Queen's face. 'It will not be easy,' she admitted, 'and will require a great expenditure of power. But the journey will be made easier if I have a pawn in place to guide me. You have the ability to pass between worlds. It should enable you to move freely between the game squares as the natives do. But that gift will be most valuable in helping me penetrate the last and most obstinate barrier surrounding the Crown, one which I understand even the natives cannot cross. Remember, if you help win me the Crown, I will cure your affliction.'

'Thank you, Mistress,' Alice said.

She was not sure how far she could trust the Queen, but at the moment it was the best chance she had. And even if the quest failed she would be down in the Boardland where she might be able find a more conventional remedy.

'Speed of travel is not as essential as secrecy,' the Queen warned her. 'The enemy must not learn of your mission. But most important of all, beware the White Queen! She is a dangerous and powerful witch! Now there is the path down to the Boardland,' she said, pointing to what was hardly more than a narrow furrow that zigzagged down the hillside. 'Go, knowing my hand and eye will always be upon you!'

And for a queen you're pretty witchy yourself, Alice thought as she began to make her way carefully down the hill. That was not a blessing but a warning. But how had she come by the power to use sympathetic magic on the voodoo doll principle? Perhaps it was the myth and fairytale influence on Underland. Queens in those stories often started dabbling in magic. As the regimented order of the chess game faded perhaps another more flexible force took its place. And queens always were the most powerful pieces on the board.

Alice was near the bottom of the hill when something that had been niggling at her subconscious mind finally surfaced.

The chessboard in the Queen's tent. She had seen it in passing several times last night and that morning, and there had been something odd about it. Now she knew what it was, but it made nonsense out of the game. There were no kings left in play.

Three

As the slope at the bottom of the hill flattened into level ground, Alice came upon the first edge barrier. It was a shimmering wall that rose up out of the centre line of a small moat or ditch to reach high up into the sky. The perspective was eye-watering as it marched away in a perfectly straight line in both directions seemingly to infinity. The wall was about as translucent as frosted glass, so it was impossible to see what lay beyond.

Alice climbed down into the ditch, which was barely waist deep, and touched the barrier. She felt nothing more sinister than a slight tingle. Taking a deep breath she stepped through and climbed up the bank on the far side.

Before her was a belt of scrub and low trees. Apart from a few twittering birds nothing moved. Pushing cautiously forward, Alice found the belt was not wide and petered out into a half-overgrown path that ran the length of a field which was freshly ploughed almost to its edge.

Beyond this several other fields and orchards were visible, separated by fences or bushy hedgerows and interrupted by the occasional tall oak or ash. On her right a narrow lane wound its way towards a straggling line of red-tiled rooftops that peeked over the distant trees, suggesting the presence of a hamlet or small village. Taken in all it was quite similar to the landscape she had encountered during her first adventure, being a slice of gently rolling English countryside that hardly existed in the real world any more. Well, Underland was largely a distorted reflection of nineteenth-century rural life, Alice recalled, so that was not surprising.

A voice calling out 'Get along, there,' caused her to shrink back into the shelter of the nearest bush. Slowly coming into view along the edge of the unturned earth was a ploughman urging his team on.

As he got closer Alice saw he was a bulky figure, quite short but with broad shoulders. Long bristling ears pricked up on either side of his flat cap, while from below it protruded a blunt snout. Evidently he was a hog or boar. He walked upright and his feet were porcine trotters but, as with most of the animals she had met during her previous adventure, his hands were human. His only clothing was a sleeveless jerkin.

As he grasped the handles of the old-fashioned single furrow plough, he also held a long carriage whip. As she watched he lifted it to flick across the bare bent backs of his ploughing team. The sight of them in Alice's world would have raised disbelieving cries of shock and outrage, but in Underland it was quite unremarkable.

They were eight naked young women, harnessed in pairs on either side of a long shaft running from the plough head. They wore what looked like small versions of padded horse collars about their necks and larger ones tight about their waists so they rested on their hips. It was to these that their arms, crooked round into the small of their backs, were cuffed. Pairs of chain traces ran either side of their bodies through rings in both sets of collars, presumably so as to spread the load between shoulders and hips. The traces were linked to poles pinned transversely across the central shaft. The plough-man's whip was presumably sufficient to control them as they wore no bits or reins, but each girl did have a wire mesh muzzle strapped across her nose and mouth.

Alice watched as, with their strong thighs swelling with effort and their sweat-sheened pendant breasts swaying, they drew the plough blade through the soil. It was hot work but she did not feel sorry for them. Satisfying hard labour under the command of a firm but fair master or mistress, the company of their sister slaves, the raw excitement of uninhibited sex and the absence of those petty concerns and foolish aspirations that seemed to fill more and more of life back home, had a strange allure. Was that what had drawn them to Underland and the life of girling slaves? Was that why she was here? But where was her place in it all? In the service of the Red Queen? Thoughts of her masterful power made her feel weak at the knees.

Alice shook her head to clear her mind. All that must wait. She must concentrate on her mission.

As the plough girls passed on she considered the landscape before her. How best was she to traverse it to reach her goal?

If she tried to remain unseen all the time she was travelling her journey might take weeks. And if she were spotted despite her best efforts, such suspicious behaviour would be bound to attract attention. She could travel more quickly if she proceeded boldly in plain sight and made no attempt at concealment. Well, she certainly had nothing to hide, she thought with an inward giggle. Alice Brown – The Naked Spy! Hopefully she would simply be taken for a girling doing a chore for her mistress, which was more or less the truth.

The plough girls were evidence that girlings were used here as beasts of burden in a similar way to the rest of Underland. If she could pass herself off as one of them then nobody would take any notice of her. But if she was supposed to be doing a chore or running an errand, what was it? She didn't want to keep having to explain herself to people. What she needed was a prop, something that would make her purpose self-explanatory.

Wary of the ploughing team, she began searching along the field edge, hoping for inspiration. After ten minutes all she found were a couple of discarded lengths of heavy string of the sort that might be used to tie straw into bales. At first she could think of no use for them, then inspiration struck.

Retreating into the cover of the trees she began breaking off lengths of some of the drier brushwood. By the time the ploughing team had passed by twice more, she had accumulated a pile of long slender sticks. These she made up into as neat a bundle as she could manage and secured it with one of the pieces of twine. The second length she tied to the ends of the bundle, leaving enough slack to slip it over her head and one shoulder so that the cord ran diagonally across her front between her breasts. It helped steady the bundle, but it was still awkward to carry. She pushed a thicker stick through the base of the bundle so its ends projected from each side. With the bundle on her back she could reach back and grasp the improvised handles, keeping it from slipping and spreading the load a little. She found she had to bend forward to keep her balance, which was useful as it gave her a reason to lower her head and avoid eye contact. The bundle was not comfortable to carry, but then it would be inappropriate if she looked as though she was enjoying herself.

Alice moved back through the bushes towards the field to check on the ploughing team. She wanted to be sure they were well out of the way while she made for the lane. She did not want anybody to see her emerge from the trees so close to the border in case they wondered where she had sprung from.

The team was just plodding into view. As they came level with her the boar ploughman called out: 'Whoa . . . rest.' The girlings immediately sank to their knees and straightened and wriggled their backs with sighs of relief.

Annoyed, Alice shrank down into the cover of a bush and held still. Why did they have to stop now with only a few furrows to go? She was anxious to get going.

The boar walked towards the bushes and Alice stifled a gasp of fear, thinking he had seen her. But his objective was a bush a few feet away. He pulled out a thick pizzle from the tangle of hair between his thighs and directed a stream of urine into the undergrowth. Alice grinned in relief. He was just answering a call of nature.

Shaking off the last drops and tucking his member away, the boar returned to his plough, uncorked a canteen of water that hung from its handles and had a drink. Then he made his way along the line of harnessed girlings, slipping their muzzles down to allow them to take a few swallows each. Alice saw the muzzles had a rubber bar across their insides, which would act like a bit when it was in place. No doubt it provided something for the girls to bite on as they strained at their task and also served to remind them of their place. As the boar went he patted their heads and murmured words of encouragement that were kindly enough but did not invite a reply. It was the way that one might address dumb animals.

'Well drawn, soon be finished,' he said. 'Then it's back to the barn for you and a good rub down . . .'

When he reached the last girling, a sturdy brunette with her hair tied back in a ponytail, a grin split the boar's great snout. After he had watered her he replaced her muzzle, then lifted her to her feet by her collar. As he clasped and squeezed the girl's heavy breasts in his large rough hands, he said, 'Needed a few flicks to keep you going today, didn't I, Brownie? But nothing you can't take. I think you enjoy the odd tickle. Did I make that arse of yours red? Let's have a look.'

He moved round behind the girl and bent her forward so he could inspect her bottom cheeks. He patted and slapped them with evident pleasure. Alice saw his pizzle was rising into something resembling a large red carrot. This he rubbed against the cleft of the girl's buttocks a few times then said with a chuckle, 'Open wide, Brownie.'

Alice found she was holding her breath, knowing what was to come. Memories of her time in Topper and Lepus's training yard came back to her. She had watched girlings casually taken like this dozens of times with a mixture of fascination and apprehension, never sure if it would be her turn next. Her fingers slid between her thighs and found warm slick wetness bedewing her cleft. And when her turn had come she had responded with the same helpless arousal she was feeling now.

Obediently the plough girl spread her legs and pushed her rear out towards him, opening her buttocks and her red-slashed, thickly haired pubic pouch. He clasped her hips firmly and drove his pizzle between her cunt lips. The girl's face screwed up as he entered her, grunted about her muzzle bit, then relaxed into a faraway expression as she resigned herself to the rough pleasure of his thrusts. The other plough girls looked round at her with mild interest and a couple sniggered behind their muzzles, but otherwise they appeared content to take the opportunity to rest a little longer from their labours.

Yes, she really was back in Underland, Alice thought as she crouched behind her bush and her fingers worked busily in her own cleft. Here it was the normal way of things for animals to use girlings for their pleasure. Evidently, however, she was less jaded than the plough girls. Had she always been potentially so easily turned on or did being back in Underland heighten her responses?

The brunette impaled on the boar's pizzle was making little quavering noises now. The muscles in her thighs stood out as she braced herself against his thrusts, which sent shivers through her body and set her breasts jiggling. With a growling grunt the boar came, pumping his essence into the girl, who in turn thrust her hips desperately back onto him again and again, trying to bring herself off before he withdrew from her. Suddenly she squeaked in delight and shuddered, her eyes rolling and knees bowing weakly. She had made it.

Pulling his glistening rod from the clinging embrace of her cleft, the boar let the girl sink to the ground. Grasping her ponytail and pulling her lolling head backwards, he used a fistful of hair to wipe clean his pizzle. Releasing her to slump onto her face, the boar took another drink from his canteen, then picked up his whip.

The leather flicked across the teams' shoulders and they scrambled to their feet with a clink of chains, even the still trembling and glassy-eyed brunette. 'Last couple of furrows. Put your backs into it!' their master commanded. Taking up the strain, the eight girlings, one with sperm beginning to trickle down the inside of her thighs, set the plough blade slicing through the earth once more.

Feeling frustrated, Alice removed sticky fingers from her cleft and watched the team move off to the left. It had been over too quickly for her to come and now there was no more time for self-indulgence.

Picking up her bundle she made her way along the belt of trees in the other direction until she reached the corner of the field. Here she found the lane was of well-compacted gravel but looked little used. Of course, there would no through traffic this close to the edge, Alice thought. The further she got along it before anybody saw her the better she would blend in. She set off.

Despite her load, Alice soon felt the calm of the perfect day overtake her. Along the hedgerows butter-flies flitted between violets, foxgloves, startling red poppies and cow parsley that dotted the picturesquely lush verges. The sweet musk of blackberries filled her nostrils. She picked a handful of the rich dark fruits from a tangle of heavy canes that spilled onto the lane and gulped them down with delight. There was nothing like walking naked in the open, as she had discovered on her first trip to Underland, and feeling the warm air caressing her body. It was one of the bonuses of being a girling and made her feel vitally alive.

After half a mile Alice reached the outskirts of the village. She smiled when she saw that its name, displayed on a signpost, was 'Uffish'. That was one of the nonsense words from the Looking Glass story, so it was not surprising to see it put to practical use. Soon she was walking down its twisting high street past a few small shops. A dozen or so inhabitants, both human and animal, were going about their business at a leisurely pace. Alice kept her eyes low, walked in the gutter and tried to look resigned and slightly bored. She sensed a few eyes on her swaying breasts and rolling buttocks, but otherwise she passed by unnoticed.

The locals were all oversized as she had come to expect, so that by comparison she was about the height of their children, a pair of whom she saw bowling a hoop along down a side road. All the animals she could see were of similar height or smaller than the boar ploughman. There was a familiar mix of species but fewer of what she thought of as the 'cuddlier' types, which was perhaps in keeping with the Looking Glass story's slightly darker mood.

A crossroads marked the village centre, beside which was a pub – The Cross Bells. High up on its outside wall, supported by iron brackets, a heavy black wooden X-shaped cross leaned out over the pavement. Chained to it was a spreadeagled girling. Her mouth was closed by a broad strap gag held in place by narrower straps that ran under her chin and over her nose, joining to cross her head from front to back. Wide resigned eyes stared out from over the gag. She had long blonde hair platted into two braids. These had rings tied into their ends which had been hung over hooks screwed into the side of the upper arms of the cross, pulling her braids tautly up and out from her scalp. Perhaps this was to help keep her head up but it also made it impossible for her to hide her face, should she still harbour any lingering trace of shame about her circumstances.

To represent the rest of the pub name, three golden bells about the size of large pears hung from her body. Two were suspended from rings that pierced her nipples, the firm rotundity of her breasts lifting the bells outwards and allowing them to dangle freely. The third hung between the girls widespread thighs from a ring that pierced both her plump shaven outer sex lips. Alice wasn't sure how heavy the bells were, but she could see the girl's nipples were stretched into long points and her labia pulled down in a taut pout.

Knowing from personal experience how exposed and humiliating yet also desperately exciting it was to be a living sign, Alice felt a fresh stirring in her loins as she wondered what it would be like to swap places with the girl. But she had to keep going.

Not wishing to appear hesitant, Alice boldly took the road leading away from the cross that seemed to be heading in the right direction. After a few minutes the houses and gardens became sparser, merging into another belt of open fields. After a mile or so this cultivation gave way to more open ground with scattered dwellings interspersed by spinneys and clumps of thicker woodland. In the far distance beyond the largest wood, like some vast curtain falling from heaven, was the hazy wall of the edge barrier dividing Uffish's square from the next.

Her back aching slightly under her load, Alice continued on along the road until it began to bear steadily to the left, looking as though it was going to run parallel to the barrier. It might change its way further on, of course, but how far that might be she had no idea.

Alice paused in the shelter of a tangled hedgerow, shrugged off her bundle and pulled out a few sticks to lighten it. While she considered which way to go she squatted down and peed, delighting in the freedom to perform the act in the open so naturally, then wiped herself off with a handful of soft lush grass.

The road was the easiest route but longer, while the straightest course over the common land might be slower going. If only she had a map to guide her. She began to realise how incredibly unprepared she was for her journey. For all her powers the Red Queen had given Alice nothing to help, even though it was in her best interests that she should succeed. Perhaps the Queen was too involved with the great game to wonder how a naked, ownerless girling was going to cross seven Boardland squares without money, food or detailed directions. Or perhaps, being royalty, such mundane considerations had simply not occurred to her. Alice had been too overawed by her mistress's presence to wonder if she could be as impractical and single-minded as any other Underlander. Well, it was meant to be a mad place.

But which way to go? Her 'disguise' had held up well so far, but perhaps it would not be a bad idea to leave the road and cut across country, where there was less chance of meeting people. So she set off over the rolling meadow towards the far woods.

An hour's steady progress as best she could estimate without sun or watch, took Alice to the edge of the big wood without encountering any creature larger than a few perfectly ordinary non-talking rabbits. Away from the fields and village the land seemed almost deserted. It was what she had hoped for, but it was also disconcerting. There were few places in her own England where you could walk so far without crossing a road or at the least seeing an aircraft passing overhead. She looked up at the pearly bright sky, wondering how long she had until dark. If she could reach the barrier while it was still light she might scout out the next square before deciding where to make camp. The nights never got very cold so a simple shelter should serve. As for food there was usually something to be found. She would not risk mushrooms, but fruits were usually safe. Nuts and berries from hedgerows would keep her going, though she might begin to miss a proper meal after a few days. Dare she try stealing some if the opportunity arose? No, that did not feel right. Was it possible for an itinerant girling to pay her way as she went in the Boardland? But what would she pay with? she wondered, then smiled to herself. It was obvious what she would pay with. The idea of what she might have to do suddenly excited her. Well, that was being true to her nature, wasn't it? It would be a challenge to avoid such situations, and even more of one to endure them when inescapable. Though she had to come back to Underland, there was no reason why she should not enjoy the adventure, with all rewards both dark and light.

She had begun well, crossing most of the first square in good time and without mishap. If she could use the same trick again then at this rate, allowing time for rests and finding food one way or another, the whole journey might take less than a week. Of course, as she had seen from the hilltop, some of the squares contained more land than others and so might take longer to cross, but hopefully this would average out.

The wood proper closed about her as she walked between the towering shafts of beach and oak, their canopies merging overhead so that only slivers of the sky remained visible. The leaf-littered ground between the great trunks was broken here and there by the dark glossy greens of holly trees and rhododendrons. Where pools of light did penetrate to the woodland floor, thick clumps of fern sprouted.

A small stream meandered between the trees over a bed of sand and stone. Alice put down her load, took a drink and splashed her face. The water was clear, cool and perfectly pure. Refreshed she continued on. Not far to go now, she told herself.

Then she came upon a distinct path worn into the ground. Beside it somebody had erected a sign crudely knocked together from scrap-wood. There were two boards on the post each pointing in the same direction. The top read, in roughly painted capitals: THIS WAY, and the one below it: NO, THIS WAY.

More Underland madness, she thought. But the path did lead in the direction she wanted to go, so she followed along it cautiously. She passed more signs: TOVES GO THIS WAY and then MOME RATHS A;SO. All pointed in the same direction. She recognised the names as belonging to fictitious creatures from the book, but wondered what purpose they were meant to serve.

Ahead of her the path wound between a holly bush and a large mass of rhododendrons. Between them something brightly coloured was lying on the ground. As she got closer Alice saw it was an old-fashioned painted wooden baby rattle. Somebody must have dropped it. Since it was right in the middle of the narrow path she stooped to pick it up . . .

It was only as she touched it that she felt the ground giving way under her with a snap and swish of dry sticks and leaves. She made a desperate sideways leap, clawed at a crumbling edge of earth, which came away in clods in her hands, and then slithered into a concealed pit.

Alice landed on her back in a shower of dirt and leaves on the remains of the pit cover, her own bundle snapping and gouging her painfully. For a few seconds she lay there, shocked and winded and hardly daring to move in case she found she had injured herself badly. But apart from the scrapes in her back she seemed to be in one piece. Slipping off her bundle she cautiously got to her feet and looked around her.

Though it had proved an effective trap, the pit was in fact not very large. She reached up and found she could just get her hand over its edge. It should not be too difficult to climb out. Perhaps it had been intended to trap some sort of animal rather than a person. A tove or mome rath, possibly? She saw the rattle lying in the debris and picked it up ruefully, only to find it was trailing a length of string with a freshly broken end, which had apparently snapped during the fall. Looking round she saw the other end dangling from a small pipe protruding from the side of the pit. Since it had not triggered the collapse, what was its purpose? Then it came to her. It must be part of an alarm system; presumably to alert whoever had dug it that the trap had been sprung. And how long would it be before they came to see what they had caught?

Anxiously she began to scrabble her way out of the pit. If she could just get a firm hold of the edge . . . But the earth was too soft to provide enough grip to pull herself out and kept breaking away in her hands. It was so frustrating. If only she had something to give her a leg up. Her bundle of sticks! She picked it up and wedged it against one corner of the pit, using it as a crude step. The broken ends jabbed into the sole of her foot but she gritted her teeth, lunged upwards, hauled the top half of her body over the pit edge, gave a final kick with her legs and slithered onto firm ground . . . only to find herself staring at two pairs of black leather shoes.

She raised her head, looking up the length of cream-coloured trousers that swelled out to encompass ample waists, short tight brown jackets with double rows of buttons, large shirt collars and finally two plump, young/old faces with wide mouths, snub noses and round, slightly bulging eyes. These peered suspiciously down at her from under the brims of small striped peaked caps.

Alice sighed. She recognised the pair, of course. As with her first adventure, it looked like she was going to encounter characters from the book as she went. That, apparently, was the way what passed for chance operated in Underland.

'I thought we'd caught a tove, Dee,' one of the pair said petulantly.

'Contrariwise, I thought it was a mome rath, Dum,' his twin replied. 'But it's just a silly girling.'

This description of herself annoyed Alice. She climbed painfully to her feet and said angrily, 'Did you dig that trap? I could have broken my neck falling into that. Can't you play your games somewhere else?'

The pair did not appear in the least repentant. Ignoring her protest, Dee looked her up and down and then said calculatingly, 'Maybe there'll be a reward for rescuing her.'

'But you didn't rescue me,' Alice said.

'We did if we say so,' Dee snapped. 'You're just a girling, nobody'll believe what you say. Who do you belong to?'

Alice took a deep breath, quelling her anger. She was trying to pass through the country as unobtrusively as possible and arguing with the locals, even these wizened boys, was no way to go about it. 'I'm from over there,' she said, pointing vaguely. 'Nobody you'd know. I was collecting wood. Now I've lost it down your hole. I'll have to find some more. Goodbye.'

'She's very rude for a girling,' Dum observed.

'And she hasn't got an owner's name on her collar,' Dee pointed out. 'Very contrary.'

Why did they have to have such sharp eyes? Alice thought. Trying to sound a little humbler, she said: 'Sorry . . . young masters. It must have been the fall. Made me forget my manners. Do excuse me.'

She began to back away around the pit, only to give a yelp as she pricked her bottom on a branch of the holly tree that flanked one side of it. Even as she looked about for a different escape route the twins hemmed her in, moving disconcertingly in step. They were as tall as she was and much bulkier. Reaching out they each caught her by an arm. Alice tried to wriggle from their grasp but they were too strong. A sick sense of fear began to well up inside her.

'Maybe she's not a proper girling at all,' Dum suggested, then added grudgingly, 'Though she's very pretty.' With his free hand he clasped and squeezed her right breast, as though testing a melon for ripeness. Alice bit her lip but said nothing. Maybe after a bit of a grope they'd get bored with her. 'Her titties are bigger than that girling Old Mr Meles has.'

'Remember the trouble we got into about playing with her,' Dee said. 'P'raps we should let this one go.'

'But this one's different,' Dum insisted. He pointed at Alice's pubes. 'Look, her cunny's got feathers all over it where it should have hair.'

'Bet they're not real.'

'They look real.'

Dee reached down, took hold of one of the larger feathers in the middle of her pubic delta and with a swift jerk plucked it out of her. Alice gave a shriek of pain. Dee held up the golden feather, which had a smear of blood on its quill.

'They are real,' Dee agreed. 'And it's pretty.'

'I want it,' Dum said.

'This one's mine. Get your own.'

Alice whimpered as Dum pulled a second feather from her pubes. 'But what is she?' he wondered as he admired his prize.

'Maybe we should pull out some more until she tells us who she is?' Dee suggested.

'No, please don't!' Alice said quickly.

Their big mouths turning up into malicious grins, they pushed a squirming Alice further back into the holly bush. A hundred spines pricked her soft skin, making her yelp and bite her lip.

'So tell us who you are, girling,' Dum said.

'It's true,' Alice gasped. 'I don't belong to anybody. Not on the Boardland, anyway. I'm working for the Red Queen. She wants me to find something for her.'

Dum and Dee exchanged curious glances, then frowned at Alice. 'You're lying,' Dee said. 'The chess-people are all gone. Nobody's seen them in years. We learnt that at school.'

'Only we don't go to school any more,' Dum added. 'School's stupid. Now we do what we want. So as long as nobody's going to come looking for you then, contrariwise, you belong to us.'

They were pressed against her, holding her close to the tormenting holly sprigs. She felt bulges growing in their trousers beneath their fat bellies and could almost smell their growing sense of power over her, even as her own resolve was melting away.

A broad unpleasant smile split Dee's chubby face, which sent a shiver down Alice's spine. 'You mean we can do what we like with her? Have fun, punish her, like Old Meles's girl but more? The way they do with other girlings?'

A mirror of the smile now distorted Dum's features. 'That's right. Finders keepers, losers weepers. We keep her and make her weep. What's your name, girl?'

'Alice Brown,' said Alice in a faint voice.

'Say "Master" when you speak to us,' Dee said, giving her nipple a pinch. ''Cos we're your masters now, and you've got to show proper respect.'

'Yes, Master,' Alice said wretchedly.

Between them they dragged Alice away from the pit. As they went Dum began to chant. The rhyme was all too familiar but its words were no longer nonsense. Instead they presented an ominous vision of Alice's immediate future.

'The time has come for Alice Brown,
To learn the way of things;
Of games her masters like to play,
And how much holly stings;
Or why a beating makes her hot,
And all the tears it brings.'

Dee took over.

'We'll take her to our secret place,
And teach her to obey;
After swishing sticks and many pricks,
She'll do anything we say;
Our slave she'll be, for otherwise,
Her pretty flesh we'll flay.'

Holding Alice firmly between them, the pair pushed their way into a great mass of rhododendron and emerged into a small natural clearing at its centre. The space was littered with carelessly scattered tools, wooden boxes and odd lengths of rope and chain. In the midst of this, assorted boards, scraps of tarpaulin and old fence posts had been nailed and lashed into a rickety hut. painted over its sagging door were the words: HEADQWARTERS (SECRET). Beside it was an equally rough and ready cage made out of slatting and chicken wire, with straw strewn over its floor.

'We made that to keep a tove in,' Dee said, as though inviting Alice to admire their handicraft skills.

'Or a mome rath,' Dum added.

'But now it'll do for you,' Dee continued.

'It's very nice, Master,' Alice said automatically,

thinking wistfully of the fine cage she had shared with her lover Valerie.

'Alice'll be more fun to have than a tove or a mome rath,' Dum said. 'We can do girling things with her and also teach her tricks like a pet.' He prodded Alice. 'Can you learn to do tricks, girl?'

Alice found her mouth working without conscious thought as her instincts took over. 'I'll do whatever you tell me, Master.' There was no point in protests now. She felt a frisson of dark excitement run though her as her senses heightened and her loins stirred in anticipation of what was to come. There would be pain and pleasure and she would embrace both to the full while keeping a small part of herself aloof from it. She was a helpless girling and that was her only power.

'It'll be dark soon,' Dee said, 'but we can have some fun with her now and start training her properly tomorrow. Get some rope and we can tie her up.'

'You get the rope, I want to have her first,' Dum said, pulling Alice towards him.

'No, I'll go first,' Dee said. 'The pit was my idea.' And he jerked Alice back.

'But I dug more of it than you!' Dum retorted, hauling the other way.

'But I hid it so well she didn't know it was there!' Dee shouted.

Red-faced, they were each gripping her arms with both hands now, throwing all their considerable weight into a tug of war with Alice stretched between them like a living rope.

'But it was my rattle I put there to lure her!' Dum screamed. 'My old rattle, do you hear?'

'You can keep your mouldy old rattle,' Dee hollered back. 'I'm having first go with her!'

Alice cringed at the rage and spite washing over her. However old they actually were, the pair were behaving like selfish children and might pull her apart before either one would give way. She took a deep breath and shouted, 'Masters, please! You can both be first!'

That got their attention. Their plump faces screwed up in frowns of puzzlement. 'You've only got one cunny hole,' Dee snapped. 'One of us has to be first.'

Alice gulped queasily at the thought because the pair repulsed her, but she continued doggedly. 'No, Master. A girling can give pleasure with her mouth as well as her cunt . . . I mean, cunny. A lot of men like it.' She looked round the debris of construction work. 'If you tied me face down across that saw horse over there, then one of you could have me from the front while the other had me from behind both at the same time.' Even as she spoke she knew she was orchestrating her own double rape, which was somehow appropriate for a masochist. And this way at least she wouldn't have them lying on her.

The pair were silent for a moment, weighing up her suggestion, then they grinned.

They dragged her over to the horse and pushed her across it, so that her stomach rested on its crossbar. With odd lengths of rope and string they tied her wrists and ankles to the ends of the saw-horse legs, then found a piece of rusty chain which they looped around the crossbar and over her back, securing her firmly in place. Alice winced as the coarse ropes and rough metal links scraped and dug into her skin, but the pain seemed only transitory. Her nipples pulsed with blood as they hung under her hot, heavy breasts, her heart was thudding and her swollen pussy lips were slippery with lubrication. She was helpless, aroused and ready.

The twins stepped back to admire their handiwork, savouring Alice's naked and bound form. Dee rubbed his bulging crotch, then feverishly unbuttoned his flies and released a thick rod of pink flesh that sprang out stiffly, projecting beyond the bulge of his belly. Alice's eyes widened in alarm and she hastily licked her lips. It looked painfully large.

'Look, mine's bigger than yours,' he said, massaging it proudly.

Dum pulled out his own cock, rubbing it into its fullest erection. 'No, look. Mine's bigger,' he said.

They stood side by side, each thrusting out his hips to try to make his penis stick out further.

Not another dispute! Alice thought desperately. Anticipation was fast becoming urgent need. How quickly she became a hot shameless slut with so little persuasion. Aloud she said: 'Please, Masters, it doesn't matter. I . . . I think you're both too big for me. You'll split me open. Please let me go!' And she tugged theatrically at her bonds, even as she secretly delighted in their confining strength.

That caught their attention. They were advancing towards her when Dum said, 'Wait! We need a stick or something. We've got to beat her before we have her. You've got to make them cry first or else they don't do it properly. Everybody knows that. Isn't that right, girl?'

And Alice found herself saying: 'Yes, Master. Hurt me, Master, make me cry, Master . . .'

Dum found a couple of lengths of garden bamboo and, with their straining cocks bobbing stiffly in time with the swings of their canes, the pair laid about Alice's bound body. Her bare back, outthrust bottom and spread thighs were inviting targets and they covered them in red stripes, making her flesh shiver and jump. Alice yelled and shrieked and blubbed. Tears ran down her cheeks as she writhed on her wooden mount and strained at her ropes.

The sight of her abused body was so exciting that it brought a rapid end to the chastisement. Dee and Dum threw aside their bamboos and hunkered down over Alice, Dum positioning himself between her thighs while Dee knelt in front of her. Grasping her hair he jerked up her head. Her mouth gaped open ready . . .

'What if she bites me?' Dee wondered.

Dum's cocktip was pressed to Alice's hot wet cleft, his eyes glazed with lust. 'She won't dare bite,' he snapped.

'I promise I won't bite!' Alice gasped, blinking away her tears.

'But she might by accident,' Dee protested. 'And don't you start before me,' he warned his twin.

'Put something in my mouth to hold it open,' Alice sobbed desperately. 'Just please hurry . . .'

'What?' Dee asked foolishly.

'Hurry up!' said Dum.

Hell! Alice thought, do I have to arrange everything? 'Get a short piece of that thick rope . . . yes, that bit. Now tie two knots in the ends . . . yes. Now put it round the back of my head and pull the ends round into my mouth between my teeth so the knots hold it in place . . . glumpth . . . uhh.'

The rope cut into the sides of her mouth, pulling her lips back and tasting musty. The knotted ends lodged between her back teeth and her mouth was wedged open.

Dum rammed his rod into her cunt from the rear without any consideration for her comfort. Her gargling yell of surprise and pain was stifled by Dee's shaft as it was pushed into her gaping mouth with equal lack of ceremony. The fat flesh plum drove past her lapping tongue and down her throat, making her neck bulge. She was penetrated front and back.

Her oral skills were not required. Her gullet was simply being used as a hot wet hole for him to spend himself inside. But Dee was not withdrawing. He was savouring the moment. Alice's eyes grew rounder. She couldn't breathe. He had hold of her hair and she could not pull away. Didn't he realise he was choking her with his cock? Why should he? He'd never had oral sex before.

The twins withdrew together and Alice desperately sucked in air past Dee's cockhead as it paused for a moment resting on her tongue, even as Dum's was still lodged in her nether mouth wet with her juices. Then both plunged into her again, stifling her squeals. In, out, in, out. They were shafting her in rhythm, making full use of their pet, their helpless slave bound to a screwing horse. It was careless and selfish and incredibly exciting.

They came quickly, like boys might in such a situation, almost before she was ready. Twin jets of sperm were pumped into her like the spouts of water pistols as her own orgasm erupted. She jerked wildly against her ropes and spluttered on choking ejaculate as it slid down her throat. She heard them laughing at her struggles as she mindlessly licked and sucked and slobbered the last traces of come from the softening shaft. Then she slumped limply over the horse, drained and utterly exhausted.

Alice was distantly aware of being freed from the sawhorse, having her hands rebound behind her back and secured with another cord round her waist, then being dragged into the cage and the door being bolted behind her.

'There's water in there,' she heard them say. 'We'll bring you some food in the morning. Then we'll see what else we can do with you.'

By the time she had recovered from her post-orgasmic swoon the camp was deserted and the skylight was dimming. Her skin still smarted from her beating and her vagina felt bruised. She squirmed across to the metal bowl in the corner and lapped water from it as best she could, washing the taste of come from her mouth. There was nothing she could do about the same substance oozing from her well-used cleft except try to rub it off on the straw bedding.

Finally she curled up in a corner, trying to get as comfortable as possible while confused thoughts tumbled through her mind. What she had suffered at the hands of the twins had satisfied the masochistic side of her nature, but she also knew she had to get away from them. It was not entirely because they looked so gross, but because deep down they frightened her.

Underland had turned Tweedledum and Tweedledee into malicious, self-centred adolescents who would perhaps never grow up. To them she was no more than a new toy. Who knew what they might do to her tomorrow?

Four

Alice awoke, stiff and aching, to the sound of banging on the wire of her cage.

'Get up, girl!' Dum, or possibly Dee, was saying. Both the twins were standing by the cage. 'It's breakfast time.'

A tin plate had been pushed inside. On it were two slices of marmalade on toast, a shelled hard-boiled egg and a dollop of porridge.

Alice blinked the sleep from her eyes, squirmed awkwardly round into a sitting position and forced her mouth to work. 'Masters, please can you untie my hands so I can eat?'

They grinned at her. 'No, you've got to eat like you are. You won't need your hands for anything we want to use you for, and you're our pet now, so you'd better get used to it. Hurry up or you'll get nothing.'

Everything was cold but Alice cleared the plate, picking up the pieces of food as neatly as possible between her teeth. Denying her the use of her hands was basic slave indoctrination, as it made her more helpless and dependent on her masters. Fortunately she had gained some practice at eating without using her hands at Topper and Lepus's, where the trainee girlings' food had been served in what had closely resembled a pig trough.

As she ate she wondered where the food came from. Dum and Dee must have a house somewhere nearby, but did they live alone or with parents, assuming they ever had any? She suspected a lot of things here had not come into existence by normal means. Just because the pair still dressed like schoolboys didn't mean much in Underland. Pity their parents if they did have any, though.

This was not simply idle speculation. She knew she must either escape from the pair or else wait for them to get bored with her, which might take a long time. The more she learned about them the more chance there was of discovering something she could use to her advantage.

She finished her meal by licking the last of the porridge from the plate like a good pet. It would do no harm to make a show of obedience. Besides, she did get an illicit thrill at being made to eat doggy fashion. If only they were nicer, and she was not on such an urgent quest . . .

They let her out of the cage and clipped a chain leash to the ring of her collar. She remained on her knees but sat back on her heels, looking up at them plaintively. 'Please, Masters, I need to go to the toilet.'

There was a spade amongst the scattered tools, and with this the twins dug a small latrine pit. Even this simple task they managed to argue over while Alice watched on, squeezing her thighs together in rapidly growing need.

'She could dig this herself,' Dum said.

'But we said she wouldn't need to use her hands, so that would make us look wrong if we changed our minds,' Dee pointed out.

'But she's our slave.'

'But we've got to mean what we say, or else . . .'

'Or else what?'

'Or else, contrariwise, what we say doesn't matter.'

Eventually the hole was dug and Alice squatted over it, gratefully emptying both her bowls and bladder. She was very aware of their curious eyes on her but there was no way she could hide anything and she had to keep her legs wide to balance, so they saw all that she voided. Like all boys, and indeed most men, she suspected, they were fascinated to see where a girl's pee came from. They watched the hissing stream twinkle merrily from her nether mouth with wide eyes. Fortunately, during her previous time in Underland, she had become used to the fact that girlings had no privacy, even to perform their so-called 'private' functions. Dum and Dee's attention almost made her smile, even though it also generated a little nervous shiver as a reminder of her complete vulnerability. In Underland a girling was an animal who lived to serve the whim of her master.

Of course, once she was finished, the pair argued about who was going to clean her, neither wanting to wipe her bottom.

'But it's got to be cleaned. We don't want her smelling of poo!'

'Let her do it.'

'But we said she couldn't use her hands.'

Alice listened patiently as they ran through the same argument as before. Eventually they settled it with a round of paper, rock, scissors, which Dum lost.

As Alice meekly went down on her knees and leaned over to rest her head and shoulders on the ground so her groin was conveniently exposed for cleaning, she wondered at the way they either behaved in close synchronisation or else complete disagreement. Their counterparts in the book had also been prone to histrionics. She might be able to make something of that.

When the job was done, and Dum had run to the stream and back to rinse off his own hands, they bent Alice over the sawhorse once again. Their caning of her was a little more leisurely and not so fierce, and Alice made a satisfying show of shrieks and groans of pain, which greatly amused them. This time Dum took her in the mouth while Dee availed himself of the pleasures of her vagina. Again they thrust into her simultaneously but she was ready for it and managed not to choke on Dum's cock as it slid down her throat. He discovered he could play with her freely dangling breasts while he screwed her, which was quite nice until he began twisting her nipples too hard. This time she came before the boys, and her orgasmic writhings spurred them on to fill her with their seed. As they rested, panting, slumped over her so she was squashed between their bulky bodies, Dee asked, 'Do they always do that when they come?'

'Girlings can't help it,' Dum declared confidently. 'It's how they're made.'

They hardly allowed Alice time to recover before they set her to work. Overnight they had evidently put some thought into humiliating ways of using her, and perverse smiles came to their faces as they brought out a besom broom and explained that she was to do some sweeping. But of course she had to hold the broom without using her hands.

With her still bent over the horse they forced the thick handle of the broom up into her bottom hole. Alice squealed as the roughly trimmed handle slid into her, her anal ring stretching and rippling over its bumps and knots, and forcing her pliant rectum to conform to its unyielding contours. She was trembling when they allowed her to stand up, feet spread wide and hardly daring to move. The broom jutted out from her rear like a bizarre tail dragging on the ground. There was no way she would be able to move it, she thought. It was far too heavy for her anal muscles to hold.

But the boys had apparently thought of that. They tied a cord round the middle of the broom shaft and the other end round her bound wrists. This at least enabled her to support its weight. By bending forward and pulling her wrists further up her back she was able to lift the broom end off the ground.

'Now begin sweeping all these leaves up,' they told her, indicating the litter on the camp floor.

Alice gulped and, keeping her legs wide, shuffled round, let the broom head down and tried to make a sweeping motion with it. But she dug it into the ground too hard and only succeeded in twisting the broom end painfully inside her. The boys laughed at her agonised expression and the tears that sprang to her eyes.

'Go on,' they said, 'get sweeping.'

Biting her lip, she tried again. This time the bristles hardly touched the ground at all and she had to twist round to stop the momentum of the overswing hurting her almost as much as her first attempt.

The third time she got it right and managed to brush a few leaves across the ground. The boys retired to the cluttered interior of their ramshackle hut and began reading comics, watching her through its open door and unglazed window and laughing from time to time at her obvious discomfort.

There was little need to keep a close eye on her in case she tried to escape. With the broom stuck up her rear she could hardly manage a hobble.

She attempted to work methodically, shuffling along a straight line while looking over her shoulder to see how she was doing. Slowly a pile of leaves began to accumulate.

As the exhausting morning began to blur into a test of endurance between her back and rectum, a recollection ran through her dulled mind that 'besom', apart from a bunch of twigs from the bush of the same name used for sweeping, was also an old word for a low woman. Well she was certainly that right now. A besom in every sense of the word.

She suspected that in her world she might be at risk of seriously damaging her tender rectum doing something like this. But none of the variety of things that had been pushed up it during her time in Underland had ever done any lasting damage. For that matter the bamboo welts on her back from the previous night's thrashing, though still sore, had been healing amazingly rapidly. If it hadn't been for the latest batch they might have faded completely by the end of the day. The marks from the worst beating she had ever experienced, at the command of the spiteful Queen of Hearts, had completely vanished in a couple of days. Why this was so she had no idea, but she was very grateful.

For Alice the ordeal gradually took on its own peculiar twist. The broom handle ground away inside her, painful and yet insidiously stimulating as the pressure of the rotating tip transmitted itself through the relatively thin membrane dividing her front and back passages. Soon her loins were warm and her pussy lips wept in mock sympathy for her suffering, partly with Dee's sperm and partly with fresh lubrication. That was both her burden and her reward for being who and what she was.

Finally the job was done. All the leaves were in one neat pile and the shack and cage were surrounded by a ring of swept earth. As the twins inspected her work, Alice sank carefully to her knees, the broom still sticking out of her, and bowed her back until she could rest her head on the ground.

'It's all right, I suppose,' Dee finally conceded, much to Alice's relief.

They untied the cord and pulled the handle out of her, grinning at her whimpers as it came free with a sucking pop, then watching intently as her well-stretched anus slowly contracted. Dum looked thoughtfully at the end of the broom handle, now stained dark by her secretions.

'If there's room to stick this up her bumhole,' he said slowly, 'what would it be like to put our prongs up there?'

Alice hung her head. She was afraid they might think of that. At the same time she wondered how much experience they had actually had with girlings if they were only now thinking of anal sex.

'It would be dirty!' Dee objected.

'We could wash her out with a hose first. It looks tighter than her pussy hole. It might be fun.'

Dee peered at the crinkled pucker of Alice's anus, prodding it thoughtfully. By reflex her sphincter tightened then relaxed as though pouting at him. Dee grinned at the sight. 'We can try. And it looks like its tender, so she'll squeal a lot.'

Alice quickly spoke up. 'Please, Masters, put some grease or lubricant in me first. Anything will do.'

Dee grasped her by the hair and lifted her head so that she stared into his puggish features. 'Have you done this before, girl?' he demanded.

'Yes, I've been sodomised,' Alice admitted.

'What's that?'

I'm going to be the first girl they ever do anal with, Alice thought. What an honour I could do without! 'Having a girling up her rear is called sodomy,' she explained patiently, 'and if you grease me properly you'll enjoy it more because then you can go deeper, where I'm really hot and tight.'

Dee let her head drop and beamed at his twin in anticipation. 'We'll do it! It's lunchtime now. We'll bring the things after we've eaten.'

They did not put her back in her cage, but chained her to a ring set in the shack doorpost. While they were gone she examined both the chain and the ring in case there was any weakness in them, but they were regrettably solid. If her hands had been free she could have simply unsnapped the spring clip from her collar ring, but with her wrists tied behind her back and the rope round her waist preventing her from sliding them down and stepping out of them, it was impossible. Alice flexed her fingers and rolled her shoulders as best she could as she wondered how long it would be before she was permitted to use her arms properly again.

She explored as far as her chain and bound hands would allow in case there might be anything of use to her. They'd bolted the shack door, but she looked in at the unglazed window. Inside was a rickety table littered with garishly printed pulp paper comics, two old armchairs leaking stuffing and a peeling cupboard with an open shelf top half-filled with the assorted junk juveniles might collect. Pinned to its side was a crudely drawn picture of a naked woman bent over a four-legged frame, and another picture showing her standing with something projecting from her rear. Alice blinked when she realised they were meant to be her. She had already become the boys' pornographic pin-up. Terrific!

By the side of the shack she did find the stub of an old pencil and a rusting two-inch nail, presumably left over from the construction work. The pencil she could see no immediate use for, but she might possibly be able to sharpen the nail enough to cut through her ropes. Even so it would hardly make a decent blade. If she used it on the rope it would be more like fraying it strand by strand. Still it was a tool of sorts. There was just enough slack in her chain to allow her to tuck both items out of sight under the bottom slat of her cage.

When the boys returned Alice was sitting innocently by the side of the shack. As she ate lunch from her tin plate, a mash of potatoes, veg and sliced meat, the boys laid out the items they had brought with them.

There was a bucket of water, a towel, a bar of soap, a short length of thick black rubber hosepipe, a jar of what Alice fervently hoped was Vaseline and, slightly alarmingly, an old-fashioned leather bellows.

When Alice was finished they bent her over the sawhorse once more and tied her ankles wide. Then they rubbed some of the soap, which was quite soft, into the water and worked it up into lather. Dee applied some soap round Alice's anus, then daringly slipped his soapy finger inside her and tickled. He laughed as she squirmed. They plugged the tip of the bellows into one end of the hose, dipped it into the bucket of soapy water and sucked some up inside. Dee guided the end of the hose into Alice, feeding a good foot through her rectum, and then Dum pumped the bellows. Alice shivered and gasped as the cold soapy water was forced into her entrails, making her stomach swell. It was too much, they'd burst her! Then the hose was withdrawn. As the tip came free from her bulging anal ring, Dee pinched it closed between his thumb and forefinger.

'Please, Masters,' Alice begged, 'let it out.'

Dee grinned and released his grip. A fountain of brownish soapy water spurted out of Alice's rear into the bushes as she gasped in relief. The flow slowed to a trickle and then just a few bubbles blowing out of her anus. The boys laughed uproariously at the sight. Dum chanted:

'With soap and water Alice was flushed
To open the way to her prize.
I'm hot and tight within she said and
She'd better be telling no lies.
Because when she's wiped and clean as a pin,
She's going to be sodomised!'

Dee added another verse:

'When her hole's washed out and all of a pout,
With grease we'll anoint her rear.
Use plenty she begged if you want to go deep,
Of that she need have no fear.
Cos she's due to be riddled like never before,
Then Alice can shed a tear!'

They found the whole process so amusing they did it three times.

When the stream from her bottom ran clear and they were satisfied that Alice was perfectly clean, they smeared her anus with Vaseline and worked a large gobbet up inside her, much to her relief. At least I've been properly prepared, she thought, as she felt herself warming in anticipation.

They put aside their things and Dee loosed his flies and positioned himself behind her.

'No, I go first this time,' Dum said. 'You had her mouth first. I should have her bottom first.'

'But I wanted her cunny slot,' Dee protested.

'But it was new and this is new, so it's fair I use it first. You can have her mouth again. It's your turn anyway.'

'But that was turns between mouth and cunny,' Dee persisted. 'This is different. It won't be even any more!'

Alice listened to the petulant exchange with mounting frustration and wonder. Only in Underland could two, for want of a better description, young men, argue over a helpless slave girl like this when they could just get stuck into her!

'We'll take her turn about,' Dum suggested. 'I'll have her bottom because I'm almost here already, and you have her mouth. Next go you can have her cunny and I'll have her mouth. Then you can have her bottom and I'll have her cunny.'

'Then we'll both be at the same end of her!' Dee exclaimed. 'But we can't have her cunny and bottom at the same time!'

Alice said nothing, knowing it was physically possible but shrinking from the thought of doing it with them. With three orifices to choose from they seemed to be getting confused. Perhaps they were compelled by their nature to mirror each other as closely as possible. They even screwed in sync. But two into three did not go.

Then the outline of a plan struck her.

'Masters, please don't argue over me,' she said, trying to sound reasonable. 'You can't both have had me the same number of times now you've got my bottom as well as my mouth and, er, cunny, to chose from. Not if you want to use all my holes properly and because two into three gives you a remainder, but it doesn't matter as long as it adds up fairly and evenly at the end, does it?' Her head was beginning to spin trying to keep up with her own explanation, but she ploughed on: 'What you must do is keep a record, a tally chart, of which of you has had me in what way, then at the end you can add it all up and whoever hasn't used a bit of me as many times as the other can make up for it. You see?'

They were scratching their heads and nodding slowly. As long as they didn't ask when the 'end' would be, she thought.

'Does that sound right, Dee?' Dum asked.

'I think so,' Dee said. 'Better than fighting.'

They fetched a crumpled sheet of paper and a pencil from their shack and then looked at Alice expectantly.

How can they spin rhymes off the top of their heads yet need help drawing up a simple chart? she wondered. Were they idiot savants, or was it simply different rules for different worlds?

'Draw two columns down the page and put "Dum" at the top of one and "Dee" at the top of the other,' she told them. 'Then draw three rows across the page and mark them "Mouth", "Bottom" and "Cunny". Good. Now fill in all the ways you've had me so far, one tick for each . . . That's right, you've both had me once each in my mouth and in my cunny' – and now its written down in black and white for all to see, which is sooo weird! she thought – 'now, why don't you pin it on my cage where it's clearly visible. What about on the door frame so you'll see it each time you open it to take me out . . . good. That way you can't go wrong and you won't have any more arguments.' She felt an urge to cross her fingers at that point, but instead rushed on. 'Now, Master Dee was going to have my nice hot, greased bottom,' she said, leaning forward over the horse and wiggling her backside provocatively.

71

'But what about me?' Dum said.

'You can have your turn afterwards, Master Dum,' Alice said. 'Now we've got the tally chart it's all perfectly fair.'

Before Dum could argue further Dee clasped Alice by the hips and drove his hard cock into her anus. There was a ludicrous farting squeal of air escaping through layers of Vaseline as his shaft forced its way up her rectum until it was lodged in her to the hilt. Alice's secret smile of triumph was wiped away by a gasp of anguish as he filled her tight back passage. Shit but he was big, she thought. This had better be worthwhile.

With a sucking sound Dee pulled back a little and then thrust into her again. Alice squeaked and groaned, saw Dum look on with a scowl on his face and forced a smile. She was going to break them apart whatever it cost, she promised herself. Then she stopped worrying and let herself enjoy being sodomised.

When Dee had spent himself in her, Dum used the hose and bellows to wash her clean before taking his twin's place. He was of course just as big and hard, and Alice strained to accommodate him in her rear. When he had finished Dee said he had enjoyed Alice's rear so much he wanted another go. Not to be outdone, Dum also used her a second time.

Whether it was because she was putting on such a convincing performance or else because she simply couldn't help herself, Alice had four orgasms. With weary satisfaction, however, she noted that each time they used her, the boys made a point of marking a bold tick on the chart.

When they finally let her crawl back into her cage that evening, it felt as though she still had a red-hot cock up her rear. She just wanted to sleep, but there was something she had to do before the light faded.

She waited until she was sure the boys had gone, then squirmed about and retrieved the pencil stub from its hiding place. Then she edged over to the door, turned her back to it and slid her fingers through the gap between the frame and the badly fitting door itself. Her fingers closed on one corner of the tally sheet and carefully she curled it back through the gap until half of it hung inside her cage. She sat on her heels and slid her roped hands down until she felt her feet and carefully pushed the pencil into the gap between the big and first toes of her right foot. She swivelled round on her bottom, reached out with her left foot to steady the paper as it hung against the inside of her cage and, with the pencil clasped between her toes, carefully added a tick to the chart. When it was done, she replaced the pencil in its hiding place, carefully slid the paper back out of the cage and, finally, allowed herself to curl up and go to sleep.

The twins didn't notice her addition the next morning until after they had each used her, Dum in her mouth and Dee in her pussy. She was grateful they seemed to be giving her still sore bottom a rest. It was only after they had rebuttoned their flies, with Alice still bound over the horse, that they went to make their ticks on the chart. Dum hesitated with pencil in hand.

'How many times did you have her in her mouth yesterday?' he asked his twin.

Dee frowned. 'Once, like you.'

'There are two ticks in the "mouth" row here under your name.'

'There can't be.'

'Contrariwise, there can be. Look!'

Dee blinked at the chart, then shrugged. 'Must be a mistake,' he said, and scribbled over the tick. His brother looked at him suspiciously, but said no more.

They didn't bother to ask Alice if she had been keeping count so she remained silent and concentrated on looking as innocent as possible. Why should they dream she could be responsible, with her hands tied behind her back and obviously without access to writing materials? Though ignorant of their domestic arrangements, she had gambled on the likelihood that each knew it was possible for the other to sneak out to her at night. How long before they realised what a tick in the column actually implied depended on how smart they really were? Then it would be time for her to speak up.

Deciding that Alice was in need of a bath, they took her on her leash to the stream running close by and washed her down, enjoying soaping and squeezing her slippery breasts and working the lather into those folds and crevices they had become so familiar with over the last couple of days. She wondered if they would free her hands for the process but they didn't. The ropes got wet of course and it would mean she would have some deep marks on her when she finally got free, but it did allow her to start the second phase of her plan.

They locked her in her cage over lunchtime while they went back to their house to eat, so she took the opportunity to add another tick to the chart, this time under Dum's column. Then she began working on the rope about her waist.

Once again they did not notice the addition to the chart on their return, because they had decided to rebuild the pit Alice had fallen into in the hope of catching something else. Carrying ropes and chains they led her off into the woods to find sticks of the right length to help cover the pit. They roamed some way before finding what they were after in a coppiced hazel. They set about it with an axe and handsaw and soon had a pile of long sticks to bridge over the pit. These they tied together and then harnessed Alice to the bundle to drag back to the pit.

A thick rope was tied about her waist and the end passed between her legs, through a loop in the bundle's binding, then back up and over her head, where it was passed between her teeth and tied off in a loop behind her neck. With flicks of their canes, Alice was urged to start hauling, clenching the rope between her teeth and wincing as its other end dug deep into her cleft, spreading her labia and rubbing against her clitoris.

By the time she had dragged her load back to the pit her feet were muddy and she was dripping with sweat. Saliva had run down her cheeks from between her clenched teeth and the section of rope passing through her nether lips was stained dark. This of course undid the effects of her wash that morning, but it scarcely bothered the boys. While they worked on rebuilding the pit cover they tethered Alice to the trunk of the holly tree, so she had to force herself to stand still amid the prickly sprigs.

That evening Dee noticed that apparently Dum had, unknown to him, used Alice's bottom once more than he remembered. There was another argument and the boys stomped off home early glowering at each other, much to Alice's private satisfaction. Before going to sleep she adjusted the chart to show that Dee had now used her bottom more than his brother.

Next day they seemed reconciled, however. Even the discovery of the anomalous entry on the tally did not cause them to argue for very long. They were more eager to try out the latest torment they had contrived for Alice.

For the first time they took her into their shack and sat her on the battered table. They had a three-foot length of two-by-four timber into the ends of which they had screwed two large ringbolts, while a third bolt ran through its centre. With many loops of rope they tied Alice's ankles to the ends of the timber, then lifted her legs high so that only her head and shoulders rested on the table and tied the middle ring to one of the shack's exposed beams. They pulled the table out from under her and Alice hung upside down, twirling in mid-air.

They admired this novel new view of her for a minute, spinning her round and pinching and slapping her breasts, which hung heavily inverted almost level with her chin. They tied string nooses round the trembling globes close to her chest and drew them tight, making her breasts stand out like pink balloons. Then they pulled on the ends, setting her swinging to and fro and causing the cords to bite deep into her tender flesh.

'Does that hurt, girl?' they asked, grinning at her discomfort.

'Yes, a bit, Masters,' Alice said. She felt dizzy and her head seemed thick and full of blood.

'But you know we like to see you wriggle and cry,' they said.

'Yes, Masters.'

'And do you like new things?'

'Yes, Masters.'

'And you do want to please us?'

Alice gulped. Where was this leading? But she had to act the part a little while longer. 'Yes, Masters,' she agreed apprehensively.

They tied the ends of the breast strings to a small hook. As Dum pulled the strings tight, Dee parted her labia to expose the small dark well of her pee hole nestling in its secret pink valley. Carefully, Dum slid the tip of the hook into the hole and let the weight of her breasts pull it downward, turning the hole into a dark slot as it stretched. Alice gasped. She had never felt anything like that before. It was not hugely painful but horribly intimate.

'How do you like that?' they asked.

'Very . . . clever, Masters. I hope I please you now.'

The pair exchanged a glance and shook their heads. 'You're not making enough noise,' they told her.

Alice began to groan loudly and wriggle about, but it failed to impress her audience.

'You're just putting it on,' they said. 'We don't believe you. We thought you wanted to please us.'

'I do, Masters,' Alice insisted.

They grinned again, and suddenly Alice felt a trap closing. 'Then see how many of these you can fit inside you,' they said, bringing out a box of white candles. 'Show us some proper tears . . .'

Alice whimpered. 'No, please don't do that . . .'

But of course they took no notice.

With one standing on each side of her they pried open her vagina and anus and began stuffing them with candles. Alice sobbed as each wax cylinder was slotted into her and her orifices began to bulge. Three, then four in her rear. Six . . . no, seven in her vulva.

The boys stepped back, satisfied that both her holes were well filled. Alice hung there; numbed, shivering, fearful, perversely excited. She had been turned into a novelty living candle-holder. But would they . . .? They did. A match flared into life and they lit the candles.

She felt the heat of the flames from eleven candles on her inner thighs. The boys cheered, the flames reflected in their eyes. How far would they let them burn down? How hot would she get?

The tightly clustered candles melted far more quickly than if they had been burning separately. In a minute Alice felt the first rivulets of hot wax touch the narrow tight-stretched bridge of flesh between her two stuffed orifices. Then it seemed to pour down her. It ran between her thighs and into her pubic down and into the cleft of her buttocks. The hook and string held open the upper folds of her cleft, allowing it to flow into its sensitive depths and even plug the mouth of her urethra. What was worse, the wax trickled down the spaces between the candles into the tender depths of her gaping passages and set in those moist hollows after they had passed on their stinging heat.

Alice shrieked and wailed and twisted in her bonds, to the delight of the twins. To add to her torment they brought out their bamboos and began caning her trussed and bouncing globes. Jerking away from the blows by reflex she arched her back, drawing the strings taut, pulling the nooses tighter about her breasts and dragging the hook deeper into her urethra. Her contortions splattered wax more widely, droplets decorating the insides of her thighs. Rivulets overflowed her groin and began to run down her stomach. Drips fell on the exposed undersides of her bound breasts.

Then came the final humiliation. Through her tears Alice saw the twins pull out their stiff cocks and begin masturbating vigorously, aroused by the picture of suffering she presented. As she sobbed and moaned they came over her red face, adding their splattered ejaculate to the wax that was already dripping down upon it. They found it more fun to watch her suffer than to come inside her, Alice thought miserably. She would not even get the reward of a proper climax for all her pain!

The twins let the candles burn down until her inner thighs and buttocks felt as though they were scorching and the wicks were flickering in tiny ponds of hot wax rimmed by her stretched orifices before blowing them out. Unhooking the spreader bar they carried her outside and laid her on the ground, her legs still tied wide. They left the plugs of wax in her for the rest of the day, so she lay soiled and shamed and horribly excited but unable to bring herself off. When they finally pulled them out she lost a few feathers embedded in the wax and yelped loudly. That final indignity convinced her. She dare not wait any longer. Tomorrow she was escaping!

When they came for her the next morning the first thing she did when they released her from her cage was to say, with evident eagerness, 'Thank you, Masters, to whichever one of you had me in the night. It made up for all the pain of yesterday.'

They exchanged frowns, and Dum said, 'Silly girl. We didn't come here last night.'

'But one of you must,' Alice insisted. 'It was too dark for me to tell which it was, but I know what happened.' She made a show of suddenly being struck by a new thought. 'Oh, sorry, Masters. I didn't know it was meant to be a secret.'

Suspiciously, Dee checked the tally sheet. It appeared to show that he had used Alice twice more than he could recall, once orally and once vaginally.

'I didn't make these ticks,' Dee protested.

'Of course you wouldn't put it down if you wanted it kept secret, Master,' Alice said helpfully, before Dum could respond. 'Nobody would do that if they wanted it to be a secret. There would only be a tick there if they were trying to make it look as though somebody else wasn't playing fair . . .' She let her eyes go wide and bit her lip. 'Oh, dear . . .'

The twins were standing face to face, their cheeks flushed and fists balled.

'I knew it was you!' Dum said.

'I knew it was you!' Dee retorted.

Struggling to keep her voice sympathetic, Alice said, 'Brothers shouldn't fight over a silly girling. Why don't you simply release me so I don't come between you again?'

'No!' they said together, still eyeball to eyeball.

It was worth a try, Alice thought. 'Or you can fight a duel for me, like cavaliers and knights used to,' she suggested. 'And whoever wins has me all to himself. That's the only way. Unless you want to be fighting each other for the rest of your lives.'

They looked at her, they looked back at each other, glowered then nodded slowly. 'We'll do it!'

'You'd better fight in the woods where you've got room,' Alice continued helpfully. 'And why not do it properly and dress up? Have you got swords and something that would do as armour?' If the story still had any meaning here they would improvise costumes. It would give her a little more time.

79

'Like knights?' Dum asked.

'Like knights,' Dee agreed.

They hooked her leash to the ring on the shack door and set off determinedly, marching side by side in step, but not looking at each other.

As soon as they had disappeared Alice began rubbing the nail she had clenched in her right hand against the rope that circled her waist. Every day she had been working at the spot where the rope was hidden by her crossed hands. She had chosen it because it was only one strand, whereas there were several confining each of her wrists. Even so it had been agonisingly slow going. After seemingly sawing away for most of last night she thought she was more than halfway through and hoped it would be weak enough when the time came to make her move.

The twins returned looking even larger than before with an assortment of blankets and bolsters tied about them to serve as armour. On their heads a coalscuttle and cooking pot respectively served as improvised helmets. They carried painted wooden toy swords and shields that looked absurdly small in their pudgy hands. Had they ever grown out of them? Alice wondered. Perhaps not. Nobody ever seemed to grow old here, so why should they?

'You both look wonderful,' Alice lied. 'Please may I start the battle? That would be proper. I mean I am the prize you're fighting for.'

She was worried they might put her back in her cage while they fought, which would be no use. She had to be in the open so she could make her break.

They led her out into the woods and tied her leash to a tree, then they squared up to each other. Alice realised she had to say something appropriate, but she had never refereed a duel before.

'Right, I, er, want a good sporting fight, no low blows, best of, er, three falls or one submission. No time

80

limit. Winner takes all . . . that's me. Are you both ready?'

'We are!' they said.

'Then . . . go!'

The twins charged at each other, swinging their wooden swords. There was a thump as their shields clashed, then they danced around each other hacking and stabbing with their swords. Alice winced at the ferocity of the blows, feeling a little guilty at being the cause of such animosity and the trick she had played on them. Then she remembered everything she had suffered at their hands and decided the pair would soon get over it.

Behind her back she was frantically sawing away at the rope with the nail. Crash! bang! Dum and Dee reeled about in furious motion. Alice felt the rope parting, gritted her teeth and jerked her arms sharply. The rope about her waist snapped and hung loose. She froze but, as she had hoped, the twins were too engrossed in their battle to notice.

Her elbows protested after having been twisted behind her for so long, but she forced her arms to stretch, sliding her bound wrists down over her hips and stepping through them with a gasp of relief. It was an agony to raise her arms in front of her and she whimpered in pain. Somehow she reached her collar, fumbled for the spring clip and unsnapped her leash.

She was free!

Slowly she edged round the tree until it was between her and the battle, then set off along the path she had been following almost a week earlier. She walked briskly, trying not to call attention to herself with any sudden movement. Just slip away, she told herself . . .

From behind her the clatter of combat suddenly ceased and was replaced with angry shouts. Then she began to run.

Alice raced though the forest, holding her still bound wrists awkwardly in front of her. She snatched a rearward glance. The pair were pounding along in her wake panting and puffing like steam trains, shedding blankets and ironware as they came. Despite their bulk they were gaining on her.

Ahead the path ran between a holly bush and a large rhododendron. A child's rattle lay on the ground. She hoped Dum and Dee were too angry to realise where she was leading them.

With the twins almost at her heels Alice jumped with all her strength, landing on the far side of the pit, stumbling but staying on her feet. From behind her came a crash and snap of breaking branches mingled with yells of surprise, then the thump of two heavy bodies hitting the ground.

Alice did not look back but ran on towards the barrier. The two of them should be able to get themselves out all right – eventually. And when they did she wanted to be long gone.

The woods began to thin. Ahead it seemed as though the forest had been cut through with a giant knife right across her path.

Suddenly the trees ended and there was a misty, blurred barrier before her, running down the middle of a brook a few feet wide. Alice did not break stride but sprang across the narrow channel. She felt a momentary tingling, twisting sensation as she passed through the insubstantial curtain, then she landed on a soft grassy bank, rolled onto her back and lay there panting heavily.

She had made it through the first square, she thought as she regained her breath, and it had only taken five days!

Five

After allowing herself a minute to recover, Alice sat up and took in her surroundings.

Beyond the grassy verge a tall redbrick wall ran along the length of the dividing barrier. A little way to her left the wall was pierced by an arched gateway. In the other direction Alice could see where the wall ended and the corners of four squares met, the misty barriers rising up into the sky forming a perfect right angle. For the moment at least she seemed to have the narrow strip of land to herself.

Alice got to her feet and backed up against the wall, using her teeth to loosen the knotted ropes binding her wrists while she kept a keen watch all round her. But nothing had changed five minutes later when she threw the ropes into the ditch and gratefully massaged her bruised and sore wrists. Even in Underland the marks would take a couple of days to heal. She hoped Dum and Dee had hit the bottom of their pit good and hard!

But which way now?

The gateway was so obvious she felt wary of it. If, however, she went along to the end of the wall, perhaps she could see what was round the other side first.

It did not take long to walk to the corner, but when she got there she found the wall extended into a tall thick hedge which ran at right angles to the brook, cutting right across it. The barrier marking the file boundary ran down the middle of the hedge. Alice tried to push her way through the hedge around the end of the wall, but it was just too thick. She supposed she could jump the brook back into the first square, find a way through the hedge into the square beside it, then across the continuation of the brook to the square above that, then through the hedge again to the other side of the wall. But was it worth all that trouble to spy out the land or would she run even more risk by passing through those equally unknown extra squares? What was worse, would she be permitted to make the detour? If she really was the Red Queen's pawn, was she limited only to moving forward in a straight line, as was her counterpart chessman? How closely was she bound by the rules of the game? She was not sure she wanted to find out.

Thoughtfully, Alice walked back to the gateway.

Set within the archway was a green wooden double gate, with one side invitingly open, and on the other a neatly painted sign which read: GARDENS OPEN – ADMISSION FREE. Through the gate she could see a stretch of paved path and a flowerbed overflowing with colourful blooms.

Is it just a nice garden or is it too good to be true? Alice wondered.

She continued on along the wall to check the other end, but it was a duplicate of the first. It looked like the gate was the only way to go. But as she turned back towards it she paused, frowning.

It had only taken her a couple of minutes to walk the length of one side of the wall square, yet it shared a common boundary with the Uffish square, which had been several miles across at least. How could they both fit together? Oh, of course. It must be the effect she had seen from the hillside. Different squares really did contain different amounts of ground, yet they all appeared to be the same size from without. She had not considered what it would be like to experience at first hand. Did it mean that this square was little used? Well, at the very least, if she could walk straight through, it would only take her a couple of minutes to reach the next one. Surely she could manage that.

She marched up to the gateway again and, taking a deep breath, cautiously stepped inside.

A wave of rich scents enveloped her, riding on a waft of air that was warm and tranquil. A path ran along between the main wall and a second slightly lower inner one, which was banked with more flowerbeds, interspersed with classically draped statues and ornamental urns. Bees buzzed and butterflies flitted lazily, and somewhere not far away she could hear a fountain splashing. In a daze she walked slowly along the path, wishing she knew the names of all the perfect blooms before her. She remembered, many years ago, visiting a stately home with her parents. They had walked in its lovingly tended gardens and she had been amazed by the spectacle of so many flowers all in one place. Well this was like that but more so.

Alice sighed· regretfully. All right, she must not get distracted. Where was the next path that led forward? Perhaps she could get though this place without anybody seeing her. There did not seem to be many visitors about at the moment.

She walked quickly along the path until she saw an open archway leading to some inner court. Turning into it she almost ran into a large man pushing a wheelbarrow.

Alice stepped back guiltily, but the man only beamed at her. 'There now, mind how you go,' he said mildly, with a distinct country burr. He was wearing heavy boots, shapeless old trousers, a collarless shirt with rolled-up sleeves and a battered straw hat, from under which spilled strands of red hair. His cheerfully creased face was ruddy and his expression mild.

'I'm sorry, Master,' said Alice, lowering her eyes deferentially.

'No harm done,' the gardener replied with a broad smile.

Alice blinked. His manner surprised her. Of course Underlanders were used to girlings and she did not expect him to be shocked by her nudity, but they were rarely so amiable. Even servants in Underland considered themselves superior to girlings and usually took great pleasure in letting them know it.

'I didn't mean to go where I shouldn't, but there was no other way,' she explained.

'Bless me, now.' The gardener gave a fruity chuckle. 'You saw the sign, girl? The gardens are free to all. Nobody's goin' to stop you looking round, as long as you don't mean to pick the flowers.'

'No, of course not, Master,' Alice assured him. 'They're lovely. It all looks . . . beautiful.'

'That's as it's meant to be. This is a place for lovely things to flower and be enjoyed.' He was looking her up and down. 'Dear me, you look a mite the worse for wear.'

Alice looked down at herself. She was grimed with sweat, her legs were mud-splattered and there were bits of leaf and twig in her hair that she must have acquired during her frantic dash through the woods.

'I've got a trough by the greenhouse, if you wants to wash yourself off,' he offered.

I can afford to spend a little while getting cleaned up, Alice reasoned. And the neater I look the less chance I have of calling attention to myself. 'That's very kind of you, Master,' she said. 'I'd like that.'

'Oh, I ain't your master, girl,' he said, taking up the handles of his wheelbarrow and leading Alice along the garden path. 'People just call me Ruddle. And what would your name be?'

'Alice. Alice Brown.'

' "Alice Brown." Now that has a nice ring to it. Pretty and practical . . .'

They passed under a second arch and along another path, past even more spectacular arrays of blooms, then through a gate into a yard beside a huge whitewood greenhouse. About it were neatly laid out all the paraphernalia of gardening: buckets and barrows, forks and spades, stakes and trellises. In one corner was a horse trough fed by a long-handled pump mounted at one end.

'Have a drink from the spout if you need, then climb in,' Ruddle told her. 'Its only water for the flowers, and they won't mind a pretty thing like yourself having dipped in first.'

Alice worked the pump handle and drank from the clear stream that gushed forth, then ducked her head under it to rinse out her hair. She hesitated a moment before climbing into the trough, smiling at her own reticence. In Underland she could walk around naked without a second thought, but taking a bath with a strange man looking on seemed more intimate. However, she could hardly object if he wanted to watch her and besides, she was meant to be a girling and therefore supposedly incapable of embarrassment. She got in, shivering a little as she sat down, and began rubbing at the dirt on her legs.

As she washed, Ruddle said, 'If you don't mind my asking, girl, how did you get to be here?'

'I was, um, on an errand for my mistress,' Alice explained. 'But I got caught by some boys in the square back that way. They . . . had some fun with me. I've only just got away from them.'

'What, two lads looking as though they came from the same pod? Faces like sour pumpkins?'

Alice giggled at the description. 'Yes, that's them.'

'The Tweedle twins. Bad lots. Used to have trouble with them sneaking in here and making mischief. But the last time I caught them and gave them a good hiding and haven't seen hide nor hair since. So where are you headed?'

'Brillig.'

He whistled. 'That's a fair way. Quite a journey for a girling on an errand. Won't your mistress be missing you?'

'I think she knows it might take a while.'

'That it will, if you falls foul of types like the Tweedles again, or worse. It's dangerous out there in places even for warriors like those that fought in the Great War, let alone dainty things like you. Find yourself somewhere safe to stay, that's my advice.'

'Thank you. I'd like to, but I have to do this.'

Ruddle shook his head sadly. 'As you will. Well, I'll be in here when you're done. There's no hurry.' And he turned away and entered the greenhouse.

Alice lazed back in the trough. It was tempting to dream of staying somewhere like this. Perhaps she could offer to lend Ruddle a hand in the gardens for a few days if he would put her up. No, there had already been enough delay. She seemed to hear the Queen's voice once again urging her on. Funny, but she'd hardly thought about her while she had been the twins' captive. Her hand slid down between her legs to her feathery delta. And she had her own reasons for wanting to complete her journey as soon as possible.

Feeling much cleaner, she climbed out and shook herself off. From past experience she knew she would soon dry in the warm air, which was even better than thick fluffy towels. She padded over to the open door of the greenhouse and peered inside. In the enclosed space the scent seemed rich enough to be tangible. Beyond the rows of pots and trays of sprouting seedlings and shelves laden with jars of feeds and weed killers, she saw Ruddle tending a single tall plant with the most remarkable multicoloured blooms, shaped like daffodil trumpets.

'Hello, Mr Ruddle,' she said as she walked up, the plant scent growing even stronger. 'I wanted to say thank you and . . . um, what's that called?'

Ruddle beamed. 'Ah, now this is one of my specials. It's called Nullivoluntaris musculum. I breed it for the special quality of its scent. What do you think of it?'

Automatically Alice bent her head forward to sniff at one of the blooms. As she did so the flower head seemed to convulse, puffing out a cloud of fine pollen into her face.

She jerked backwards, reaching up to wipe the powder away, only to find that her arm did not want to obey her. Ruddle caught her as her legs folded beneath her.

'Don't be afraid, Alice,' he said, scooping her up effortlessly into his huge arms. 'It only takes the control away from your muscles for a while. I'll keep you safe. A thing of beauty is always safe in my garden.'

He carried her over to one of the long potting tables and laid her carefully down on her back. Her head lolled to one side. She could roll her eyes a little but only a faint and plaintive sigh escaped her lips. She could still breathe and feel, but could not move so much as a finger. If he'd wanted sex he could have asked, she thought desperately. She would have paid her way. He didn't need to do this!

Ruddle beamed down at her, gently brushing the hair out of her eyes, his face still kindly but his eyes now deeper and sharper. He was standing more erect as well. And where had his accent gone?

'I really couldn't let you go, not such a fine specimen,' he continued. 'Your place is here, along with the rest of my special blooms. Now, let's have a proper look at you.'

He took hold of her breasts in his large work-roughened hands and squeezed and rolled them in his palms, carefully assessing their weight and the development of the glands below their soft skins. It was appreciative but not overtly sexual, and unlike any touch Alice had felt before. What was he going to do with her?

'Fine ripe fruits,' he declared. 'No problem there, I'm sure.' He prodded her stomach. 'Trim and firm. Good. But I see your pubic hair is somewhat odd.' He bent over her groin and stroked and tugged at her downy growth curiously. 'Most interesting. The result of a potion?' Alice gave a desperate throaty groan, which Ruddle appeared to take as an affirmative. 'Quite so,' he said sympathetically. 'Well, we'll just have to trust it won't interfere with the process. You appear to have lost a few feathers here and there and your groin is sore. Was it those Tweedles? Really, they are incorrigible. I hope they did no other damage.'

Ruddle eased her limp legs further apart and slid two fingers into her vagina, gently but purposefully exploring the depth and elasticity of her passage. Alice gurgled helplessly as he probed her. Withdrawing his fingers he examined them critically. 'You lubricate easily, which suggests a healthy, sensuous nature. I'm sure you will make a fine addition to the garden.' He spoke as though some honour was being bestowed upon her.

Turning her over onto her front he examined her bottom, sliding a finger, still slippery with her vaginal secretion, into her rectum. When he found how pliant her anal ring was he introduced a second and explored her passage to the depth of his knuckles. 'Your orifices have been well used,' he pronounced when he finally withdrew, 'but they retain their natural tightness. All to the good. Now, we must get that collar off.'

Tucking a rag under the back of Alice's collar for protection, Ruddle found a hacksaw and began sawing away steadily, talking to her as he did so. 'Hard steel . . . not the proper material for collars around such pretty necks. Something pliant like good thick rubber, that's the right stuff. Soon have this off you, then I'll put on a broad buckled strap, so it won't cut you but you'll be well supported. Much more comfortable . . .'

He sounds so kindly, thought Alice, silently raging against her dumb immobility, how can he be doing this to me? Her collar fell open and Ruddle removed the pieces.

As her head was turned to one side she saw Ruddle go to a slatted wooden locker and carefully lift out a tray of a dozen large glossy purple plant bulbs. Selecting one he held it out as though for Alice to admire. 'My finest creation,' he said proudly. 'Femini mutotisflos ruddeli, I've named it. It took years of experimentation and crossbreeding, but it's been worth the effort. You'll soon see. Just a little sunflower oil to ease it in . . .'

He ran some oil from a bottle over the bulb, then pried open Alice's buttocks and pushed the narrow end into her anus, forcing her muscle ring to stretch wide. Alice grunted, then the fattest part of the bulb was past her bottom mouth. Ruddle continued to push it in until it was lodged well up her rectum.

'Let it bed in for a few minutes,' he said. 'I'll just fit your frame, then I'll stake you out with the others.'

Ruddle gathered a stout post and two thinner wooden rods from the assortment outside, together with a bundle of black rubber straps with sleeve fastenings that enabled them to form double loops. He arranged Alice so that she lay straight with her legs apart and arms a little way out from her torso, then laid the post on her back and fastened it with straps about her neck and waist, leaving a good length extending beyond her feet. Holes had been drilled through the post at certain intervals, and through these he slid the rods so their ends crossed Alice's wrists and ankles, which were secured in turn. He passed two longer straps between Alice's legs so that they lay in the folds either side of her pubes at the tops of her thighs and then ran up along the undercurve of her buttocks. These straps were looped over the lower transverse rod and buckled tight.

Ruddle gathered a bottle and metal funnel from a shelf and slipped them into his pocket, picked up Alice and the frame to which she was now securely bound without apparent effort and carried them outside. There was another closed gate to one side of that through which she had entered the greenhouse yard. Ruddle produced a key, unlocked the gate and they passed through into a small walled enclosure with a path running down the middle and flower-beds on either side.

'Now this is my special garden,' he said. 'Beautiful, aren't they?'

Alice gave a despairing gurgle of amazement as she saw what was growing there. Of course they were in the book, but not like this! No . . . he couldn't be going to do that to her!

The mouth of a narrow upright pottery pipe protruded from a patch of watered earth ready to accept the base of Alice's stake. Ruddle slotted it in so she stood securely upright.

'Now, you need a dose of my special mixture to activate the bulb,' he explained as he took out the funnel and pushed its curving spout into Alice's mouth. Unstopping the bottle he poured half of some cloudy fluid down Alice's throat. She choked and spluttered but felt the bitter burning liquid course through her.

Ruddle smiled. 'It might make you feel a bit odd at first, but you'll soon get over it. I'll be back to check on you later.'

He walked out, closing the gate behind him. The dozen other flowers in the walled garden turned their heads to watch him go, then looked at Alice.

They were girlings strapped to stakes as she was, arranged in two rows along either side of the path. No, they *had* been girlings, she corrected herself. Now they were living flowers.

Their hair had become halos of coloured petals encircling their faces. Rings of smaller petals grew out of their areolae, making pretty flower heads of their prominent nipples. Fans of petals had also replaced their pubic hair. But most grotesquely of all, long thick white roots ran down from between their buttocks and burrowed into the rich earth.

Alice suddenly felt sick and dizzy and jerked feebly at her straps. The effect of the paralysing pollen was wearing off . . . but too late.

The girlflower staked opposite Alice was looking at her in horror. As Alice groaned she turned her head away and began sobbing.

'Don't fight it,' the girl beside Alice said. 'I know it's like a nightmare, but you're not going mad. You can get used to it. I did.'

Alice's skin was prickling and her bowels were hot. She felt the bulb in her rectum begin to stir and swell. Her breasts tingled. Struggling to recover the use of her tongue again, Alice said, trying to sound braver than she felt at that moment, 'I've had change potions before . . . got turned into a bird once . . .'

The other girl smiled encouragingly. 'You must tell me about it sometime.' She had clear dark eyes with well-marked brows, a firm straight nose and neat expressive lips. Her face looked bizarrely pretty within its blossom frame. There were butterflies flitting about her petal-breasts, which were not large but very rounded and prominent, with glistening pointed nipples.

Alice felt her scalp crawl as her hair began to fan out, the strands fusing together. Her nipples were pricking up as soft petals grew out from the edge of her areolae. Her pubic feathers stung for a moment, then also blossomed. The bulb was growing, pushing stems upwards and threading their way through her bowels, while a rootstalk was extending back down her rectum. She gasped as it pushed its way out of her anus with a frighteningly sensuous motion and reached downwards for the soil.

'The worst of it's almost over,' her neighbour said. 'I mean, things will still be crazy, but they won't happen so quickly.'

The root penetrated the soil and immediately began to thicken. Alice felt it swelling inside her, becoming firmer. A new tingling began in her stomach. Her head felt strange.

'Do I . . . do I look like you, yet?' she asked, trying to keep her voice steady.

The girl nodded, her delicate fan of petals gently bobbing as she moved. 'Yes, you do,' she said quietly.

Alice screwed up her eyes for a moment. I will not freak out, she told herself. I've had worse things happen to me.

'My name's Suzanne Ryder,' the girl said. 'What's yours?'

'Alice Brown.'

Suzanne smiled. 'Hello, Alice. Is your stomach turning over?'

'Yes,' Alice groaned.

'It'll settle down after a while,' Suzanne assured her. 'Meanwhile let's get the introductions out of the way. You're going to get to know us all pretty well . . .'

Still feeling sick, Alice nodded to the other girlflowers as they were introduced. The young girl opposite was Juliet. She had wide almond eyes, full lips, skin tanned a light golden brown and heavy breasts with large areolae at the centre of their petal rings. Because of her transformation Alice had no idea what colour her hair had been. Her pretty rounded face was tear-streaked and she seemed unable to look at Alice directly.

'Juliet was the last girl Ruddle brought in,' Suzanne explained quietly. 'She's new to Underland and hasn't got used to the way things work here yet.'

'I can hear you,' Juliet said miserably. 'This place is mad, it's evil! I shouldn't be here. This can't be happening. I want to go home!' Her last words came as a despairing shriek.

Alice felt sorry for the girl, but she could not even help herself right now. Suzanne called over to her: 'You know that's not possible, Julie love. You have to learn to make the best of things.'

Juliet said nothing and turned her head aside.

In a whisper Suzanne confided to Alice, 'I think it's harder for her because she's never been slave-trained. At least the rest of us are used to bondage and we've some idea of the things they can do to girlings. Juliet wandered into the garden a week ago and Ruddle caught her. She's been too confused to explain much, but as far as I can tell she'd only arrived here the day before. She won't say how but I don't think she had any idea what she was getting herself into. Most of the girls I've met were picked in some way and can fit in. She may be here by accident.'

'I can see why she's freaked,' Alice said. The wave of nausea had largely passed, though she had a sense that something was going on in her stomach. She tried not to think about it. 'Who is Ruddle? What's he up to? Does he work for anybody?'

'Not as far as I know.'

'Why does he use the old yokel act?'

Suzanne shrugged as well as her straps allowed. 'Puts people off their guard, maybe? It certainly fooled me.'

'Me too,' Alice admitted. 'He seemed so easy going. I'd never have guessed he was a head case.'

'The thing is, in a twisted way, he does care about us,' Suzanne said. 'Most of the time he couldn't be kinder. I think he really believes he's doing us a favour keeping us here like this.'

'So what happens now? Do we hang about here for the rest of our lives looking pretty for a flower freak?'

'No, it's more complicated than that. We're meant to be useful as well as decorative. You see, what happens is . . . oh, he's back.'

Ruddle came through the gate. He beamed benevolently at the flowergirls as he made his way along the rows, chatting cheerfully to them, stroking their petals and praising the fullness of their breasts. How could he be so considerate yet so blind to what he had done? Alice wondered. Finally he reached her.

'How are you feeling, Alice?' he asked gently. 'The worst of the change should be over by now.'

Alice overcame her natural desire to scream at the man for the outrage he had committed upon her and instead said levelly, 'This is wrong. You know that. Having a little fun with a few girlings who wander into your garden is one thing, but you're taking away what we are!'

Ruddle simply smiled benignly, as though excusing a child's tantrum. 'You'll get use to it, Alice. In time you'll understand that things are better this way. Ask some of the others. In the meantime you'll be safe in here.'

'Perhaps we don't want to be safe all the time!' Alice said. 'You can't hide away from the world and pretend it doesn't exist. Maybe we're braver than you are.'

Was there a slight flicker of resentment at her words? Had she touched a sore spot?

Ruddle held something up for Alice to see. 'Look what I've got you.' It was a small neat sign with her name painted on it mounted on a wooden peg.

'That's supposed to make me feel better, is it?' Alice replied sarcastically. 'You change me into a freakin' plant but it doesn't matter because I've got my name on a sign! You know where you can stick it!'

Gravely, Ruddle pushed the sign into the earth beside Alice's frame. She now saw that all the girls had similar markers by them.

'I'm sure you don't mean that,' Ruddle said. 'It's just the shock of the transformation. In a few days you'll see I was right.'

He squeezed and prodded her breasts and stomach. 'Good, you're coming along nicely. Now, I'll just stimulate your fruiting . . .'

He unbuttoned his flies and pulled out a rod of flesh already semi-hard. The frame held her at a convenient height, and all Ruddle had to do was grasp her waist and bend his knees slightly to position himself. Alice gasped and bit her lip as he plugged her to the hilt and began thrusting steadily, all the while smiling encouragingly as though she should welcome what he was doing to her.

As Alice jerked back and forth in her bonds, the frame creaking and her petalled breasts bouncing, she thought that at least this she understood. He could have had her like this if he wanted without using potions and mutating plants. All he needed to have done was to be masterful and her submissive side would have taken over. She would probably have enjoyed it.

Actually she was enjoying it even now, she realised, despite everything. Was there any limit to her perverse nature, or had the metamorphosis made her more easily aroused than usual? Her nipples, grinding against Ruddle's shirt, were hard as rocks and pulsing with blood. God, she was getting sensations from the petals that now surrounded them! It was as though her areolae were ten times as wide and twice as sensitive. Her vagina had become one big pleasure hole. She was watering the soil with her lubrication. Her clit felt as though it was going to burst. How could he do this to her?

She cried out aloud as she came, setting her petals shivering and her anus clenching on the root that now impaled her. Even after her climax, post-orgasmic tremors went on and on, coursing through her and her extended nervous system in waves of slowly diminishing pleasure. Dimly she was aware of Ruddle pulling out of her, saying, 'Good girl,' and stroking her flushed cheek. 'Trust me. Everything will be fine.'

He left the garden and she hung limp against her frame. The other girlflowers watched her with varying degrees of interest. A few smiled while others went back to chatting between themselves or turning their heads to the warm bright sky and closing their eyes. Suzanne had the patience to wait a few minutes before saying, 'Don't feel bad about enjoying yourself. Something about the transformation makes us come easily. We each get a screw like that every few days to stimulate our fruiting.'

Still breathing heavily, Alice gathered her wits enough to gasp out, 'I'd have given him that just for being nice to me. He didn't have to do all this to get regular sex. If he wants a few girlings for company he could have bought some, or even made strays work for their keep. A lot might enjoy the garden if they were given the choice.'

'It isn't just about sex,' Suzanne said. 'This is how he wants us: girling flowers he can nurture, that's one of his favourite words.'

'Well I'm not staying around here to be nurtured, not like this.' She thought for a moment. 'What's this about "fruiting"?' she asked.

'It's pretty strange, even for Underland,' Suzanne warned her.

'Tell me the worst,' Alice said.

'We produce one fruit a day. I think they must grow in our wombs, anyway they come out of our pussies, you know. They look rather like golden pears. Actually, once you get used to it, popping them out is quite nice.'

Alice was staring at her. 'You mean . . . like having a baby?'

'No, it's just a fruit. It comes out like a hen lays an egg. There's no mess.'

Alice trembled and swore under her breath. 'Anything else I should know?'

'Well . . . there's what's happening to your boobs.'

'Go on. I was also a cowling for a while. It can't be worse.'

Suzanne looked at her with surprise tinged with admiration. 'You've been busy. When did that happen?'

'It's a long story. At least this time I can still think for myself. What about my boobs?'

'They start producing nectar, I guess you'd call it. Something like thin honey, anyway.' She looked down at her own taut and shiny breasts. Butterflies were flitting round her nipple blossoms. 'You can see insects like it, and wait until a big one comes to feed! Gives you quite a high.'

'But what's it used for?'

'He has some regular customers in the next door squares who pay a lot for girlflower fruit and nectar. Sometimes he lets them in to see us and they can squeeze a bit for themselves. It's not so bad. Actually it's a change to see new faces. Otherwise we just gossip or else soak up the sun, well, the light anyway.'

'That's all?'

'There's not much else to do. We can't exactly go for long walks. Though you don't feel you miss moving about after a while. While we get plenty of food, water and light we stay healthy.'

'Like any plant!' Alice said scathingly. 'That's all we are now: plants in girls' bodies pumping out fruit and nectar for Ruddle to sell! You can't like it!'

For the first time Suzanne's bright, positive manner slipped. She bit her lip and her eyes filed with tears. 'Of course I don't! I've got a master living in Brillig. That's who I belong to, not Ruddle. I keep pretending things are not so bad to stay from going mad!'

'Sorry,' Alice said gently.

Suzanne blinked away her tears, sniffed and forced a smile. 'It's all right. I don't usually let it get to me like that.'

'I don't blame you. Listen; do you believe in destiny? A lot of weird things have happened to me here, and sometimes it looked as though I'd be stuck in some place for good. But each time I got the feeling it wasn't right, and I moved on. I know this is not where I belong, so I'm going to get away somehow. And if I can get away, so can you. In fact we can all get away!'

Suzanne was looking at her thoughtfully. 'You really believe that?'

'Yes,' Alice said firmly.

'I'd like to believe you, I really would.' She glanced at the sky and smiled wanly. 'But we're not going to get away today. It's getting dark and we're going to sleep.'

'Just like that?'

'We can't help it,' Suzanne said. 'Flowers close up at night, remember? You'll feel it in a minute. I'll say one thing, having a plant growing out of your bum makes you keep sensible hours.'

The light faded from the sky. Alice felt her breast and pubic petals slowly closing tight. The petals about her head began to fold inwards, and as they did so the energy seemed to drain out of her. She struggled feebly, frightened of being suffocated.

'Don't fight it,' she heard Suzanne say sleepily.

The petals closed tight about her face and darkness took her.

During the night a shower of soft rain fell over the garden. It trickled off the flowergirls' bowed heads and petal-tipped breasts and watered the rich dark soil in which they grew.

Gradually Alice felt life flowing back into her. She had had a weird dream that she had been turned into a flower and . . . No! She gave a reflex jerk against the straps that bound her to the frame, then forced herself to relax.

Her head petals unfolded to welcome the bright light of a new day. Stiffly she raised her head as the other flowergirls stirred about her greeting the day. She had seen something like it in an old highly anthropomorphised cartoon, but never imagined she would be one of them. Warmth coursed through her and goodness from the damp earth was flowing up through her root. Her sap was rising . . .

No!

She was a girl not a plant. This was just a temporary aberration, another slice of Underland madness – albeit a pretty large slice.

'Good morning,' said Suzanne beside her. 'Sleep well?'

'I . . . er, yes, I suppose I did.' Alice tried to stretch but her bonds didn't allow much movement. 'Strung out like this I should ache all over, but I feel OK.'

'Plants aren't big on heavy exercise, in case you hadn't noticed,' Suzanne said with a wry smile. 'They seem to keep us comfortable. Ruddle's one hell of a bio-engineer, I'll say that for him.'

'Will Ruddle come round to feed us? Oh, I suppose he doesn't have to.'

'No, we get everything we need from the soil and air now. Well, more or less everything.'

Opposite her Juliet was silent and withdrawn, but Alice exchanged a few remarks with the other flowergirls along the row. She related her adventures for them up to the point she had entered the garden. Her encounter with the Red Queen drew special interest, as some of them had heard stories about the Chess Wars. It was agreed that most of the native Boardlanders thought all the chess warriors were dead, or else had gone away long ago. Nevertheless they listened intently, hanging on every word. Though it was a good tale Alice suspected it was receiving more attention than it deserved. But then she was telling it to a captive audience. How long before they all ran out of stories and were left longing for the next poor girling to swell their numbers and

101

distract them with her life history? Alice thought of the dreadful false sense of contentment that had accompanied her cowling transformation and how she had fought against it. At least Ruddle had left their minds alone. Perhaps he wanted flowers that could talk back to him. But it left them to suffer the anguish of frustration and insidious boredom, which was perhaps even crueller.

Alice's breasts felt full, standing out tautly from her chest like true melons. Well, it had only taken them a few hours to fill with milk when she had been a cowling, so she supposed nectar would not take any longer. Her plumped-out nipples were glossy with an exudation of the golden fluid and like the other flowergirls she had attracted her share of butterflies and, a little alarmingly, bees. They did not sting her, however, but delicately collected their share. Alice was hypnotised by them, feeling them tickle her super-sensitive areolae as they fussed about her twin fronts.

Then Suzanne said, 'Here they come – the premier league.'

Alice heard a louder buzzing that became a drone. The bees and butterflies left them in a fluttering cloud as a swarm of two dozen insects the size of birds descended into the garden in a shimmer of huge translucent wings. A couple hovered in the air right in front of Alice, as though assessing her through their huge compound eyes. She flinched in alarm, but Suzanne said, 'It's OK. It only hurts a bit, then it's quite fun.'

Every girlflower had a pair of the giant insects settling on their breasts. Alice felt tiny hooked legs biting into her flesh as they landed. Proboscises uncoiled and probed the tips of her nipples, sliding delicately into them. For a moment it was like having hot pins driven into her, then the pain turned on its head as her breasts pulsed with joy at being penetrated. The garden filled with contented sighs as they gave up their nectar. Even Juliet appeared lost in the strange pleasure.

Ruddle seemed content to let the insects have their share and then harvest the rest. He came round afterwards with a funnel-ended hand pump and sucked the golden fluid from their still-plump breasts. He squeezed a little of Alice's nectar onto his fingers and licked it experimentally.

'Rich and sweet,' he pronounced with approval, and pumped her out. Afterwards he gently prodded her stomach, which Alice had felt was slightly bloated. 'Your first fruit is coming along nicely. You should be ripe by the end of the day.'

Alice watched him leave the garden feeling slightly sick.

The day wore on. Though she did not feel hungry or thirsty, Alice missed having a break for lunch. The only substitute, apart from mindless basking under the bright sky, was talking. Suzanne explained how she came to the garden.

'Martes martes, my master, is a well respected merchant,' Suzanne said, with evident pride. 'He moved to Brillig quite recently and he's doing very well there. Because the roads are improving and the railway is being extended, my master wanted to find new suppliers along the edge squares. And he took me with him. We were travelling the square next to this one by coach. I was on top with the luggage when a giant crow swooped down and grabbed me . . .' She broke off, smiling. 'I know it sounds crazy when I tell it but that's what happened.'

'Seems about right for Underland,' Alice said. 'There are myths about people being snatched by huge birds, and pterodactyls are doing it all the time in dinosaur films. I think those ideas shape the way things happen

103

down here. And there is a giant crow in the Looking Glass story, so it sort of fits.'

'Is there? I've never read that part. Anyway, the crow carried me for miles and then dropped me in its nest. But before it could eat me, or whatever it had planned, I managed to climb out and get away into some woods. The trouble was I got totally lost and wandered around for a few days until I came to the edge of the square. I didn't know what was on the other side but I hoped it would be somewhere I could get help. Unfortunately it was here. Ruddle was so sympathetic I thought everything was going to be all right. Then I made the mistake of sniffing at one of his special plants and . . .' She broke off again with a breathy gasp. 'I think my next fruit is about ready . . .'

Her stomach below her restraining strap bulged slightly, then contracted. Suzanne screwed up her eyes. 'It's coming . . .'

Alice looked on in queasy fascination as Suzanne's pudenda gaped wide and the rounded base of a soft golden fruit appeared between the stretched pink lips. Suzanne grunted and tensed herself. With an almost audible pop it was ejected from her vagina and dangled beneath Suzanne's thighs like some strange ornament. A thin trailing stalk and a few leaves slithered out after it, letting the fruit slide gently to the soft earth.

'Are you OK?' Alice asked anxiously.

Suzanne caught her breath and smiled. 'Fine. I felt sick the first couple of times thinking I'd just done the grossest thing imaginable. But now I've got used to it. I mean we are designed to do that sort of thing with a baby so this is no strain. Truth is, anything going up or coming down feels good. Maybe that's some sort of compensation.'

Alice hoped so.

That evening Alice produced her own fruit. She hardly realised what was happening until she felt it drop into the upper end of her birth canal. Instinctively she pushed and it slithered out, stalk and all, with no trouble and a faintly pleasurable sensation. It was only half the size of Suzanne's fruit. For a brief moment Alice felt slightly ashamed that she had not been able to produce something better. Even poor tearful Juliet opposite had, with a few moans of helpless excitement, expelled a lovely plump golden pear from between her pretty thighs. Then Alice caught herself. What was she thinking?

When Ruddle came round to gather the day's crop he examined her offering with a slight frown. 'Ah, well, it's only your first. No doubt you'll do better tomorrow.'

Alice watched him carry his basket of fruit out of the walled garden. With the gate only half closed behind him he paused, put the basket down and lifted his hat to scratch his head. It was only because she was the nearest to the gate that Alice noticed, and in any other circumstances it would have been an absolutely unremarkable gesture. But what she saw under his hat made her stifle a gasp.

Suzanne looked round at her. 'What's the matter?'

'Nothing,' Alice said distractedly. 'I've just realised something. I need to think it over. Tell you in the morning.'

How could she use what she now knew about Ruddle to her best advantage?

Ruddle was not her first concern in the morning, however. Alice woke up feeling sick. Suzanne looked at her anxiously.

'You don't look good. You, well . . . your petals are droopy and look sort of brown round the edges.'

'I don't feel good either,' Alice said testily, trying to cover her fear. She had never felt ill before in Underland. What was wrong with her?

She was worse by the time Ruddle came round. He examined her then shook his head gravely. 'I fear it is the residual effect of the potion you took that produced that strange pubic growth, Alice. Your body is rejecting the bulb. It will have to be cut away. I'm so sorry for you.'

She should be sorry? she thought wonderingly. For once her feathery bane was working to her advantage. She would be free of the damned plant. But what to do then? Her mind raced.

Ruddle drew out a sheath knife from his pocket, unsnapped the blade, and with a look of profound sadness, sliced through the root midway between Alice's bottom and the soil.

It seemed to Alice that she could feel the bulb begin to shrivel within her. The tendrils that had so intimately threaded their way through her body were contracting. The spray of petals about her head sagged, then began to split apart, their ends fraying into finer threads. She was getting her hair back. Her nipple petals dropped in a shower. She would never be as sensitive there again. The petals about her pubes stiffened into feathers once more. She could have done without those. Ruddle pulled on the shrivelling root trailing from her anus. Alice gasped as the remains of the bulb popped out of her and hung from his hand, withered and dead.

'Please, I feel so cold,' Alice said pitifully. 'I . . . can't feel my legs and arms. They're going dead!'

'Poor girl,' said Ruddle, sounding genuinely concerned. 'I'll take you to the greenhouse. You'll be warmer there.'

He unbuckled her supporting straps and she fell limply into his arms. With the troubled eyes of all the other flowergirls on her, he carried her across the yard and into the warmth of the greenhouse.

Ruddle laid her down tenderly on the potting table and smoothed back her hair.

'Please . . . some water,' Alice gasped.

'Of course. You just lie quietly.' He found a tin mug and went out to the pump in the yard.

Alice heaved herself off the bench and almost fell to the floor, feeling horribly weak but determined. There would only be one chance to do this. She fumbled amongst the clutter on the shelf for what she was looking for, cursing the clumsiness of her fingers. Then she staggered over to the wooden slatted cabinet.

Ruddle came back in carrying the cup. 'Here you are, Alice . . . what?'

Pale but resolute, Alice was standing with the tray of mutotisflos bulbs balanced on one arm and an open bottle of weed killer poised above it. 'Take one more step and I swear I'll pour this all over them,' she said. 'I don't know what's in it but it's got a skull and crossbones on so I guess it's not nice. What will it do to your precious bulbs, I wonder?'

'No!' Ruddle groaned in horror. 'You mustn't!'

'Just watch me!'

Ruddle's huge frame seemed to sag. He looked more like a small boy being forced to accept a scolding. He must really love these things, Alice thought.

'What do you want?' he asked faintly.

'I want to get out of here,' Alice said. 'And I don't want to go alone . . .'

In the end three of the girlflowers decided to stay as they were. Perhaps when confronted with the chance of freedom they found they no longer had the nerve to face it, or perhaps this was the right place for them, Alice did not know. It seemed a mad choice, but then this was Underland where madness was the norm. Either way there was no time to argue. They had their chance, what they did with it was not her business.

'But what's to stop him doing all this again?' Suzanne asked Alice as they watched the last of the freed girls recovering the use of their legs.

'A promise . . . and a threat,' Alice said with a determined grin. She still had the bulbs and weed killer at the ready, though her arm was beginning to ache. Ruddle stood in one corner looking on mournfully.

When all the girls were strong enough to stand, she turned to Ruddle. 'Take off your hat,' she commanded.

He gaped at her incredulously. 'What are you saying?'

'Do it!'

With a trembling hand he lifted the battered old straw hat from his head. Underneath was a gleaming red crown.

'Even though you ran away from the war, some habits are hard to break, aren't they?' Alice said. 'And the name Ruddle, I think that's another word for red ochre or something. Everybody, meet Carnelian, former king of Stauntonia!'

A murmur of wonder went up. Carnelian gazed round at them, suddenly looking very weary. 'I was so tired of war,' he said. 'The joy goes out of slaughter after a while, especially when it's the same faces again and again. You begin to wonder what the point of it all is. Once doubt crept in I began to notice how the natives were getting hurt and the land was being ravished. The more I studied them the more I found I loved beauty, whether it was the bodies of women or flowers. But there was no time for that when we had the next campaign to plan. So one day I just . . . slipped away. The King was gone and Ruddle took his place. By and by I made my way here and started to experiment. It was just a hobby.'

'Call this a hobby?' Suzanne cut in angrily.

'Yes,' Carnelian said simply. 'I meant no harm. I really didn't want to see beauty go to waste any more.'

Alice was beginning to feel sorry for him, but she had to see the thing through. 'Do you believe that once you've said a thing that fixes it and you must take the consequences?' she asked.

'Of course.'

'Then you're going to promise that in future you'll show any girlings who wander in here your special flowers first. No more knock-out plants. What happens next is up to them, understood?'

'I promise I will not trick any girling into becoming a flowergirl,' Carnelian said with a heavy sigh.

'Remember, everybody here knows who you are now. If they hear of any girlings going missing, they can tell on you. The locals still remember what your kind did to Boardland, so I don't think you'd be very popular.'

The King hung his head.

'Now, everybody decide which way you're going,' Alice called out. 'Apparently there are four exits so choose the right one. If you want to make for Uffish watch out for the Tweedle twins. Bye ... and good luck!'

The girls milled about and began to file away out of the gardens. Suzanne stood by Alice. 'I'm going to try to get back to Brillig. Are you still going there?'

'If I can.'

Juliet was standing alone looking lost. 'I just want to go home,' she said hopelessly.

'You'd better come with us,' Alice said. 'I won't promise, but I'll see what I can do to get you back.'

For the first time Juliet smiled. 'Thanks,' she said.

'If you want to help, pick up three trug baskets from the yard, and three of the widest support straps you can find.'

'Why?'

'You'll see.'

Now there were only themselves and the King left.

'I'll put the bulbs down outside the north gate,' Alice told him. 'You can pick it up when we're gone. One more thing. In case you have any idea about breaking your promise, the "mistress" I'm running an errand for is your wife. Now you wouldn't want me to tell her where you're hiding, would you?'

Leaving Carnelian looking very pale, they joined Juliet in the yard and the three of them jogged along

109

paths until they came to a gate like the one Alice had come through three days earlier. Beyond it was another brook and the barrier guarding the next square. So long to get so not very far, she thought bitterly.

Alice put the tray of bulbs down and said, 'Jump!'

They sprang over the brook and through the shimmering curtain.

Six

On the other side of the barrier was another idyllic forest. It seemed to Alice that Underland had an endless supply of such settings, but its greatest appeal at that moment was that it appeared to be quite deserted.

She looked at Suzanne. 'You're the guide. Which way now?'

Suzanne ran her fingers through her newly restored shoulder-length dark brown mane. She carried her slim figure with a light step and her small nipples stood up cheerfully. Alice guessed she was a couple of years older than herself.

'I don't actually live around here, remember, but I know there's a small town called Gyre somewhere in this square because I passed through it with my master. Trains run to Brillig from there, but we'd need money for tickets, and I don't think they'll allow girlings to travel unaccompanied.'

'We'll work round that when we get there,' Alice said. 'I suppose we'd better find a path or track and see where it takes us. You all right with that, Juliet?'

The third member of their party had been looking about her in silence. Her girlflower petals had turned back into long curling mid-brown locks, the ends of which she was twirling nervously about her fingers. She was even prettier than Alice had thought, with an attractive remnant of puppy fat about her waist and

rounded bottom, contrasting with breasts only a little
smaller than Alice's own, capped by large brown
nipples. Her face however was clouded and she looked
at them anxiously.

'Can we find some clothes first, please?' she asked. 'I
don't like walking round with nothing on.'

Suzanne and Alice looked at her in surprise. 'Girlings
don't wear clothes in Underland,' Suzanne explained.

'But I'm not a girling!' Juliet insisted.

'You are here,' Alice told her firmly, 'so you'd better
get used to it. If we want to travel inconspicuously we
must look the part of properly owned and collared
girlings running an errand. That's why we've brought
the baskets and straps.'

'Oh, I wondered why you wanted them,' Suzanne
said. 'Now I get it.'

'You mean, we've got to wear collars?' Juliet exclaimed. 'But we've just got out of those horrid straps.'

'And now they'll pass as collars,' Alice said, picking
one up and buckling it about her neck. Suzanne did the
same. Juliet fingered the remaining strap while biting
her lip, then with great reluctance put it on.

'See, it's not so bad,' Alice reassured her. 'We'll carry
a basket each and pick a few flowers or something, so
that if we meet anybody they'll see what we're doing and
won't bother us. If they do just keep your eyes lowered
and try to look humble and you'll be fine.'

'I hate this,' Juliet said. 'I shouldn't be here.'

'We know you've had a bad introduction to Underland,' Suzanne said. 'What happened in the garden was
OTT even for this place. But it can be wonderful, trust
me. I'm sure you'll find out where you fit in soon enough.'

'I don't fit in anywhere here,' Juliet said sharply. 'I
just want to go home!'

Alice and Suzanne exchanged helpless glances. 'First
let's find a station,' Alice said.

* * *

112

They came upon a fairly well-used path running through the woods, which led to a lane that wound on between open fields. In the distance they saw a cluster of rooftops which they hoped was Gyre. As they went they picked bluebells, berries and a variety of nut that Suzanne said was safe to eat. These added convincing variety to their baskets and also doubled as rations.

Along the way they passed a weasel farmer driving a team of four naked and heavily harnessed girlings who were drawing his haycart. Alice, Suzanne and Juliet kept to the side of the lane with their heads bowed and he went by with hardly a glance. Once he was behind them, however, Juliet twisted round to gape at the cart and its straining team.

'He's an animal . . . and he's using those women like horses!' she said in amazement.

'Of course,' Suzanne exclaimed. 'Didn't you listen to any of the gossip in the garden? Half of it was about how well or badly our masters treated us. In Underland we do the work animals do, or did anyway, in our world. Here we're usually bigger than they are so it makes sense.'

'And there are no female animals, so we fill in there as well,' Alice added.

Juliet looked from one to the other of them in horror. 'But . . . you couldn't let an animal do that to you!'

'Well, you don't usually have a choice,' Alice said with a grin, trying to sound offhand to allay the girl's evident concern. 'It's strange at first, but you get used to it. In fact it can be very good. Remember, animals are people here.'

'I'd rather have sex with the right animal than the wrong person,' Suzanne declared boldly. 'Didn't you realise my master's a pine marten? He's lovely. Sometimes he can be strict, of course, but mostly he's very kind . . . and right now I miss him more than you know, and if you can't say anything nice about that, then be quiet!'

Juliet looked at her in disbelief. 'You're . . . filthy! And this place is mad!'

They walked on for a while in strained silence, with Juliet trailing behind the other two. Eventually Suzanne said quietly to Alice, 'I've never seen anybody react this badly before, at least not for so long. Whatever new girls say you can usually tell they're really excited underneath.'

'That's how I was at first,' Alice agreed. 'I thought everybody who came here belonged, even if they didn't know it. Either they find their own way or they're brought by somebody like the White Rabbit who can sniff out submissives. You're sure you don't know how she got here?'

'I couldn't get a straight answer out of her about it. Of course she was pretty off her head about the flower thing. I suppose that's what's caused the trouble.'

'If something has gone wrong and she really doesn't belong here, then she must feel she's in a nightmare,' Alice said.

'I'll do all I can to help her, but I'm not going to be ashamed of what I am,' Suzanne stated. 'I know where I belong.'

They hid in a convenient spinney on the outskirts of Gyre while Suzanne went on alone. A single girling was less likely to attract attention than three together, and she was most familiar with Boardland ways. While she was gone Alice took the opportunity to talk to Juliet.

'I know all this must seem very strange to you,' Alice said. 'But I'm sure you'll get used to it.'

'How can I? This place is mad and people do filthy things to each other.'

'Well, it was shaped by the original Wonderland stories,' Alice said carefully, 'so it's normal to be a bit mad. And I think it changed into Underland as more permissive ideas have filtered through, but the link is still there. In fact some of the girls who came here were reading the Alice book just before they made the journey. Was that what you were doing?'

Juliet gave her a startled look that turned into an angry grimace. 'No I wasn't! I was with my family. We lived in a lovely house and I had everything I wanted. That's where I belong. Now please stop asking me stupid questions!' And she sat against a tree with her back to Alice.

Suzanne returned within an hour.

'It is Gyre and the station's there all right,' she reported. 'Trains to Brillig leave every other day. The trouble is full fare tickets cost three and six each, and even shipping a girling at livestock rates is a florin.'

'Is that a lot of money?' Juliet asked.

'It doesn't matter, because even if we had it you'd still need a local to arrange everything,' Suzanne said. 'It means we'd have to have somebody to ship us off, and who could we trust to do that? I'm afraid you can't get far here without a master.'

Juliet looked disgusted at this last remark. 'You keep on about "masters". If this one of yours is so wonderful why can't you just phone him and tell him where you are?'

'Because there are no telephones in Underland.'

'Well, what about a sending a letter?'

'We've still got to raise the price of a stamp and a letter from somewhere. Then it would take a few days and my master might not be there to receive it immediately because he's travelling.' A new thought seemed to strike her. 'He might still be looking for me along the border . . . or else he thinks I'm dead.'

'Then we'd better walk to this Brillig place.'

'It's four squares away and there's some dangerous country in between,' Suzanne said. 'The train's safest. Even then it's a full day's trip because it makes a detour round the Slithy Woods. I've heard that's the worst square.'

Alice had become thoughtful. 'Maybe we can take the train.'

'You mean sneak onboard?' Suzanne said. 'It'll be risky.'

'No, I mean get on quite openly.'

'And how do we afford it?'

'We earn the money.'

'But we need to have a master to work for, and once he has us why should he let us go, or pay us anything?' Suzanne pointed out.

Alice grinned. 'No, we just need to seem like we've got a master. What's Gyre like otherwise?'

'Well, pretty busy. As I said, the edge squares are being opened up now the railways are spreading. Why?'

'I've got an idea how we can pay our way and maybe even get some clothes for Juliet.' Alice made a wry face. 'It means having a bit more to do with flowers, I'm afraid. How much do you think we can sell posies and buttonholes for?'

'Flowers, Mistress? Lovely fresh picked today.' 'What about a buttonhole, Master? Let me pop it in for you . . . very smart!' 'You want that one I've got down there? What, with my scent on it? Want to pick it yourself? Naughty, sir . . .'

Pretty naked girlings with buttercup and daisy chains around their heads and necks, and larger blooms apparently sprouting amid their pubic hair and the clefts of their buttocks were obviously a novelty in Gyre. Small posies sold for a penny, buttonholes tuppence, larger posies for thruppence, bunches for sixpence. After consulting with Suzanne, Alice suggested they concentrated on selling to animals, as they appreciated the attentions of girlings even more than the local humans did.

Obviously they had been sent out to make money for their master, but nobody wondered who or where he was amid the bustle of the growing town. Nevertheless, all the time they were on the streets Alice looked out anxiously for any sign of a policeman marching up to tell them they were trading without a licence or something, but nothing of the kind occurred. Nor did they see any rival flower sellers. Presumably human women or slaves gathered flowers at times, but the commercial florist trade did not appear to have come to Gyre yet and they did brisk business.

That afternoon they sold out. With some of the money they bought a little food and a large blanket, then retreated to the spinney outside the town where they arranged branches into a rough shelter. A hollow between tree roots provided a cache for their precious earnings. As they huddled together under it gazing up at the blue twilight, Alice said tiredly, 'Up early tomorrow to pick them while they're fresh.'

'Do we have to sleep out here?' Juliet asked. 'We've got some money now. Can't we stay in a hotel or something?'

'It's going to take us at least a week to earn what we need living cheaply,' Alice explained. 'If we blow it on luxuries it'll take a year.'

'But we only need one set of second-hand clothes and three tickets, and two of those are cheap ones, you said.'

'For the livestock pen in the goods van,' Suzanne murmured.

'But we'll also need to buy proper collars, leashes and cuffs for us,' Alice pointed out.

'You really need to wear all that?' Juliet wondered.

'Yes, otherwise they won't let us onboard. It still comes to less than buying three tickets and two more sets of clothes. Why are you complaining? You'll be travelling in comfort.'

'Won't you mind being locked up like animals?' Juliet asked tentatively.

'You really didn't listen to much of anything in the garden, did you?' Suzanne said. 'We like being treated that way, most of the time, anyway. I mean it makes a big difference who's got the key to your collar, but usually it's a turn-on.'

'I wouldn't do this sort of thing back home,' Alice added, 'but it's natural here. It's part of everyday life.'

'So, you're both masochists, or submissives, or what?' Juliet asked, sounding slightly embarrassed.

'Probably a bit of both,' Alice said. 'Those are Overworld terms. In Underland being a girling includes all of that and also being a slave, a pleasure toy, a working animal . . .'

'Ughh! How can you do that? It means you don't have any choice, any freedom.'

'I'm free if I'm honestly being who I am,' Alice replied.

'But you wanted to get away from Ruddle's garden.'

'Because I didn't want to be a flowergirl for the rest of my life. Also he was too obsessive for my taste and I had enough of that with the Queen of Hearts. If he'd told me about the flower thing and I trusted him, and had time, I might have tried it for a while. Or if he just wanted some S&M he could have kept me around for a day or two and had a bit of fun. A girling expects to get treated like that.'

'You really like pain?'

'As part of being dominated or foreplay, it can be fantastically exciting. Sex is much more intense here.'

'I saw you come a few times in the garden when Ruddle was stimulating fruiting,' Suzanne said to Juliet. 'And what about when the insects took your nectar? Don't pretend that didn't feel good.'

'But I couldn't help myself!' Juliet exclaimed defensively.

'Exactly. You were just following your instincts. Well it's the same for us, for all the girlings down here as far as I know. I just want to be with my master and please him. If it doesn't hurt anybody else, who are you to judge?'

'But how can you like being the slave of an animal better than your old life?'

Suzanne twisted round to face Juliet. 'Shall I tell you about my old life? I left home for a boy I thought was going to be my partner for the rest of my life. But inside a year he'd left me without friends, self-respect or money. I got so low I took an overdose. As I was slipping away I thought I saw a dodo wearing a waistcoat and carrying this big old watch come into my room. He said if I really wanted to give up responsibility for my life then he knew a place where at least I'd be some use to other people. All I had to do was follow him through this door. I knew I must be hallucinating, but I got up and followed him because I had nothing to lose.

'Of course it wasn't an ordinary door and it led here right into a girling trader's house. They flushed the drugs out of me, broke me in and trained me. And gradually I realised I valued myself more as a girling than I had back home being free. I was giving pleasure, I was useful, I felt alive! Martes bought me when I went to auction and I've never been happier.

'Maybe I did die of that overdose or I'm in hospital in a coma and this is all a dream, but I don't want to go back and find out. Life is right for me here and that's all I care about. So don't you dare tell me what I should or should not like, understand?'

And Suzanne turned away from Juliet and cuddled up to Alice, resting her head on her breast. Juliet said nothing else for the rest of the night.

As she drifted off to sleep, Alice wondered how many Underland agents there were roaming her world looking for suitable girling material. And who made those dimension-twisting watches they used?

The next day's trading went even better. They had customers from the day before who came back not just for flowers but for the banter that went with it. Even Juliet, who had been nervous about being naked before so many people, seemed to draw repeat attention. Her shy manner had its own appeal, apparently.

That night, tired but well satisfied, they huddled down in their makeshift shelter once again. Alice felt Suzanne's warm body next to hers and smiled. Then, with lithe grace, Suzanne slid on top of Alice so that their breasts flattened into plump pancakes against each other and kissed her invitingly on the lips. For a second Alice hesitated, then realised there was absolutely no reason why she should not respond and kissed her back with equal passion. Suzanne giggled and slipped her hand between them to where their pubic mounds pressed together.

'Does having feathers make it feel different?' she asked softly.

'I don't know. Why don't we find out?' Alice suggested.

'What are you doing?' exclaimed Juliet.

Alice sighed in exasperation as Suzanne sagged limply over her. 'What do you think we're doing?'

'You're lesbians as well?'

'No, we're girlings,' Suzanne said impatiently. 'I like Alice and I think she likes me, so we're going to have some fun together. Either keep quiet or join in, but don't criticise.'

Juliet rolled over until her back was turned to them.

'Right, where were we?' Suzanne asked.

Alice guided her hand. 'You were about here,' she said.

As Alice lost herself in the uncomplicated, friendly freedom of girling sex, she hoped Juliet would come to terms with realities of life in Underland soon for all their sakes.

Afterwards, lying under the blanket with Suzanne asleep in her arms, Alice thought of Valerie, the lover she had met during her girling training. Valerie had found her perfect master in the shape of Atheling, the Nave of Hearts and apparently the only sane member of his family. Would she ever be as lucky? If she sorted out her current problems, should she try to find out how they were?

She fell asleep trying to plan the journey.

The next day Alice had an unusual customer.

They sold flowers to a few women, but mostly they attracted men and animals. But then a dumpy lady in a white skirt and jacket came up to her. She had a chubby, unlined face with small sharp pale eyes, and was carrying a rolled umbrella and a hatbox that dangled from its string handle.

'And what have you to offer today, girl?' she asked, fixing Alice with an amused stare.

'Pansy posies, bluebells and primroses, Mistress.'

'And how much is that?' the woman asked, pointing to where a bright pink orchid grew impudently from Alice's pudenda.

'Thruppence, Mistress,' Alice said quickly.

The woman dropped the coin into Alice's basket and before Alice could pre-empt her, plucked the bloom from its moist cleft.

'What novel pubic growth you have,' she observed. She raised the orchid to her nose, passing the stem under her nostrils. 'And what a pretty scent as well. It says so much about you.'

And with that she walked briskly away.

That night in their hideaway, as Suzanne kissed Alice and ran her fingers through her hair, she drew back slightly and said, 'I think your feathers are longer than they were yesterday.'

Alice examined herself and frowned. 'You're right, they are.'

'But why are they growing again so suddenly?'

'Maybe it's a delayed reaction to Ruddle's plant food mix,' Alice speculated. 'It took a few days after the whole rejection thing for them to recover. I hoped I'd get this quest finished before they got too bad. If feathers start sticking out of my head people are going to notice.'

Juliet, who had been silent up to now, said, 'I don't know if they have hair gels here, but if you can get some cream or Vaseline, you could slick your hair back, so the feathers won't show as much.'

'It might help,' Alice agreed. 'Thanks. I don't want anything to get in the way now we're doing so well. The sooner we're on that train the closer I am to a cure.'

'Are you sure the Red Queen will keep her promise?' Juliet asked.

'I think a promise counts for a lot here, but I don't see what choice I have,' Alice replied. 'I came to the wrong part of Underland, but it took me a few days to realise it. The first story is full of magic mushrooms and potions, so what happened to me fitted in. But now I can't think of any mention of that sort of thing in the Looking Glass adventure. I was so desperate to get here I didn't think the rest through.'

'But Boardland isn't quite like the book,' Suzanne said. 'What about the Red King becoming Ruddle?'

'I know. If only he wasn't so plant crazy he might have been able to concoct something to cure me. Maybe there's somebody else out there that's into animal potions, but I haven't a clue where to look for them. So I'm stuck with the Queen's offer.'

'Well, I'm glad you came here,' Suzanne said, gently kissing Alice. 'Otherwise I'd still be in Ruddle's garden with a plant growing out of my bum.'

'Me too,' Juliet said. And, shyly, she pecked Alice's cheek.

They were in their hideaway four days later, before the light faded from the sky, when they totalled their money.

'I think we've just got enough,' Alice declared, carefully replacing their modest hoard in its hiding place. 'Right. Tomorrow Julie buys clothes at that cheap shop – not for yourself, remember, but your "master's daughter" who's about your size.'

'I know,' Juliet assured her.

'Don't forget a strip of cloth to bind your tits down. And some flat shoes. You've got to look young and innocent. And also buy travelling food for yourself and us. Meanwhile I'll get the harness items and Sue buys the tickets. We all change in that back alley, then Julie, now looking like a young local girl, takes us to the train and sees us loaded onto the goods van. Remember to write your ticket number on our collar labels. If anybody asks you're taking us to Brillig to be sold. You ride in a carriage and try not to speak to anybody. Bring us some food at lunchtime because we won't be able to feed ourselves. In Brillig collect us from the van and Sue will lead the way to her master's house. All clear?'

'Yes,' they said in chorus.

The three snuggled down together.

'I'm just glad we don't have to pick any more flowers tomorrow morning,' Suzanne said sleepily.

The plan went more smoothly than Alice had dared hope.

Just before the train was due to depart at nine thirty, Juliet, now in a bonnet and pinafore dress and looking quite the part as an Underland girl with her long hair spilling out over her collar, led them into the station. Alice and Suzanne now wore leather collars with labels

123

tied to them, and their hands were cuffed behind their backs and secured with a waist strap. Once again Alice felt herself succumbing to the helpless reassurance being in harness gave her. All she had to do was accept its constrictions and obey the orders of the person holding her leash. What a wonderfully simple life it could be.

Juliet handed over their leashes to the train guard, who led them through the sliding side door of the goods van. Inside, between the stacks of baggage and parcels, was a barred cage with sawdust on its floor, a metal bowl of fresh water in one corner and a bucket in the other. The guard pushed them inside with a pat on their bottoms, clipped their leashes to hooks set low on the wooden rear wall of the cage, stepped out and bolted the door.

Alice and Suzanne sat down with their backs to the wall and waited patiently as girlings learn to do. A few minutes later they heard the clatter of closing doors and then a whistle blowing. There came a distant hiss and chuff of steam and a jerk as the couplings engaged. They looked at each other and grinned. They were heading for Brillig.

After about an hour of steady travel, Alice felt a slight shiver run through her as a blurred wall passed down the length of the goods van. Suzanne said, 'That was the barrier. We're into the next square.'

'That was easy. What's in it?'

'Nothing much that I can remember. Wasteland, a few scattered villages. Just before we reach the far side the railway turns west to avoid the Slithy Woods.'

'You mentioned them before. Why doesn't the line go through them?'

'Apparently it's because of the Toves and Mome Raths that live there. They make so many burrows it would undermine the rails.'

'I suppose that would be a problem. Where does the line go then?'

'It goes west then north again through three squares, stopping at a town called Gimble on the way, then it turns east back into the square beyond the woods. There's a small station there called Wabe, I think, then the next square is Brillig. We should be there by this evening.'

'Great. You're sure your master will put us up?'

'Oh, he's very nice. When he knows how you helped me I know he'll be grateful.'

Alice smiled. 'You really love him?'

'I know he's the only master for me. I belong with him, it's as simple as that.'

'I envy you. I still haven't found where I fit in down here.'

'What'll you do after we get to Brillig?' Suzanne asked.

'Meet with this Sir Rubin and he'll call the Red Queen somehow and then we'll go after the Crown. Have you heard anything about it, or the square north of Brillig?'

'No, I don't think so. Of course we haven't lived there that long. I'm sure my master can find out, if it'll help.'

'Thanks.' Alice frowned. 'I wonder what the time is. I hope Julie doesn't forget to feed us.'

Just then the door leading to the next carriage opened and Juliet appeared.

'Here she is . . .' Suzanne began, then the words died on her lips.

Juliet's face bore an anguished expression. The front of her dress had been ripped open exposing her breasts, and loose binding tape hung about her waist. She was being pushed forward by an angry-looking conductor. Juliet cast them a helpless aside but said nothing as she was hustled past and into the guard's van.

Alice and Suzanne hardly had time to exchange horrified glances when Juliet and the conductor reappeared with the guard now in tow.

'. . . a lady passenger said she recognised her as a girling she had seen on the street only yesterday,' the conductor was explaining rapidly. 'As soon as I challenged her you could see the truth of it, so I brung her through here.'

'I know her,' said the guard. 'She's travelling with those two.' He jerked a thumb at Alice and Suzanne, who were looking on helpless silence, knowing there was nothing they could say or do that would save Juliet now.

The conductor frowned at them for a moment. 'Well, at least they're wearing collars and you can see they're girlings,' he said. 'We'll report them all when we get to Gimble.' He looked back at Juliet, who cringed away from his angry face. 'But she's not going any further looking like that and pretending she's one of us.'

He literally tore the dress off Juliet, who yelped and tried to cover herself in a futile attempt to preserve her temporary return to modesty. The guard laughed at her evident embarrassment, caught hold of her wrists and pulled her arms up high so she could not conceal anything.

'That's better,' said the conductor, looking Juliet up and down appreciatively. 'A clothed girling's not natural.'

'Shall we put her in the cage?'

'Maybe later. First we should teach her a lesson. Got any rope?'

'There's some baggage cord over there.'

They tied Juliet's wrists over one of the exposed iron frames that supported the van's curved roof, so that she had to stand almost on tiptoe. Alice swallowed at the sight of her taut young body. She looked beautiful, frightened and vulnerable, dressed only in her girlish white socks and sandals, which for the moment they had left on her.

The two railway officials also appeared to be assessing Juliet. The conductor pinched her left nipple and pulled it and her full breast out into a stretched cone, making her whimper.

'Are you sorry for what you've done, girl?' he asked sternly.

Alice thought Juliet would protest and beg for mercy, but instead she said tremulously: 'Y . . . yes, Master.'

'You know you've got to be punished?'

'Yes, Master.'

The conductor unbuckled his belt and slipped it loose, then doubled the end around his fist.

The smack of leather against flesh echoed round the van, rising above the regular clickety-clack of the wheels on the tracks. Juliet's shrill cry sounded eerily like a finely modulated train whistle. She twisted wildly under her bound hands, her fingers clawing, her face contorted, tears running down her cheeks, but there was no escape. In numbed silence, Alice and Suzanne watched the conductor methodically apply his improvised strap to her breasts, belly, back, thighs and buttocks, until her torso was shaded in crimson and pink. After a dozen blows Juliet went limp, her head dropped forward so that her chin rested on her chest, her tears dripping onto her trembling scarlet breasts, her softly rounded stomach palpitating, her knees bowed outwards by her boneless collapse.

The conductor pulled her head up by a fistful of her hair and said, 'Now that's what you get for boarding my train out of your proper place, girl!'

He let her head drop again, slipped his belt back on and left the van. The guard had watched Juliet's punishment in appreciative silence and with a growing bulge in his trousers. Now he stepped forward and lifted Juliet's head again.

'We're not quite done with you yet, girl,' he told her with a smile.

He found two more lengths of baggage cord, tied them round her ankles, then pulled them up and outwards. Juliet gasped as the tormented flesh of her bottom and thighs was stretched to its limits. He tied the cords to the iron frame well to each side of her wrists, leaving Juliet hanging doubled over and splayed wide open in midair, her knees almost level with her shoulders, inner thighs taut, her dark pubic triangle split through where her soft pink inner lips gaped wide in enforced invitation. Even the dark little pit of her anus was on display.

The guard grinned at the sight and unbuttoned his flies. Juliet watched him with curious, misty-eyed resignation.

His prong of hard flesh bobbed free and erect, its slot-eye seeking its haven. He cupped his large hands under the tight curves of her buttocks to raise her slightly, then slid himself slowly into her, savouring the spreading of Juliet's lovemouth by his cockhead, the filling of her sheath, the widening of her eyes. He began pumping in and out of her, setting her body swinging from the iron beam like a bell.

Alice gulped, hypnotised, her masochistic side aroused and fascinated by Juliet's ravishment even as she ached for her friend's suffering. It had been her idea – she should be there now, not Juliet. God, she was perverse! She wanted to be there. But like Suzanne, she could only watch helplessly.

The guard was grunting though gritted teeth, his thrusts setting Juliet's heavy breasts jigging. Her eyelids were fluttering and she was making little throaty gasping noises. Suddenly she tensed, for a moment seeming to ride the impaling shaft, using her bonds to lift herself and bear down upon it. Then she convulsed wildly, yelling aloud and throwing her head back.

'Good girl!' Suzanne said under her breath. 'You enjoy yourself!'

Slowly Juliet subsided, oblivious to the pistoning cock which still reamed her insides, shivering and twitching and going limp. The guard spent himself in her with desperate urgency, his breath sounding harsh. After a moment he withdrew his glistening shaft and rebuttoned himself. Brushing down his jacket he grinned at Alice and Suzanne.

'Maybe I'll have you two before we reach Brillig,' he warned them. Then he left through the other door back to his van.

Juliet dangled from the roof frame, her head lolling on her slowly heaving chest, sweat glistening between her breasts. The guard's sperm and her lubrication began to drip from her flushed and pouting labia to the scuffed wooden boards beneath.

'Julie, love, are you all right?' Suzanne called out anxiously.

Flushed, confused, her eyes glazed and dreamy, she raised her head. She blinked and focused on them, slowly returning to reality. Then she gave a little sob.

'Did he hurt you?' Alice asked fearfully.

'No . . . it's not that. I didn't do anything wrong . . . pretending to be a girl, I mean. She knew who I was all along.'

'Who?'

'The one who told on me to the conductor. A woman in white.'

'In white . . . Oh shit!' Alice swore.

'Do you know who she is?' Suzanne asked.

'Yes, it's the –'

Just then he door opened and a large man came in. He had flaxen hair and wore a frock coat that strained across his massive shoulders. He looked about the interior of the van with suspicious eyes, then stood aside. The dumpy woman orchid fancier came in, still carrying her umbrella and hatbox. She smiled serenely at Alice and Suzanne and raised an amused eyebrow at Juliet's suspended body.

The big man turned a crate on its side and she seated herself primly upon it. Before they could speak she raised a warning hand.

'If all you are going to do is protest at my actions, then spare your breath. It must be a disappointment after all your strenuous efforts at raising the funds for your tickets I know, but I really could not allow you to proceed further. That would conflict with my plans.'

'I was going to ask,' said Alice trying to keep her voice level, 'if you keep your crown in that hatbox?'

The woman hesitated, then the smile returned to her lips. 'You are more perceptive than I thought, Alice Brown. Yes, I am Lilian Argentia Canescence Pearl Alabastrine, and I do keep my crown in the box.'

'The White Queen,' Alice said.

'I am also known by that name,' she acknowledged. 'When I realised I could only travel about the Boardland by acting the part of a native, by feeling as they do towards the barriers, I found I could remove my crown. Nonetheless I like to have it close by. Such things are more nearly parts of us than you can imagine. To remove it is almost a denial of what we are, but in war one must make sacrifices.'

'I suppose your spy insects put you onto me.'

'Yes. Magenta was not as successful in eliminating them as she supposed. I knew the route you would take so moved to intercept you.'

'And your bugs also told you where the Crown of Auria is?'

'Naturally. After all these years it will finally be over. I suppose I should thank Magenta for that piece of intelligence.'

Alice looked at Suzanne and Juliet. 'Don't hurt them. I'm the one you want to keep out of the way. They're only with me by chance.'

'A noble gesture, but unfortunately I cannot agree to it. Firstly they might tell others who I am, which could impede my progress as the natives still harbour some resentment for my kind. Secondly, I have need of one of your companions. Ideally I would take you, Alice, and

130

utilise your remarkable ability to pass between worlds to breach the final barrier. Magenta was really quite astute in recognising your potential. Who would have imagined common girlings could be so useful? But she has bound you to her and I really could not trust any control I may exert over you.

'I have spent the last few days in Gyre observing you three, while I waited for Albinous here to join me. Consequently I have decided to take this one, Juliet, I believe she is called.'

Still dangling helplessly from the roof frame, Juliet twisted her head round to stare at the woman who was so calmly appropriating her.

'She may not quite have your power but she is the most malleable,' the White Queen continued. 'I also sense she has only recently arrived in Underland, and so still does not fully belong here. With suitable encouragement I think she can be shaped into the best key to unlock the final barrier.'

Juliet was shaking her head and tugging at her bonds, but the White Queen only smiled at her briefly before returning her gaze to Alice. 'I have spoken to the conductor and a certain sum of money has changed hands. Consequently the railway is pleased for me to take all three of you off their hands, and relieve them of your embarrassing presence. This way by the end of the journey, Juliet will be my girling and you two will be gone, so there will be no awkward report to make.'

'And where will we be?' Suzanne demanded.

'You will shortly be leaving the train. We are passing through a rather desolate spot. Assuming you survive your disembarkation, by the time you reach any significant settlement it will not matter what you do or say because I will have what I desire. Albinous, open the side door and throw these two out.'

'No, you can't!' Juliet screamed, wriggling and tugging at her bonds, 'they might be killed!'

131

The Queen rose, stepped up in front of Juliet's twisting splayed body and jabbed upwards with the tip of her umbrella. With uncanny accuracy the ferrule sunk into the dancing bull's-eye of Juliet's exposed anus, causing her to freeze with a sudden yip of surprise as the shaft of the cold metal spike penetrated her. There came a crackle and tiny blue sparks danced about the stretched ring of muscle. Juliet's eyes and mouth widened into "O's" of horror and her body shivered and twitched as the electric fire coursed through her. A thin high-pitched shriek of pain issued like a siren call from her gaping mouth.

The Queen withdrew the umbrella tip and Juliet sagged, trembling feebly and dizzy from shock.

'If you are to serve me, you should know that I do not permit slaves to speak out of turn,' the Queen said. 'Do you understand?'

Crushed, Juliet could only nod dumbly.

'Good. Continue, Albinous.'

Albinous unlatched the loading door and slid it backwards, letting in a rush of air and whiff of engine smoke. Trees and bushes flashed past. He unbolted the cage, unclipped Alice and Suzanne's leashes and hauled them out. They kicked and struggled, but with their hands still bound behind them they could do nothing to prevent themselves being dragged to the doorway.

Alice gritted her teeth. Whatever happened next, there was one question she had to ask. And at this one moment she might be rewarded by a straight answer. 'Why is this Crown of Auria so important?' she shouted at the Queen. 'The Red Queen just said it was powerful. How? Is it a weapon of some kind? Is it really worth all this?'

An odd light came into the Queen's eyes. 'It changes things, that is all. My kind has great powers, but we cannot alter the way we were made. Why should I live in envy of the beauty of lesser beings? I don't care about the war any more; I simply want to be as perfect as Magenta. Is that such an unreasonable desire?' Her last words bore a hint of defensiveness.

'It depends how many people you hurt to make it come true,' Alice retorted.

But the Queen had turned away, waving her hand dismissively. They had a last glimpse of Juliet's frightened face, then Albinous gave them a shove and they tumbled from the train.

Seven

Alice and Suzanne crashed through a thin screen of bushes, narrowly missing a large oak on the way, and landed on a steep grassy embankment. Down this they tumbled helplessly, hands still bound behind their backs, yelling and gasping with every roll and bump, over and over. Their descent ended amid the rushes and duckweed of a shallow pond into which they plunged. Here they flopped and wriggled about like stranded fish as they gasped for the breath that had been knocked out by their fall and then denied them by the pond water. Finally, bedraggled and smeared with mud and weed, they struggled to the bank and collapsed into limp and trembling heaps. The puffing of the train faded away into the distance and silence returned to the boggy hollow, broken only by the girls' ragged breathing.

When Alice finally steadied her heaving chest long enough to speak, she panted, 'Are you hurt?'

Beside her Suzanne rolled onto her side and spat out some pondweed. 'I don't think anything's broken. You OK?'

'Just a few scratches and bruises, I think. I'm so sorry . . .'

'What for?'

'I got you into this. And Juliet. I'll never forgive myself if something happens to her.'

'You haven't got anything to be sorry about,'

Suzanne said firmly. 'You didn't plan to bump into the White Queen.'

'But we've got to try to get Juliet back.'

'Of course we will, but not because you feel guilty about a bit of bad luck.'

Alice smiled into her friend's mud-streaked face. 'Thanks,' she said simply, and kissed her.

'Ouch!' Suzanne exclaimed. 'Mind the lip, I think its split.'

'I'll take a look at it, but first we'd better get these cuffs off. Good thing I only bought the cheap ones.'

They wriggled around until they were back to back and began working on the securing buckles. Soon Alice got one wrist free and the rest was easy.

When she was loose Suzanne gratefully unclipped her trailing leash and made to throw it and her cuffs away, but Alice said, 'Let's keep them. You never know if they might come in handy, and I don't want to have to sell ten more baskets of flowers to buy another set.'

Leaving their waist straps on, they tied the cuffs to them with their leashes, so they hung over their hips. Then they circled round the pond to find some undisturbed water and washed themselves off. Cool dock leaves were found and pressed to the worst of their scrapes and bruises.

As they performed this minor first aid, Suzanne asked, 'What'll we do now?'

'We head for Brillig as fast as we can,' Alice said determinedly. 'That's where the White Queen's going. It's next door to the crown square.'

'Yeah, but it'll take days to get there following the railway line. By then she might have got this Crown and gone off who knows where, taking Juliet with her.'

Alice had been looking round as Suzanne was speaking. The hollow they had landed in was bounded on one side by the railway embankment and on the other by a thicker line of trees. Rising beyond them was the softly shimmering curtain of an edge barrier.

'What's on the other side of that?' she asked, pointing at the barrier. 'I never know which way I'm looking without a sun to help me.'

'It must be the Slithy Woods square,' Suzanne said. 'The railway curves round to avoid it, remember. They must have thrown us off when we were already heading west.'

'So, as the crow flies, that's the direction we want to go.'

'Yes, but it's supposed to be dangerous.'

'Who says so? Just because it's not right for a railway line doesn't mean we can't walk through it.'

'But what about those odd animals that live there?'

'Well, according to the book, toves were sort of half-lizards-half-badgers with corkscrew snouts who nested under sundials and lived on cheese. Raths were green pigs and borogoves birds with big beaks and long legs, a bit like storks.'

'You really read up on this place, didn't you?' Suzanne said, impressed.

'I was trying to fix the feel of it in my mind. I'm not sure how much it helps, because things have changed so much down here. But they don't sound so bad, do they?'

'No, I guess they don't. OK, we'll give it a go. It might save us a day or so. At least we won't be so far behind.'

Alice was frowning. 'Wait a minute, let me get something straight. The train's going to go through three other populated squares, and stop at Gimble, to get round the Slithy Woods, right?'

'Yes.'

'But if no people live in these Slithy Woods, or not much goes on in it, maybe it's only a small square when you're inside, like Ruddle's garden. If we cross it quickly we might even get to Wabe before the train!'

Suzanne blinked for a moment, then a smile spread across her face. 'You could be right. I sometimes forget how crazy this place is. But if we manage it, how do we get back onboard again?'

'I don't know yet. We'll think of something. But are you on?'

'Of course!'

They set off for the trees at a brisk walk.

The brook running along the line of the barrier cut through the belt of lush greenery in a die-straight line. No details of what lay on the other side were visible through its distortion, but Alice got the impression it was dimmer than on this side.

She looked at Suzanne, who nodded. They took a step back and then leaped across.

They landed on a clearing littered with dry sticks and dead leaves. About them was a darker forest of tall straight trees filled with shadows. Ahead the ground rose in a gentle slope. All was still and silent, with no sign of any exotic wildlife.

'OK,' Alice said, her voice unconsciously lowering, 'I suppose we just keep going straight ahead.'

'I'm right behind you,' Suzanne said with unnecessary emphasis.

They set off along a hollowed path between the exposed tree roots. The bare earth was well worn, as though by the passage of many feet. The tall trees closed around them. As they went they began to notice burrows in the sides of the path and exposed banks of earth. Their numbers increased as they progressed. Alice, who was leading, suddenly felt the ground giving way under her foot and had to skip aside as a section of the path gave way, dropping into a small dark tunnel beneath.

'You can see why they wouldn't want to put the railway through here,' she said with feeling. 'The place is like a Swiss cheese.' She picked up a long stick and prodded the ground before continuing.

They made their way carefully up the low hill. Suzanne tapped Alice's shoulder and pointed to the interlaced branches above them. Several large nests were clearly visible, though they appeared to be empty.

'Maybe they've all died out or left or something?' Alice wondered.

'I don't know,' Suzanne said. 'I've got the feeling we're being watched. Let's get out of here as soon as we can. This place is seriously creepy!'

The trees began to thin and they found themselves on the edge of a clearing at the top of the small hill. In the middle of this grassy lawn was a curious structure which Alice took to be a sort of monument. There was a paved circle ringed about with a dozen oddly arranged pairs of stone blocks. At the centre of the circle was an upright column capped by a flat stone disc. As they got closer Alice saw there was a small triangular upright piece of metal set in the centre of the disc. Suddenly she laughed. 'Well, there's a sundial.'

'I suppose a sundial in a land without a sun makes a kind of mad sense,' Suzanne said. 'But what are these other things for?'

They examined the ring of paired stone blocks. The inner block was a knee-high upright rectangular slab with a shallow convex top with two scallops cut out of its inner face. Below the scallops were some faded dark stains. At the bottom of each side, bolted to the stone was a hinged metal half-cuff, hanging open. The end of the second stone slab butted up against the lower outside face of the upright. It was like a low pedestal, narrower than the upright. On either side of its other end was another pair of open cuffs.

For a moment the arrangement baffled Alice, then she realised how it could be utilised. 'OK, I think I can see what these are for. Maybe we'd better keep going.'

'I think you're right.' Suzanne turned, then grabbed Alice's arm. 'Too late. We've got company.'

Alice looked round. As they had been inspecting the stones a circle of perhaps two dozen animals had silently formed around them.

There were the toves – slim, striped badger heads and front paws merging into reptilian hindquarters and long tails. Some rested on all fours while others stood upright, holding their paws neatly tucked in. Their improbable tapering corkscrewed snouts undulated sinuously as they regarded Alice and Suzanne with their sharp little eyes. Beside them were raths, who were indeed green pigs with large ears and mobile snouts like small elephant trunks, though she could not tell at that moment if they were feeling particularly mome or not. Finally there were the borogoves; shaggy balls of feathers balanced on stalk-like legs with long hooked beaks giving them an air of constipated self-importance.

It was disconcerting to be the focus of so much silent interest. Alice licked her lips and said, in case they could understand, 'Hello. Didn't mean to disturb you. We're just passing through. Um, nice sundial . . . we'll be going, then.'

But as they started to move off the silent crowd closed about them. Alice saw a knowing depth in their eyes. They might not talk, but they could think. Alice and Suzanne were edged back until they stood beside two of the paired stone blocks.

'You know what they want!' Suzanne said nervously.

'What most animals down here seem to want, I guess.'

'Can you think of any way out?'

'We could probably outrun them.'

'But we'd have to get past them first. Have you seen the claws on those badger things? And those beaks look pretty sharp.'

'Then we'd better get it over with,' Alice said resolutely. 'Come on, we're girlings. We're supposed to like this sort of thing.'

'But there's so many of them!' Suzanne's fine white teeth caught over her bottom lip. 'Since I was sold my master's the only one who's ever had me, except Ruddle. Sorry, I'm a bit scared.'

Alice felt equally fearful. These were half animals. Did they know the rules? But she tried to sound assured when she said, 'It's OK. A little fear spices it up, right? Just get yourself warmed up and let it happen.' She made a show of licking her fingers and rubbing them into her cleft. 'Get the juices flowing. Good thing we didn't screw last night. I was feeling a bit horny anyway. Twelve each, maybe, we can handle that.'

Had she managed to convince herself or was her body priming itself regardless? She was not sure, but she could feel her nipples swelling and the familiar slick warm wetness filling her cleft. With two fingers she scooped some of the lubrication out and rubbed it into her anus, just in case. Then, heart thudding, Alice knelt down over the upright stone and straddled the lower slab, so that her legs were parted and calves were pressed against the sides while her ankles lay in the open cuffs. She bent forward so that her chest rested in the hollowed top of the slab and her breasts nestled in the scallops on the other side. Her arms she placed against the sides of the block and her wrists in the invitingly open cuffs. Beside her she saw Suzanne adopting the same position on her blocks, then she looked up expectantly at the animals.

Two toves shuffled purposefully forward, circling round them, their weird snouts rippling curiously, making small snuffling sounds. They reached out with their front paws, which Alice now saw had opposable thumbs, and deftly closed the cuffs about their wrists and ankles. Suzanne gave a little whimper and Alice instinctively tugged at the cuffs but she was firmly secured. No going back now, she thought.

Now the borogoves stepped up, strutting importantly. They subjected both girls to a beady-eyed examination, but seemed to find Alice particularly interesting. The cream she had been using to slick back her hair for the last few days had been mostly washed out by her dunking in the pond. Now her feathers were pushing out clear of her scalp, forming a golden halo over her head and beginning to smother her remaining hair. The borogoves investigated this growth with their beaks, delicately picking at the feathers. Alice winced at their touch, horribly aware of the sharpness of their hooked tips, but they did not hurt her. It was rather like being meticulously combed.

'I think they're preening me,' she said nervously.

'That's good, isn't it?' Suzanne replied. 'Maybe they think you're a distant cousin or something.'

The borogoves stepped back, apparently satisfied with their work, and stood in front of their prisoners for a moment with their heads tilted back as though lost in thought. Then one of the birds right in front of Alice swayed forward on its ridiculous legs, stabbed down with its beak and jabbed her painfully in her right breast.

Alice's yelp of pain mingled with that of Suzanne who had suffered the same sudden assault from a bird standing before her. Before Alice could recover, another beak jabbed down, then another. The two girls were gasping and squealing in chorus as their breasts were systematically pecked, punching tiny neat triangular holes in their soft flesh. Some of the deeper pricks oozed blood and a few trickles ran down their breasts and over their perversely erect nipples, adding their stains to those left by who knew how many suffering girlings before them.

Alice managed to gather herself enough to gasp through her tears: 'Please don't ... eek ... do that! What do you ... ahh ... want us ... ahww to do? Uhh ... you can ... ugh ... have us ... oww.'

And they both wiggled their out-thrust backsides in desperate invitation.

The pecking stopped. Almost immediately Alice felt a moist blunt-ended snout snuffling between her legs and investigating the ripe fig of her pubes and the cleft of her buttocks. Despite the stinging pain in her breasts she had to stifle a giggle. It tickled! Twisting her head round she saw Suzanne also had a rath admirer. It was probing her intimate parts while standing on the slab that parted her legs and ducking its head. Alice groaned and licked her lips. The snout was getting playful.

Suddenly it was withdrawn and a potbelly bore down on her buttocks and trotters scraped along either side of her ribs. The rath was mounting her by standing on its hind legs on the slab. A hard pizzle was jabbed two or three times into her crotch before finding its goal in her anus, which it forced its way into and began to sodomise with rapid thrusts. Beside her Suzanne was gasping under a similar assault. Alice wailed as the pumping shaft up her rear drove the breath out of her, even as she was infused with a wonderful sense of utter perverse delight. She was being buggered by a green pig!

All too soon it came inside Alice, and with a few reflex thrusts its weight was lifted from her. But she had no time to recover before a tove had taken its place on the slab between her legs, its sinuous snout worming its way into her pouting vagina. And in and in. How far could it go? Then its snout began to twirl and corkscrew within her and she cried out aloud as her hot wet clenching passage was bored out. She orgasmed wildly and it eagerly licked and slobbered up her outpourings. It withdrew and another rath took its place.

After that her impressions became vague as she surrendered to pure sensation. She recalled Suzanne coming with a wild-eyed yell as another rath used her rear. She was brought back from post orgasmic swoons by warning pecks on her breasts from the borogoves. She recalled peeing helplessly when the pleasure of her next orgasm became too great to maintain control, but eventually all this dissolved into a relay of mobile wickedly pleasurable snouts and thrusting pizzles, sharp beaks, and herself at their mercy coming again and again . . .

An unknown period of time later, Alice became aware of Suzanne helping her to her feet. Her legs felt stiff and useless and her crotch was one big reamed-out dull pulsing ache, dribbling sperm and intimate juices from both orifices. But her mind was still high with the afterglow of half a dozen orgasms and she didn't care.

She looked around her with bleary eyes, but the clearing was deserted. 'Where . . . have they gone?' she asked stupidly.

'I don't know. When they finished with us they undid the cuffs and wandered off. We'd better get out of here before they change their minds and come back for seconds.'

An odd insight struck Alice as she staggered along rubber-legged beside Suzanne. 'They won't bother us again,' she said with conviction.

'Why not?'

'Because we've paid our toll, haven't we? This place is a short cut, but the locals make sure you know who's in charge, and you have to give them something they want for the privilege of using it.'

'Couldn't they have charged sixpence like anybody else?'

'Then we wouldn't have been able to pay, would we? It's lucky we've got something that's always welcome . . . like a good credit card.'

For a moment Suzanne stared at her in confusion, then she began to laugh and Alice joined her.

They tottered down the far side of the small hill and through the dark wood until they reached the next brook. They did not jump it but waded across through the barrier and sat on the other bank, shielded by a screen of rushes from whatever lay beyond, washing themselves off and scooping cooling water into their sore groins. Their labia and anal rings were scarlet with the vigorous use they had undergone. As they tended them, Suzanne said, 'You're amazing, you know that?'

Alice frowned. 'What do you mean?'

'I think a few of those raths had seconds with you. I always thought I liked sex, but you must have come six or seven times.'

Alice shrugged. 'I know I turn into a pretty hot slut when I get forced into it. That's my sub-masochist side coming out. I can't help it.'

'But the rest of the time you look so . . . well, fresh and innocent.'

'Butter wouldn't melt between my legs, sort of thing?' she said with a grin.

'Not quite. A little naughty, perhaps, just starting out, one careful boyfriend, etcet.'

'That was me a few months ago. A lot's happened since then. But I think you came a few times as well, and you don't exactly look like an old slag.'

Suzanne grinned. 'Only after I let myself go like you said.'

'You OK with what happened?' Alice asked gently. 'You know we had to do it.'

'Like you said, we're girlings, we expect that sort of thing. I'll be fine . . . but I'll be glad to get back to my master. He's the only animal I want to screw me ever again.'

'I envy you,' Alice said simply.

Suzanne broke the silence that followed by saying briskly, 'Anyway, I'm glad we won't ever have a "Who Can Come Most" competition, because you'd beat me hands down.'

Alice blinked and shook her head to clear it. ' "Beat"? Did they screw our minds too? We were taking a shortcut to beat the train. How long were we in there?'

Suzanne suddenly looked anxious. 'I've no idea. We'd better get going.'

Beyond the brook were fields and meadows populated by ordinary-looking sheep and cows, all peacefully grazing. They ran through them until they came to a lane where a helpful signpost pointed the way to Wabe. There was no time to find props to explain their presence so they hurried along it, trusting they would be taken as local girlings if anybody saw them. After a mile or so they found the lane dipping down into a shallow valley along which ran the railway line, passing through the outskirts of Wabe itself. On the opposite side of the line was the station platform with its green board awning, waiting room and booking office, while on the near side was a small cottage whose woodwork was painted in the same green. A neat walled garden extended out from the back and in it they could make out a figure digging over a small vegetable plot. He was in shirtsleeves but had on a blue peaked cap.

Alice and Suzanne ducked down behind a hedge.

'If he's the stationmaster or porter or something, he ought to know if the Brillig train's been through,' Alice said.

'But we can't just walk up and ask him,' Suzanne pointed out. 'And even if we're in time, how do we get back on the train with him around? And if we do, what's to stop them throwing us off again if they catch us? The Queen bribed them, so they're not going to admit to what happened, are they, not to keep a couple of girlings happy.'

Alice frowned thoughtfully. 'Maybe we can get him to help us.'

'How?'

'By telling him most of the truth and making as much fuss as possible, so that he has to confront the Queen when the train stops here. I mean even though we're only girlings she shouldn't have had us pushed off the train. That has to count as cruelty to pets, or something.'

'And then?'

'Then we threaten to tell everybody her real name if she doesn't hand Juliet over. That should shake her up a bit.'

'But who'll take our word against hers?'

'We tell them to look in her hatbox. Who else carries a crown around with them? If we get away with it we ask to be taken on to Brillig. I mean we did pay for the tickets and we'll all travel in the cage if they want. When we get there we contact your master and hope he'll help.'

Suzanne looked doubtful. 'I suppose it's the only chance we've got.'

'Can you think of anything better?'

'No.'

'Right. First let's get these cuffs back on. We should look as helpless as possible to start with . . .'

Five minutes later they stood at the back gate of the cottage calling out plaintively to its tenant: 'Master! Please help us.'

The man in the peaked cap left his gardening and came over. He was of large, squarish build and had a light grey beard. His eyes were pale and his expression as he walked up to them was of mild surprise.

'Now what's this? I don't recognise the pair of you.' His eyes narrowed as he took in Alice's feathers. 'I'm sure I'd recall one like you.'

'No, Master,' Alice said quickly, 'we're not local. Something terrible has happened to us. But please, are you the stationmaster and has the train to Brillig passed through yet?'

He touched the badge on his cap. 'I'm Deputy Stationmaster Hoar and –' he consulted the watch hanging on his waistcoat chain '– the Brillig train's not due for another hour and a half. But what would it be to you?'

Alice and Suzanne exchanged relieved glances, and Alice said, 'Thank you, Master. You see we were on that train, but we fell off.'

'And we've had a terrible time getting here, Master,' Suzanne added. 'We had to go through the Slithy Woods and look what they did to us ...' and she pushed her perky breasts out so he could see the mottled peck marks that adorned them.

'Fell off the train? Slithy Woods?' Hoar scratched his beard in agitation. 'Maybe you'd better come in and tell me about it.' He opened the gate and they trotted in.

Hoar led them through his back door into a small but neat kitchen, warmed by a black-leaded range set into one wall.

'Are you thirsty?' he asked.

'Yes, Master,' they replied.

He filled a bowl of water and put it down on the floor where they knelt over it and lapped away gratefully. Alice appreciated his consideration and did not for a moment resent being treated as one might a stray dog. What more could a girling expect, after all? Hoar opened a tin and offered them a biscuit each, which they neatly took from his hand, tipping back their heads as they ate to help them go down, as one learned to do with cuffed hands. How simple to live like this at knee level, Alice thought. To be a favourite pet – playful, obedient and loyal, and occasionally pampered as a reward.

Alice shivered, reminding herself where she was. She had a job to do.

Hoar sat down at the table and Alice and Suzanne quickly knelt before him, resting back on their heels with their knees submissively wide.

'Now tell me what's been going on with the pair of you,' he said.

Alice took a deep breath. Hoar seemed kindly enough so she would risk telling him most of the truth.

'There were three of us on the train, Master; Suzanne here, myself, I'm Alice, and Juliet. Suzanne belongs to a merchant in Brillig, but she got lost on a trip to the edge squares and is trying to get back to him. Juliet and myself are new to Underland and don't belong to anybody. We got to Gyre and earned money selling flowers to buy our tickets to Brillig. Sue and I travelled in the goods van, but because we had to have somebody to mind us, Juliet dressed as an ordinary girl. She travelled in a carriage. It didn't hurt anybody and we did pay for our tickets. See, we still have the numbers on our labels.'

Hoar examined the now stained pieces of card and nodded.

Alice continued. 'Everything was fine until a woman who we had sold flowers to recognised Juliet and told the conductor. But instead of just putting us all in the goods van, the woman bribed him to let her take Juliet as her slave. Thinking we might tell, she then had us thrown off the train! Please, you mustn't let her get away with it. I'm frightened what she might do to Juliet.'

Hoar scowled as she concluded her tale, scratching his beard. 'Well, you shouldn't have done what you did, but neither should this woman have bribed members of the railway staff. That's a serious offence. And there's certainly no cause to throw pretty things like yourselves off a train. It's such a waste, not to speak of the trouble it might cause if you landed on somebody. This will have to be looked into.' He looked at them both sternly. 'You know the penalty if you're lying?'

'Yes, Master. It's all true, Master. We can prove it.'

'Well, I'll have to talk to this woman for a start. Do you know her name?'

Alice hesitated. 'I don't know if she's using her real

name because it's very long. She might be using something shorter.'

'Well, what might that be?' Hoar demanded.

'Um, Lilian Alabastrine, maybe . . .'

She trailed off because of the expression on Hoar's face. He had gone deathly pale as a look of horrified disbelief spread across it.

'Oh . . . no,' he grated. 'Not her, not here! Not after all this time . . .'

Alice scrambled to her feet and lunged forward. Before Hoar could stop her she grasped his cap between her teeth and pulled it off his head. Beneath, nestling on his silver-grey curls, was a platinum crown.

'Not another one of you!' Alice said in dismay.

The White King looked shrunken and much older as he tried to explain. As he spoke he fiddled with his cap, as though unsure whether he should put it on again.

'I loved her the way she was,' he said bleakly. 'But she was never truly happy. She threw herself into the campaigns as a distraction, I think. What a strategist she was, what a warrior! But then the Boardland changed and stories of the Crown began to spread. It was a powerful thing, too much for the natives to handle. But we were different. We knew it had to be a means to break the stalemate; the last gambit of the last game. But as soon as Lilian heard of it she had a different idea. She became obsessed with tracking it down, however long it took. And so I lost her. Eventually I just left. Well, what was the point in remaining in play? The rules had changed. Nobody needed me any more. But I couldn't go back home alone, without wife or army. So I took to living amongst the natives. It has its rewards. I like the simple regularity of trains, you know. Something you can count on. And the only battles to fight now are over first or third class tickets and lost luggage.'

'But you still can't take your crown off,' Suzanne pointed out.

'Oh, I will . . . someday. I mean there's no rush, is there?'

'As long as your wife doesn't recognise you as she comes through here about an hour from now,' Alice pointed out.

'No, she mustn't!' the King wailed. 'I'm sorry for what she did to you, but I can't help.'

'All right,' Alice said. 'You won't face up to her, but can you at least get us back on the train so we have a chance to rescue our friend?'

'But what good will it do?' he said. 'They're bound to recognise you before you can save her.'

'When's the next train for Brillig?'

'Not for two days.'

'We can't wait that long,' Suzanne said. 'There must be some way of disguising us.'

The King scratched his beard. 'Well, I suppose you could travel parcel post. Nobody would see your faces then.'

'What?' Suzanne exclaimed.

'It's just started. It only operates for live packages over short distances, of course. In fact there are three girlings parcelled up for Brillig in the baggage room.'

'Perhaps you could show us the way?' Alice asked politely.

They peered in at the little baggage room. Amongst the other goods, propped up against the wall like brown paper mummies were three girl-shaped parcels neatly tied up with string. She could see their chests slowly rising and falling as they waited with enforced patience. They had labels tied round their necks that declared they were bound for POPERT AND PELUS PROMOTIONS, FRUMENTY STREET, BRILLIG.

Only in Underland! Alice thought. Yet it had its own mad logic and there had to be worse ways to travel.

'Right, you wrap us up and address us to Suzanne's master, and we won't tell anybody who you really are,' Alice said to Hoar briskly. 'Agreed?'

'Unfortunately this service is only for goods to be collected from the station,' he explained. 'It'll be no help to be left in the parcel office because your master doesn't know you're there.'

'Can you add us to the order for Popert and Pelus?' Suzanne wondered. 'At least that way we'd get collected.'

'Yes, I could do that,' Hoar agreed.

'Do you know anything about these people?' Alice asked Suzanne.

'No. Maybe they're also new. Though Brillig is quite a large town, so I might not have heard of them.'

'I suppose as soon as they unwrap us you can give them your master's name,' Alice said. 'No reason why they shouldn't send for him.'

'I think it's our best chance,' Suzanne said.

Alice took a deep breath. 'Right. Find some brown paper and string, Your Ex-Highness. You've got two girlings to wrap.'

Until she was completely cocooned, Alice did not realise how perversely exciting being turned into a parcel would feel. The King cut a small hole for her nose so she could breathe, but otherwise she was completely enclosed.

Her arms were confined to her sides, held in place by several turns of string binding that steadily moulded the sturdy, crackling paper to the contours of her body as it was looped and tied around her. Ankles, knees, hips and wrists, waist and elbows, diagonally across her chest between her breasts, loosely about her neck, firmly over her mouth and then, changing direction, under her chin and across the top of her head. Then she was rolled onto her front and longitudinal cords were run down her back threading through the circling bindings and around her feet. Rolled over onto her back again, they were run up her front in the same way to tie to her neck loop. But even as she was constricted she was also supported. She had wondered how the other three girlings had stood so straight; now she understood the way the paper and bindings combined to brace her almost rigid. It was an absurd waste of time and string, but deeply exciting. She had entered the realm of total helplessness once again, but this time with a thin paper skin between her and the unseen outside world.

Alice felt the heavier string handles being tied through the other loops. Then she was lifted off the table. So well was she bound that she only bent slightly in the middle. The renegade King propped her up against the wall and went away to start wrapping Suzanne. Curiously Alice felt no urge to try to speak, even if her bindings would have allowed it. Very strange. Were her senses expanding or contracting? She was a parcel without desire. Her label said it all. She awaited handling.

A little later Suzanne was propped up beside her. She felt the warmth of her body penetrating her cocoon.

'The train's due soon,' the King whispered to them. 'Good luck to you . . . and don't blame Lilian too much for what she's done.'

Then all was quiet and incredibly peaceful.

At some point the train must have come, because Alice remembered being carried into the goods van and being placed in a rack with the other girls. Ropes were strung across their chests and knees to hold them in place. A hand briefly squeezed her breasts through their brown paper wrappings and then vanished. She had no idea if Juliet was in the cage only a few feet from her, but her strange new circumstances seemed to have induced both extraordinary patience and fatalism. She would find Juliet when she reached Brillig and not before. Meanwhile there was nothing she could do about it.

There followed a couple of hours of gentle swaying motion, ending in the clank and bustle of a larger station. She was unloaded with the rest into an unseen room with the other baggage. Soon she became aware of a conversation between faceless voices:

'I was told there'd be three of them.'

'Well, there's five here. Are you complaining?'

'No. They can sort it out. They need as many as they can get anyway.'

'Going to be a good show, is it?'

'One of their best. Got your tickets yet?'

She was picked up and loaded into a cart with the others, enjoying an intense tactile sensation at being carried over a man's shoulder like a roll of carpet. Had Cleopatra got high like this? Was she wet enough for it to soak through the wrapping over her groin? How embarrassing. The cart rattled through the streets until it turned into some sort of yard. Another little high as she was hauled off to be stacked with the others, warm flesh in brown paper.

There came a man's voice, tantalisingly familiar. 'He said he'd send us three, not five.'

'Has he charged for five?' said another voice that she also thought she should know.

'No.'

'Well, it's his loss, then. Let's get them undone.'

The sound of ripping paper came nearer, then a knife cut the string about her head and fingers tore the wrapping away. She blinked in the sudden light. Two faces were peering at her, one from up high, the other low.

'Alice Brown!'

It was Topper and Lepus.

Eight

'You caused us a lot of trouble back home, girl!' the March Hare said once again. 'After your escape the Queen never forgave us for bringing you to Underland. As news of her disfavour spread our customers deserted us. Together with scares about the revolution your friends were planning, it made it impossible to keep trading as girling brokers.'

'But I was never really part of the revolution, Master, it was all a mistake . . . aah!'

Lepus had flicked the small cane he carried across the smooth swell of her stomach, causing her to flinch painfully.

'As a consequence we had no choice but to move here,' Lepus continued, uninterested in hearing her excuses. 'It's not been easy building new reputations, you know.'

'I'm sorry, Master,' Alice replied contritely. At least it explained why the pair were now living in Boardland under assumed anagrams.

'You will be,' he said.

Alice shivered. 'Yes, Master.'

His whiskers bristled and his snout wrinkled into a frown as he peered more closely at the cowl of feathers where Alice's hair had been. Then he reached out a small but perfectly formed hand and plucked at her pubic down. 'Where did you get these from?'

'It's a long story, Master,' Alice began. 'You see I . . . uhh!'

Lepus had switched her again. 'Then save it for another time,' he said.

Alice wanted to ask what had happened to the White Rabbit who used to work for them, how the revolution was progressing and if her friend and one-time lover, Valerie, was safe. But now was clearly not the best time, so she merely said, 'Yes, Master.'

The premises of Popert and Pelus Promotions appeared to be a converted warehouse. A rack of hutch-like cages along one wall housed a good two dozen girlings. Beside them were deep shelves stacked with crates, tins of paint, jars of nails, bolts of cloth and canvas, and coils of rope and chain. In addition there were racks of assorted timber and three workbenches. Off-cuts of fabric, sawdust and wood chippings littered the paint-splattered floor and several large unidentifiable objects lurked under dustsheets. The general impression was of a place of considerable activity that had just finished work for the evening, but Alice had no idea what it was all for. What did 'promoters' actually do anyway?

After her recent experiences she supposed she should not be surprised at running into Topper and Lepus again. The laws of chance in Underland, as with so much else, clearly did not operate rationally. Meeting two runaway kings within days of each other was proof of that. Actually, she now recalled, her fictional counterpart also met them in the book, though in very different circumstances. And had not the Hatter and Hare also made brief appearances under slightly different names? She shivered. Was every event in Underland shaped by words written over a century ago?

Alice and Suzanne, who had been identified as the other girling superfluous to order, stood with their arms stretched above them and wrists manacled to long chains dangling from roof beams. Topper – tall, powerful and surprisingly handsome despite his prominent nose – paced about, frowning at Alice in between sharp low-toned exchanges with Lepus. Alice caught a few words.

'. . . and I tell you she's bad luck . . .' Lepus was saying.

'But we're well away from all that now,' Topper countered. 'We can make good use of her.'

The only hopeful sign was that, after Suzanne had given her master's name, they had sent a messenger to inform him of her return. Suzanne leaned towards Alice and whispered, 'They don't seem very pleased to see you, do they? When my master comes I'll tell him about you. I'm sure he'll offer to take you off their hands if they don't ask too much. You haven't cost them anything, so they should be pleased to get rid of you at any price.'

'Thanks, but I don't think those two will see it that simply. Because of me they were hauled up before Queen Redheart's court and had their reputations trashed. I think they might want a bit of revenge first before they think of selling me.'

'I'm sorry.'

'I'll survive.'

A small door set into the larger double service doors opened and a new figure was ushered in. At the sight of him Suzanne called out excitedly, 'Master!'

The newcomer ran over to Suzanne who twisted round in her chains, arching her back and parting her knees as though trying to kneel before him.

'There you are at last, girl!' he exclaimed with feeling, patting and stroking her affectionately. 'I thought I'd lost you for good!'

Martes was, as Suzanne had said, a pine marten and evidently well to do. He wore a black top hat and well-cut tailcoat, a short waistcoat, white shirt and bow tie. Like other sentient Underland animals his snout and keen black eyes displayed that peculiar degree of mobility and expressiveness that set them above their common kindred. In addition he had a distinctly commanding and assured manner, and though he only came up to Suzanne's nipples, there was no doubt about who was the master.

Topper and Lepus came over to the happy pair. 'Good evening, sir, I am Mr Pelus,' Lepus said, 'and this is my partner, Mr Popert. I'm glad to see you received our message, and I take it this is indeed your girling?'

'Of course she's mine,' Martes said impatiently. 'I can produce my ownership documents if you doubt me.'

'Not at all,' Topper said quickly. 'Clearly she belongs to you. Now there is just the small matter of stabling, transportation costs –'

Martes cut him short. 'I posted a reward of ten pounds for her safe return.' He took out a wallet and unfolded a large, elaborately engraved banknote. 'I understand she has only just come into your possession, so I should imagine that will be adequate compensation for any slight expense you have incurred.'

He's no fool, Alice thought. She saw Suzanne looking at her master in starry-eyed gratitude, and realised that ten pounds was a lot of money here. He really did care for her.

'Most generous of you, sir,' Topper said, taking the note. From the faint look of surprise on his face Alice suspected he had been planning to ask for less.

'Now release her,' Martes said.

The cuffs were unfastened. Immediately Suzanne went down on her hands and knees and kissed Martes's sturdily clawed feet. He patted her bowed head. 'Good girl. Now chin up. See, I remembered to bring your favourite leash.'

Suzanne lifted her head and he clipped a leash of braided red leather to her collar ring. 'Now let's get you home,' he said.

She leaned forward and whispered urgently to her master, glancing at Alice as she did so. After a moment, Martes looked round at Alice, then Topper and Lepus. He took out his wallet again. 'I understand this girling is also recently arrived and you have no legal claim to her. I will pay you five pounds for her.'

Alice's heart lifted momentarily and she smiled her thanks at Suzanne. Then she saw Topper's expression set.

'I'm afraid the girl is not for sale,' he said. 'Besides which we do have an old claim on her and, like your good self, we can produce the declaration she signed of her own free will. She escaped from our care after we spent considerable time and money training her, so I believe our moral right is inarguable.'

Martes looked regretfully at Suzanne and put away his wallet. 'You will permit my girling to say goodbye to her?' he asked.

'As you will,' said Topper.

Suzanne embraced Alice and kissed her on the lips.

'Don't worry about me,' Alice said. 'You look out for Juliet and the White Queen. There's a good chance they're still around here somewhere.'

'I will. And I'll try to see you again.'

'Bye.' Suzanne kissed her once more, then was led away by Martes.

Alice watched them go. She was pleased for Suzanne. How such bonds formed between beings so different she could not explain, but clearly they belonged together. Lepus's next words brought her back down to earth.

'Now, how should we punish this ungrateful girling?' he wondered aloud.

'Wait a minute,' Topper said thoughtfully. 'She might be more use to us unmarked. She does look most distinctive now, you must admit.'

'What of it?'

'We still need a special feature for the big event. She might provide it.'

'How do you mean?'

Topper smiled mischievously at Alice then drew Lepus aside and they talked together for a couple of minutes. When they turned back to her, Lepus looked amused.

'You're lucky, girl,' he said. 'We have something in mind that requires you to be presented before the public at your best. This limits the severity of the punishment we may inflict. However, you shall not escape without a token of our displeasure to cherish. A ride on our pogo-pricker is called for.'

From the racks at the back of the chamber, they brought out a curious device that did indeed look a little like a pogo stick. It consisted of a stout rod about waist high, crossed at right angles by two hinged and spring-loaded arms close to its bottom end. On the ends of these arms were what appeared to be combination ankle cuffs and stirrups. On the upper end of the vertical rod were mounted twin phalluses ringed by integral prongs. Just below them was an array of thinner upward curving springy metal arms, on the ends of which were spiked wheels, each free to rotate. Linking rods connected them to the lower pair of sprung arms.

With Alice still suspended they cranked the winch that controlled her chain, lifting her a little higher. Then they pulled her legs apart and slid the twin phalluses up into her vagina and anus, plugging her tightly. Placing her feet in the stirrups they secured them with the ankle cuffs.

Suddenly letting go of Alice she wobbled and swayed, pulling on her manacled wrists while trying to balance on the lower end of the pogo rod, which was capped by a rubber ferrule, even as its forked upper ends impaled her. As she did so she discovered painfully the function of the spiked wheels. As she twisted about, pushing down with her left or right feet, the motion was transmitted through the connecting rods to the upper set of arms, which caused the wheels to run their spikes up and down the tender inner flesh of her thighs, around the heavy undercurves of her buttocks and even the feathered pout of her pubes. After a minute of gasps and whimpers she managed to find her balance, controlling her swaying and thereby reducing the spiked wheels at least to static points of pain.

Of course they did not permit her to remain like that. Bringing out broad rubber paddles, Topper and Lepus gave her a thorough smacking, working methodically across her breasts and stomach, back and bottom, front and back thighs. Her flesh shivered as it took on a bright rosy hue. Alice cried and yelped as she swayed and twirled about on her cruel mount.

The relentless pricking of the rolling spikes, the plunging and sucking of the twin phalluses and the stinging of her abused flesh had its inevitable effect. After what she had been through in the Slithy Wood earlier that day she would not have believed her body could still respond so readily, but somehow it did. She felt the excitement bubbling up from her loins and surrendered herself to its rising tide.

Alice came loudly, appreciating as she did so the irony of the situation. She was chained and helpless, suffering pain and pleasure at the hands of Topper and Lepus. After a long and very strange journey she was right back where she started when she had first come to Underland.

Topper rested his arm, admiring Alice's helpless writhings and the discomfort she was inflicting on herself. 'At least you haven't lost your taste for this sort of treatment, girl,' he said with a smile.

'We said when we first imprinted you that you'd never forget it,' Lepus reminded her.

Toper found a gag and stuffed it into Alice's mouth. 'You'll stay like that till morning,' he told her. 'And tomorrow you'll tell us how pleased you are to be serving us once again.'

They left the big room through a back door, dimming the lights as they went. As Alice balanced precariously on the pogo-pricker, she could hear a few whispered conversations from the girling hutches, but soon they faded away. How she envied them their comfortable beds of straw. She thought of Suzanne, who even now might be happily chained to some even grander bed while her master reasserted his dominance over her.

Hours dragged by. A few times she actually dozed off as tiredness overcame her, only to jerk awake as she shifted her position and set the spiked wheels moving once again. She felt her inner muscles clutching and squeezing at the phalluses she was mounted upon as though by reflex. Was it perhaps no longer possible for her to have anything pushed up her front or rear passages without wanting to feel it moving inside her, whatever the consequences?

Slowly, marvelling at her own perversity, she stimulated herself bit by bit with little wiggles of her hips until the inevitable happened. This time her spasms were accompanied by a stream of urine as her full bladder, already compressed by the phalluses stuffed within her, could no longer be contained. Naturally the gag-stifled outpourings of her orgasm dramatically upset her balance and began the cycle once again. It was a long night.

Stiff and aching, Alice was woken from the depths of utter satiated exhaustion by a few brisk slaps from Topper. It was morning and the other girlings were already being taken out of their hutches. Alice was ungagged and the pogo-pricker unbuckled and pulled out it of its now red and sticky twin sheaths. The chain was lowered and Alice slumped to the floor, her legs incapable of supporting her, while her arms were numb and useless. Nevertheless she was made to squirm on her belly over the floor, still wet with her own pee, and kiss Topper and Lepus's feet.

'This poor girling begs forgiveness for all the trouble she has caused you, Masters,' she said, thrilled by her sense of humiliation even as she spoke the shameful words. 'Please make use of me in any way you wish.'

She was fed with the other girlings, chained by the collar to a long trough into which food was tipped, which they ate without using their hands. It reminded her of being fed in Topper and Lepus's house at the start of her first visit to Underland. The food had been provided by the Dormouse, she recalled. She hoped he had not come to Brillig as well, as he'd been a mean-minded and spiteful creature.

After breakfast the other girlings were assigned their tasks, and Alice realised they were not merely pleasure slaves but labourers. Under the supervision of Topper and Lepus, together with a couple of other animals, they were soon hard at work cutting fabric, painting canvas and measuring wood. It was a strange sight to see half a dozen naked girls industriously hammering nails or sawing timber, some chained to their workbenches. She suspected this was one workforce that would never contemplate going on strike.

Alice was given a much more demeaning task, which she suspected was a continuation of her punishment.

The first part was easy. It soon grew warm in the big shed and as the girls were working hard they soon began to sweat. Alice was fitted with a hobble chain and given a large can of water and a tin cup, which she was to take round to give to any girls who needed it.

The second part was less pleasant. In one corner was a raised tiled plinth into which were set six squat toilet holes with buckets underneath them. At certain fixed break times the girls were allowed to use this simple facility to relieve themselves. Of course all this took place in plain sight of anybody else in the workshop, but then girlings did not expect privacy. This was different from the old arrangement Alice recalled where each hutch had a toilet bucket, or else the Dormouse had gone round with a can and a funnel into which they could pee. But then they only had half a dozen or so girls in training at any one time. This way was no doubt more practical.

But since girlings often had their arms secured by harnesses, they could not clean themselves afterwards, and even if their hands were free they had been ordered not to attempt to wipe themselves. It was, Alice knew, another way of increasing their dependency on others. However it meant somebody had to wipe their bottoms like babies, and that task now fell to her. She stood on the floor behind the toilet plinth watching the squatting girls and, as each finished, made sure she was clean and dry.

Alice soon decided, in an attempt to be philosophical, that there were worse things in life than rubbing a wad of tissue paper into moist plump pubic mounds or tightly puckered bumholes set between smooth soft rear cheeks. This and her water-carrying duties also enabled her to snatch a few moments' gossip with the girls as she worked. She had wondered about the odd assortment of items they were making and where the cart, which shuttled in and out of the yard beyond the big double doors, took them when each was completed. Piece by piece she found out what was going on.

In two days' time, Topper and Lepus, alias Popert and Pelus, were putting on a big event in Brillig's Central Hall featuring commercial displays and stalls of girling-related merchandise. There would also be various novelty girling contests, but its concluding event, and star attraction, would be a boxing match between the lion and the unicorn to determine the supreme champion of all Boardland. The 'Fight of the Century' they were calling it. Of course, Alice thought as she heard this, she was caught up in a twisted version of the Looking Glass story again. They were re-enacting the battle that went with the old nursery rhyme about the lion and the unicorn fighting round the town. But presumably it would be a more serious affair than it had been portrayed in the book.

She also tried pumping the girls for any information about events back in Redheart country, but they knew little apart from vague rumours about unrest. One girl did pass on something she had overheard Topper and Lepus discussing. They had mentioned a friend called 'Ory' whom they had learned from a traveller had been officially denounced as a ringleader in the continuing underground movement to overthrow Queen Redheart.

This startled Alice. The Latin for rabbit was oryctolagus cuniculus, from which was derived 'Ory', the White Rabbit's Underland nickname. But how had such a timid, and often drunken, animal become mixed up in the revolution? What had got into him?

In a frantic last minute flurry, which involved several girlings' bottoms being tanned to encourage them to work faster, the preparations were completed in time. As the tired workers, who would also perform in the great event, snatched a few hours' sleep, Alice was bathed and groomed for her role. Seeing herself in a mirror for the first time in weeks she had to admit she looked striking.

Golden feathers had entirely replaced her hair now, even down to her eyebrows. A crest swept back from her forehead in a smooth graduation from the smallest and finest to the largest and thickest, which hung down over her shoulders. Her pubic feathers had also thickened into a fluffy delta, and a line of them was growing up towards her navel. In addition a small triangle of feathers had appeared on her sternum just above the divide of her cleavage. Slowly but surely, superficially at least, her bird transformation was re-establishing itself.

It was not uncomfortable, but it did not feel right to her, even in Underland where it was merely a curiosity.

She had feathers while she flew as a bird, which had seemed perfectly natural to her adjusted instincts, and it was almost trivial in comparison to what Ruddle had done, but she was a girl now and wanted to stay that way. However, for the time being she would have to accept her hybrid form. And it was true that it had tempered Topper and Lepus's revenge, which she supposed was something to be grateful for.

As the morning of the great fight dawned, Alice was locked into a new collar, ball gag and cuffs all made of gold, or at least some golden-seeming metal. Then she was loaded into a cart and taken off to the Central Hall.

Though she had been there for three days, it was her first chance to see Brillig properly. As the cart trundled along wide streets flanked by three- and four-storey buildings with tall roofs, some half-timbered and others of brick, she realised it was more like a small city and by far the largest settlement she had yet seen in Underland. There was a sense of energy about the place and it bustled with life. No wonder Topper and Lepus had come here. Where there were people there was money to be made.

The Central Hall was a grand affair with a fine portico entrance guarded by tall columns. There were people already queuing to get in, but the cart went round the back and Alice was led in through a rear door. Inside the main hall was bustling, and Alice could see how all the signs, banners, screens and display podia made in the workshop had been put to use. Mingling with the crowd were girlings from the workshop now prettily chained and handing out leaflets, or else decoratively on display mounted on the walls between the hanging banners.

Topper and Lepus, both now wearing top hats and dressed in smart suits, took turns leading Alice round to greet people and show her off. As many eyes looked her over with varying degrees of approval and desire she felt her nipples pricking up in excitement and helpless anticipation, though of what she had no idea.

'Yes, she is unusual, isn't she?' her masters said in response to several enquiries. 'But then originality is the hallmark of all Popert and Pelus promotions. I do hope you enjoy yourself . . .'

There were many stalls ranged about the sides of the hall, whose products all in some way related to girlings.

Alice was led past an apothecary selling what he called 'Girling love philtres', which he demonstrated on his captive girls. Within a minute of being made to swallow the drug, one girling was squirming with lust, which she only relieved by masturbating herself frantically on a large floor-mounted dildo, much to the onlookers' amusement. A second girl, strapped spread-eagled to a frame and unable to touch herself, got so aroused and frustrated that she began pleading with the crowd to put her out of her misery. All it took was a few strokes from her master for her to orgasm, producing a remarkable quantity of lubrication, which almost sprayed out of her.

The love philtres reminded Alice of the special cakes Topper and Lepus had used on their girls, except these seemed much more potent. She examined the stall hopefully for any sign that the apothecary dabbled in metamorphic potions, but saw none. If any existed this would be the place to find them. It looked as though the Red Queen's offer was still the best she had, but how was she to rendezvous with her or Sir Rubin now?

There was a harness shop stall, exhibiting numerous ingenious means of restraining and controlling girlings. Half a dozen female bodies stood, lay or hung within tight webs of leather, chain and rope. Next to it was a furniture maker of corrective devices such as stocks and racks. An unfortunate girling was strapped to a chair supposedly designed to 'stretch her orifices for deeper penetration'. The seat was cut away under her crotch, and through this gap large wooden screw plugs could be inserted. Her gag-muffled cries were already quite loud and the plugs were not yet halfway in. A whip maker had racks of different implements designed to inflict various degrees of pain close to or from a distance. A girling had been strung out on a frame for demonstration purposes. A liberal number of blushing stripes and blotches already patterned her body and her eyes were moist with tears. What would she be like by the end of the day, Alice wondered? Then came an agricultural equipment manufacturer selling girling ploughs, yokes and other devices. There was a carriage maker displaying a beautiful team of six girlings in full harness with plumes on the headbands. A pet shop was selling girling-sized baskets and bowls. For a consideration an artist could paint a portrait of your favourite pet. Training courses were available to teach discipline and unusual tricks. The more wealthy owners could purchase girling body jewellery from a specialist supplier. A very beautiful olive-skinned girl with the most soulful eyes Alice had seen was on display within a slowly rotating cage. She had been pierced through her ears, nose, lips, nipples, navel and labia with jewelled rings, which then supported hanging baubles or fine chains linking them together. Some owners were having pets they had brought with them fitted on the spot, and their brief shrieks and whimpers of pain rose above the background hubbub.

After a while Alice noticed the smell of warm flesh and female arousal seemed to permeate the hall. How could all this be for girlings, supposedly the lowest creatures in Underland? Was it an inversion of values according to the crazy logic of the place, or was there actually a rational explanation? Perhaps humans here were inhibited from keeping non-sentient animals as pets while rubbing shoulders with their larger talking and thinking cousins, so girlings were a logical substitute. And sentient animals kept girlings because, as she had discovered during her first adventure, for some mysterious reason there were no female animals so naturally the males wanted some release for their sexual urges. But underlying all that, there was always the desire to control and dominate others, common to a greater or lesser degree in most beings. Girlings, specially selected for their submissiveness, were admirably suited to fill such positions.

The centre of the hall was given over to something resembling a large stepped trading pit, on the floor of which a raised platform very much like a conventional boxing ring had been erected. In the middle of the ring was a large colourfully painted wooden disc, mounted on a frame that was in turn suspended by chains from one of the heavy ceiling beams. The face of the disc had straps and buckles bolted to it laid out in a large 'X'.

Although it was still some hours until the fight, the lion and unicorn were already in the ring to promote the bout. They were limbering up, shadow boxing, talking to admirers and even signing autographs. Half expecting something close to the illustrations in the book, Alice found them instead very impressive. They were both big, powerful animals, as large as the local adult humans. Both walked on their hind legs, of course, and had human-shaped hands. They wore loose silk gowns and boxing shorts, the lion in red and the unicorn in blue, which might have made them seem ridiculous but somehow did not. In fact they looked like serious fighters. Nobody would dare drum them out of town, as in the rhyme.

Topper and Lepus led Alice up a flight of wooden steps and into the ring. The lion and unicorn broke off from their glad-handing to take up positions on either side of the promoters. Somebody rang a bell until silence descended on the hall and all eyes turned to Topper.

Raising his hat, Topper bowed to the assembly. 'Ladies and gentlemen, Popert and Pelus Promotions welcomes you to the Fight of the Century!'

There was an enthusiastic cheer. Topper continued, his powerful voice filling the hall. 'May I present to you, the champion of West Boardland, Panthera "Leo" Leonus!'

The lion stepped forward and raised his huge arms above his head to tumultuous applause.

'And the champion of East Boardland, Equus "Spike" Monoclonius!'

The unicorn received his accolade in turn.

'Remember,' Topper said as the noise died down, 'the fight is due to start at five o'clock, ticket holders only. Novelty events begin one hour earlier. But in the meantime we thought we would show you, and our contestants, the prize purse.' He drew out a heavy leather pouch from his pocket and shook it so that everybody could hear it clink. 'One hundred sovereigns!' he boomed. 'And in addition, the winner will receive this rare golden birdgirling slave!' He pulled on Alice's leash, jerking her forward so everybody could see her. 'But where should we put the money and the girling for safekeeping?' he asked rhetorically. 'Gold with gold, perhaps?'

As he spoke, helpers freed Alice's hands only to push her back against the wooden disc and strap her to it, arms and legs spread wide, with thicker bands going round her neck, waist and knees, so she was firmly secured. With a smile Topper turned to her.

'Will you hold this for us, girl?' he asked, but of course Alice could only grunt helplessly from behind her gag.

'Oh dear,' he said, winking at the audience, 'she doesn't seem to have any pockets. Perhaps if we look at the problem from another angle ...'

Grasping the wheel, he gave it a heave, sending it spinning round and round. Alice groaned as the world tumbled dizzily about her. Suddenly the wheel stopped with Alice hanging upside-down, her breasts bouncing and swaying to rest almost brushing her chin. Topper poked an exploratory finger between Alice's widespread legs.

'Ah, now here's a little pink purse we can use, hiding amongst these feathers. But I think its mouth is a little narrow. Mr Pelus, if you please . . .'

Lepus had a large glass funnel ready. As Topper pried Alice's vagina open, he thrust the spout into her, a ring on its upper rim hanging over a small hook screwed into the disc between her thighs to hold it in place. Alice shivered as her inner sheath was exposed to the open air. No, surely they weren't going to . . .

But Topper was already tipping the golden shower of coins into the funnel, through which the watching crowd could see them pouring into Alice's gaping passage, now serving yet another function it had never been intended for. As the onlookers loudly applauded, Alice gasped and bit on her gag as the rich cold metal filled her, its weight making her passage bulge unnaturally and press on her inner organs. There was no room for the last few coins inside her, which clogged the funnel spout. But apparently they had anticipated this problem and Lepus handed Topper a small ramrod, the clothball end of which he pushed down into the funnel, forcing Alice's sheath to stretch wider so as to accommodate the remaining coins. Alice shrieked and slobbered round her gag, tears pricking her eyes as the mass of tight-packed coins expanded within her under Topper's ramming.

At last all one hundred coins had been forced inside their hot wet living pouch and the funnel was withdrawn, now filmed with her juices. Her pudendum was swollen with riches and the wet pink cleft between her feathers literally brimmed with gold.

'Now our little cuntpurse is full we must make sure it doesn't spill open,' Topper said, pinching together her elastic inner labia to seal in the treasure. In his other hand he held up a solid-looking padlock. 'Our thanks to Messrs Corvus and Pica for kindly donating this patent self-piercing fleshlock. '

Alice's eyes widened in horror.

There came the snap of a released spring and Alice felt a hot–cold stabbing sensation as the sharply pointed tip of the curving bolt passed through her tender sex lips and clicked home. Her wail of pain was stifled by her gag as a few drops of blood welled up from between her stapled flesh leaves.

They spun the disc, turning Alice right way up again, bringing forth a renewed mew of pain as the weight of coins within her stretched her cruelly sealed lovemouth. Topper was holding up a small key. 'The winner shall receive this key, to unlock all that is within and without!' he announced.

Chains rattled and the disc was hauled up into the air until Alice dangled high over the ring, her pain and humiliation displayed for all to see. And there she would remain until the winner of the great fight claimed her as his own.

Nine

The disc hung tipped forward slightly, so Alice could gaze down on the people in the hall as she rotated slowly in the air. In turn of course they could stare up at her and her bulging pubes and the dangling padlock that locked her up tight as a chastity belt would. Look, up in the sky – a bird stuffed with gold!

As always, pain and humiliation was now giving way to excitement. The weight of the coins was pressing on her clitoris from the inside, and she hoped her pubic feathers concealed its erection. It did mean that the few drops of blood her piercing had spilt were now mingling with the juices of her arousal. With a shameful blush she actually saw a couple of them fall to the ring and just hoped nobody else noticed.

Below her the pre-fight showmanship continued. She watched the contestants taking turns sparring lightly with a few amateur hopefuls. Only in Underland could a fight between two great heraldic beasts be reduced to a contest between 'Leo' and 'Spike', she thought. And by the end of the day she would belong to one or the other of them. Alice shuddered in her tight straps at the thought of those powerful beasts mounting her. Maybe it was good that her vagina was being pre-stretched.

Lifting her eyes she determinedly went back to watching the crowd, hoping Martes might have brought Suzanne along to see her. But in the crush she might easily miss them . . .

She blinked, seeing a familiar face, but not the one she sought.

The White Queen was staring up at her with a mixture of bafflement and anger. Alice could not see Juliet anywhere. Could she have escaped somehow, or was she merely being kept secure out of sight? But Albinous very visibly loomed by the Queen's side, also scowling.

The humour of the situation suddenly struck Alice. She could not tell on them and they could do nothing to her on public show as she was. In mutual frustration they were reduced to staring mutely at each other. If only she had been ungagged she would have stuck her tongue out. As it was she tried to convey the impression she was smirking. Perhaps she succeeded, for after a few moments more the Queen turned her back on Alice and melted away into the crowd.

But why was the Queen still in Brillig? She had arrived three days ago. Surely that was ample time to make any preparations she needed before continuing on to the crown square, and she would certainly not delay without good reason. It could only mean she was waiting for somebody else to join her party. How many other pieces did she still have on the board? Alice wondered. And what did she expect to face in the final square that required more than her own power and Albinous's brawn to handle?

By mid afternoon, as the traders' business slackened off and seats about the ring began to fill, the novelty girling contests began. Under Alice's dangling body naked girls battled each other in boxing matches with overstuffed gloves, or else wrestled singly or in teams. Blindfold girls were sent out against each other with their hands tied behind their backs and rubber phalluses strapped to their waists, the idea being to get under their opponent's phallus and penetrate her first. Girls of slighter build

173

rode piggyback on more muscular girlings and fought against each other in mock jousts with short padded lances. Hits were recorded by ink soaked into the lance tips which left highly coloured stains on their opponent's body. A pursuit race was staged around the outside of the large ring with girlings hobbled and chained so that they could only move on their hands and knees. Each had a rod strapped to her head on the end of which was a phallus, and the idea was to chase round the ring until one girl got close enough to push it up the other's bottom. Bets were made on all these contests, of course, and the crowd vigorously booed or cheered the girlings along according to preference.

When the novelty fights were over there was an intermission while the exhibitors closed up their stalls and the audience changed over. As the light filtering through the tall windows began to dim lamps were lit. Alice was briefly let down, given a drink of water and allowed to pee into a bucket, which she needed to do badly. The sensation of her water having to force its way through her urethra squeezed by her gold-packed vagina, and thereby further stimulating her clitoris, did nothing to reduce her state of simmering arousal. As the serious fans and aficionados began taking their seats, she was hoisted aloft once more. The moment to decide who was champion of all Boardland had finally come.

Spike and Leonus (Alice could not think of such a magnificent beast as 'Leo') entered the ring, both looking sober and thoughtful, raising their arms to acknowledge the applause, but no longer playing up to it as they had earlier in the day. Alice could feel the tension building. This was going to be a genuine fight, she thought.

Topper himself was the referee and announced the rules.

'This shall be a contest of unlimited rounds each of five minutes' duration,' he said. 'The winner shall be determined either by a knockout, or by one of the contestants yielding to the other and withdrawing. A knockout shall be declared if one contestant remains down for a count of ten while the other is standing within the marked area.' He indicated a circle painted in the middle of the ring. He turned to the contestants. 'I want a clean fight, break when you're told. Back to your corners and wait for the bell, then come out fighting.'

The two animals touched gloves, then stepped back. A hush fell over the hall. Suddenly it felt to Alice that, though she was suspended above them naked and in full view, her hair turned to feathers and cunt stuffed with gold, she had become invisible. The attention of everybody in the hall was fixed on the two fighters. Then a fleeting eye contact with a tall man in one of the back rows spoiled her grand generalisation. Why was he alone looking at her so intently? And then the bell rang and she lost sight of him behind waving arms.

For a minute the pair circled round sizing each other up. Then Alice winced as the first punches were thrown, driven piston-like by rippling biceps to the accompaniment of cheers and shouts from the audience. Half a dozen rapid blows were traded and blocked, then the two seemed to dance apart with remarkable agility for such large beasts. She would have thought Spike's equine jaw would have made an easy target, but his long neck held it up and back. To strike it Leonus would have to get dangerously close.

A medley of grunts and thuds reverberated round the hall as they closed in again and got down to the serious business of the contest. Their great bodies trembled with the impacts. Alice doubted an ordinary human boxer would have lasted two minutes in the ring with either of them. But somehow they absorbed that ferocious energy and gave as good as they got.

The first round ended with neither looking as though they had yet inflicted any serious injury on the other. A minute's rest in the corner, a wipe with a sponge, a drink of water and then they came out again to resume their brutal business.

As the clamour of the audience grew louder a voice inside Alice's head was reminding her that she did not approve of boxing. But she hardly heard it. She could not tear her eyes away from the two figures circling below her trading pile-driver punches. Was she learning to appreciate the elegance of ringcraft? Possibly the raw primal energy of it had touched her. Or perhaps her new-found fascination stemmed from the fact that she was part of the prize they were fighting for.

By the sixth round both contestants were bleeding from minor cuts and were clearly beginning to tire. But neither looked as though he wanted to give up. Why were they doing this to each other? Alice wondered. For the applause, the celebrity, to own Alice or even more likely the gold stuffed inside her, or simply the desire to prove he was the best? She might never know.

By round fifteen Spike and Leonus were clearly exhausted and their fancy footwork had given way to the shuffling of leaden limbs. They were being sustained by will-power alone now, locked into a grinding exchange of ever-wilder punches to see who would last the longest. The crowd had shouted themselves into a ragged chorus that echoed the fighters' weariness, and yet like them would not cease until it was over.

Alice alone, from her unique vantagepoint, saw exactly how it ended. But she never told anybody.

There was a small circle of wet splash marks about the centre of the ring that had dribbled over the hours from her excited and tormented cleft. As Spike lunged forward trying to land a haymaker punch his foot skidded slightly on her spilt juices, throwing him off balance for a split second. By pure reflex Leonus's left arm jabbed out and caught Spike on his exposed jaw. The strength seemed to go from Spike's neck, he took one half step backwards and then toppled like a felled tree, hitting the canvas with a booming thump that shook the hall.

The crowd sprang to their feet as one, roaring in excitement.

Leonus was swaying dangerously, looking as though he might join his opponent at any moment. But somehow he kept upright and tottered into the marked circle and stayed there until Spike was counted out.

The ring dissolved into a tumult as aids and supporters of both sides swarmed over it. Leonus's gloves were removed, he was towelled down, had his back slapped and hands shaken and a laurel wreath was thrown over his shoulders. Spike was revived and sportingly congratulated Leonus, who in turn held his opponent's arm aloft as the crowd cheered again.

Only when a space was finally cleared was Alice lowered from the ceiling. As she was released from the disc a leash was clipped to her collar and her hands cuffed behind her back. Feeling as rubber-legged as the boxers after her long suspension and weighed down by the gold crammed inside her, she was led over to Leonus and made to kneel before him. Topper handed the boxer the key to her fleshlock.

'It gives me great pleasure to declare you, Panthera "Leo" Leonus, the Heavyweight Boxing Champion of all Boardland!' he announced. 'Please accept this girling and all she holds!'

Then Leonus was swept away to the celebrations and Alice as his prize was carried along in his wake.

As they passed through a narrow gap in the cheering crowd, Alice caught another fleeting glimpse of the only man in the room with eyes for her alone, who held himself aloof and apart from all the wild excitement about him.

Who was he?

* * *

It was much later that Alice knelt in the best suite Brillig's finest hotel could provide. For the first time in hours she and her new master, with whom she had yet to exchange a single word, were alone.

Leonus, washed and bathed and now relaxing in a chair, delicately held a glass of wine in one large hand. Somehow she had expected a boxer should only drink beer or lager, but he seemed content with his choice.

He surveyed her through tired, half-closed eyes. 'So, bird-girl. What a day, eh? How does it feel to belong to the Champion of all Boardland?' He sipped some more wine. Even in low tones his voice held a deep resonance, though he was better spoken than she had expected. 'Do you have a name? They never told me.' He snapped his fingers. 'Come here.'

Alice obeyed as quickly and gracefully as her inner burden permitted and knelt at his feet, gazing transfixed into his slightly anthropomorphised leonine visage. She could read the play of subtle expressions into it, but there was still enough of a wild animal there to make her shiver. Even freshly bathed there was an exciting muskiness about him, and she had witnessed ample demonstration of his brute strength in the ring. In addition when he yawned it revealed the glint of huge canines. Leonus was naked, or at least as naked as a furred animal could ever be, and Alice's eyes flickered down to the thick tangle of long ruddy hair between his thighs and what it only partly concealed. Yes, it was right that she should kneel small and low before such intense male power. No wonder a warm wetness was flowing about her plug of coins and leaving its incriminating mark on the thick rug.

He reached out and pulled the gag from her mouth. Gratefully Alice licked her stretched lips. 'Thank you, Master,' she said.

'So, what's your name, girling?'

'Alice Brown, Master.'

He raised a large brow. 'An "Alice", eh? I have heard interesting tales of girlings going by that name . . . most interesting.' His eyelids drooped for a moment, then he shook himself and took another sip of wine. 'And what did you think of my fight, Alice?'

Entirely truthfully Alice said, 'It was one of the most exciting things I've ever seen, Master.'

Leonus chuckled heartily. 'It was good, wasn't it? A few times I thought Spike had me. Fine fellow, Spike, and a good sportsman, but I had the beating of him – in the end.' His head nodded slowly forward.

Fearful he should fall asleep, Alice said, 'Master, please can you take your prize money out of me?'

'What? Oh, the purse in your cunny. Uncomfortable, is it? Suppose it must be . . . where's that damned key? I put it down here somewhere . . . ahh. Come closer . . .'

Alice stood with her legs spread wide before him. Leonus clasped the padlock that hung from her inner labia.

'A clever little bauble,' he observed. 'Perhaps I'll clip your leash to it in future.'

Alice gulped. 'Whatever you wish, Master.'

He turned the key and Alice winced as the curved bolt slid out through her tender newly pierced flesh. Her lovemouth bowed wide as her stretched lips drew back and then seemed to vomit forth a shower of coins. Alice shuddered with relief as the golden waterfall poured out, clinking and jangling onto the floor between her feet.

'Now there's a rare sight,' Leonus said admiringly, as the fall became a dribble of slippery golden discs. 'Is that all of them?'

Alice sighed. 'I think there are a few more, Master.'

Leonus slipped a large finger into the dark hole of her loosely gaping vagina and hooked the last of his prize money out of its living purse. Alice trembled, literally feeling lighter now she had been emptied out, yet also aware of the void the coins had left within her.

Her lion master sniffed his finger which was wet from her secretions. 'You've a pleasant scent, Alice.' He reached out and his big hand with its claw-tipped fingers stroked her face, running down to envelop and squeeze her breast. 'I think I'm going to enjoy having you.'

Alice could see his penis stirring and rising from his pubic mane. His genitals were more manlike than leonine, and were proportionate with the rest of his physique. And in turn she was responding to him. She had been in a state of arousal all day and had not come since her night spent impaled on the pogo-pricker. For a healthy girling that was an age of deprivation.

'May I go to the bathroom to prepare myself, Master?' she asked with anxious eagerness. 'I won't be long.'

He unfastened her cuffs and patted her bottom to send her on her way.

The bathroom was a grand affair; all marble tiles and polished pipework. Apparently Boardland rewarded its sporting heroes very well. Alice quickly used the toilet, ran a basin of hot water, found soap and a flannel and wiped herself down. She would have liked the luxury of a proper bath, but she did not want to keep her new master waiting. Or herself, for that matter. On the shelf above the basin, amid an array of oils and bath salts provided by the hotel, was a pot labelled 'Girling Grease' with a self-explanatory illustration. Alice gratefully applied some to her anus. If Leonus chose to use her that way she would need all the lubrication she could get to accommodate him.

A rogue thought briefly passed through her mind to the effect that what she was actually doing was preparing for her possible sodomy by a lion-man to whom she had been arbitrarily given as a slave only hours earlier. It was obscene, perverted, chauvinistic madness! How could she possibly surrender to it?

The phantom flicker of outrage melted away as Alice grinned at herself in the bathroom mirror. This was

Underland. What else did she expect? Besides, he was the hottest-looking lion she'd ever met. She reviewed that last thought and saw a look of wonder grow in her reflection. Could he be the one?

She came out of the bathroom to find Leonus sprawled on the suite's big four-poster bed. Quickly she ran over and knelt attentively by its side. He was idly examining an array of girling restraints and a selection of short canes and lashes laid out on the bedspread.

'See this, girl?' he said with an amused rumble. 'A gift from that harness shop that had its stand in the Hall. They want to use my name to promote their wares.' He looked at her thoughtfully. 'It is said that all new girlings should have a good beating to let them know who their master is. Do I need to beat you, Alice?'

Alice felt her heart skip a beat. She opened her mouth intending to give the safe response: If you wish, Master; but somehow it came out as, 'I'd enjoy that, Master.' She clapped her hand to her mouth but it was too late. Her heart had spoken.

Leonus looked at her in mild surprise. 'Is it like that with you?'

There was no denying it now. Feeling as though she was stepping off a precipice, she said, 'Yes, Master. In the right hands, or even the wrong ones sometimes, I can't help getting turned on by pain and humiliation, especially if they're mixed with sex.'

He smiled. 'Then shall I be strict with you, Alice?'

'May I speak freely, Master?'

'Go on.'

'Be as strict as you like with me, Master, as long as you're also kind and fair, which I think you are. I'll suffer happily if I know it pleases you . . . and you care for what I'm feeling in return.' It felt as though she was baring her soul so she went all the way. 'I need to belong to somebody . . . and I hope it's you.'

181

The lion regarded her thoughtfully and she sensed a keen mind within that great head. 'Never have I heard such bold words from a girling,' he mused. 'Popert and Pelus boasted you were unique. Perhaps they were right.' He picked up a cane from the selection and handed it to Alice. 'It would hurt if I used this on you. What do you say?'

Alice carefully kissed the cane and handed it back to him. 'Use it on me, Master. My bottom is yours to do with as you want. Mark me as your own property.'

Leonus nodded. 'Bend over the bed, then . . .'

Alice yelped as he caned her, burying her face in the covers to muffle the sound, her knuckles white as her fists bunched up the cloth. The hiss of the cane through the air and the crisp fleshy cracks that followed filled the room. But as sharp as they were she knew it was only a fraction of the force he might have used. The thought of what he could do to her fired her loins, complementing the heat of her buttocks.

When a dozen stripes ran across her once pale hemispheres he lowered his arm and lifted her head, looking into her sparkling eyes. 'I've made you cry.'

'But I'm not sad, Master,' Alice said, smiling through her tears. 'Did you enjoy marking me?'

He cupped the hot trembling scarlet flesh cheeks in his palm and stroked them gently. 'Your pretty little bottom jumped about in a most lively fashion and your submission gave it an extra spice. Yes, I enjoyed caning you.'

'Then I'm happy, Master. How may I serve you next?'

He smiled. 'Begin by fastening those chains to the bedposts, you little trollop!'

She lay spreadeagled on the bed, limbs stretched out to its four corners. Leonus knelt between her widely parted thighs, the thick pole of his erection standing out from his pubic mane.

'Can you accommodate me?' he asked her.

Alice licked her lips. 'If I can't then stretch me until I do, Master. I want you all the way inside me.'

'If it hurts, you can cry out.'

'Gag me if you like, Master.'

'No, this once I think I'll let anybody hear who cares to listen. They must expect a bit of noise from a room where a man is enjoying a lively new girling. Besides, I have a reputation to uphold.'

He bent forward, the bed creaking under his weight. His great maned head loomed over her as he took up position. She felt the head of his penis pressing into her slick and eager cleft and gazed up at him with helpless longing. The hot weight of his body descended upon her. He bared his teeth in a fearsome smile, then unexpectedly lowered his head and nuzzled his snout against her mouth. In return she kissed his bifurcated lips, and whispered, 'Now, Master, please!'

He thrust with his hips and penetrated her. A choking shriek escaped Alice as his shaft filled her to the limit and beyond, testing the pliancy of her passage and forcing it to accept the entirety of its new master. So tightly was she plugged that as he withdrew for a second lunge she felt her insides being sucked after him. Then she cried again as he filled her anew. It was both frightening and wonderful, and though she was almost being crushed under his grinding weight it was the most exciting thing she had ever known. She wriggled and squirmed her small body under him as far as his bulk and her bonds allowed, offering up her total submission to her new master. By the time he began to pump his seed into her hot depths she was already lost in the throes of her own orgasm. Her wild and incoherent cries of joy were only stifled by the furry bulk of his chest as he slumped on top of her, forcing her to turn her head to one side to breathe.

So she lay imprisoned under him for a time, his weight pressing her into an Alice-shaped indentation in the soft bed. She bore the burden happily, conscious of no discomfort.

When he finally stirred she passionately kissed the fur of his huge chest and shoulder, softly murmuring, 'Thank you, Master.'

He shifted his bulk downwards slightly, withdrawing his now flaccid member from the grip of her soaking quim, and smiled down at her. 'You are a lusty little thing, aren't you?' he said.

'I hope I pleased you, Master.'

'You know you did. Is it natural with you or training?'

'A bit of both, I think, Master.'

He stroked her fan of feathers. 'And these. Were you born with them? Are there others like you?'

Alice sighed. 'It's a long story, Master.'

Leonus turned to rest on one elbow. With his free hand he toyed with her sweat-hot breasts and inflamed nipples. 'I have no pressing plans, and certainly you are going nowhere.'

Alice squirmed happily under his manipulations. 'Well, Master, it all began when I met a White Rabbit . . .'

He stopped her only once at her first mention of the Red Queen. He said: 'A Carnelian, a chessplayer, are you sure?'

'It's the name she gave, Master, and she certainly seemed to fit the part.'

'All right. Go on.'

When she had brought her tale up to date Leonus brooded in silence for a minute, then said slowly, 'The Red Queen expected you to meet her agent in this square, correct?'

'Yes, Master.'

'But if I keep you from that rendezvous, her plans will be frustrated, yes?'

'I should think so, Master.'

'Good!' he said with feeling.

'Master?'

His face was grave. 'You would not know this, but my kind have special reason to hate the chessplayers, even above the general populace. When the wars were at their height they ruled all Boardland and none dared stand before them. In between their battles they enjoyed certain sports, amongst them hunting. As so-called 'Royal Beasts', my kindred were their favoured prey. Do you wonder that I hate them?'

Alice felt sickened. 'No, Master. I'm so sorry. I didn't know anything about that.'

'I know you didn't, girl,' he assured her, ruffling her feathers affectionately. 'You've been making your own way as best you could, and doing it well. But you will be the Carnelian's tool no longer. Tomorrow we'll look for the White Queen, if she's still in Brillig, and if possible recover your friend. Then . . . well, we'll see. But if I finally rid Boardland of those gameplayers, I'll count it a sweeter victory than ever I won in the ring today!'

Alice awoke in the small hours to the sound of a heavy blow striking home. She felt the impact transmitted through Leonus's body, which lay half on top of her. She heard him moan and jerk as though to rise, then came another thud and he collapsed back to the bed. In the dim glow of the night lamp she saw a shadowy hooded figure looming over the bed holding a club aloft. She opened her mouth to scream, only to have a wad of cloth forced into it. Leonus's limp body was heaved off her and hands began to unsnap her chains. She flailed about, trying to kick at the shadowy intruder, but a heavy cuff across the side of her head stunned her. By the time she had recovered herself her arms and legs were bound tightly by the chains and she was helpless.

A hood was pulled over her head and tied about her neck. Strong hands picked her up and she was thrown over a large shoulder. As a wriggling bundle she was carried out of the room along a deserted corridor and down two flights of stairs, where another door opened onto the outside air. She was tossed over the back of a horse, her kidnapper then mounted behind her and, with a clatter of hooves, Alice was spirited away into the night.

Ten

The nightmare ride into the unknown seemed endless to Alice, though it could not have actually lasted much more than a couple of hours. Her discomfort and fear for herself was tempered by the terrible memory of her abduction. The sickening thuds as the shadowy figure hit Leonus again and again rang through her mind. Was Leonus all right? Was he even alive? It was not fair to be taken from him so soon!

Finally the horse was reined in and her kidnapper dismounted. He lifted Alice down and laid her on her side on damp earth, where she felt a warm breeze playing over her naked body. Her hood was stripped off and the cloth gag pulled from between her numbed dry lips. Blinking in the bright light of day she saw the stately trees of an Underland wood about her, while not one but two horses were peacefully cropping the grass nearby.

Alice moaned in fear and rage, rolling onto her back as she strained at her bonds. A large man clad in scarlet knight's armour was standing over her. The long peaked visor of his helmet was raised, revealing a square-jawed face, a prow of a nose and hard, penetrating eyes. She had seen those eyes before somewhere . . .

Then she knew who he was. He was the man in the hall: Sir Rubin the Red Knight and Queen's agent, whom she should have met in a wood outside Brillig. This very wood?

He was scowling down at her. 'Why have you taken so long to get here, pawn?' he said sharply. 'I can sense Her Majesty's impatience even from this distance, and do not wish it to become anger!'

But Alice was not listening. 'You bastard! Why did you have to hit him so hard? He might be dead!'

Sir Rubin looked genuinely baffled by her outburst. 'The lion? What of it? I had to get you out of his clutches and that was the easiest way. You should be grateful.'

'Grateful? I liked him! He was kind to me.'

The Knight's eyes narrowed suspiciously. 'Is your brain addled, pawn? Is it those feathers, for you certainly have more now than I was given to expect? You have the marks of a fresh beating on your rump. Did that animal not do that?'

'I asked for it! And I loved everything else he did to me!'

His lips wrinkled in displeasure. 'I believe you are some kind of animal lover. I didn't expect much from a girling, but I allowed that you might have no choice in who you served. But you actually boast of your pleasure with that creature! You disgust me.'

'And you're just a bigot! I know what your lot did here. They're people, can't you see that?'

Sir Rubin reached down, grasped her by the shoulders and lifted her upright. 'It does not matter what you like or not, girling pawn,' he said grimly. 'You have a function to serve in a noble cause. Now I must send the signal so that her Majesty can begin her move.'

He unclipped the chains still fastened to her ankle cuffs, freeing her legs, then dragged her across to where a fallen tree lay picturesquely in a small clearing. Bending her over it so that her breasts pressed into the rough bark, he kicked her legs wide and took up position behind her. Alice heard a strap being unbuckled and a rustle of cloth.

'Did he use your front passage?' Rubin asked in a tone that did not invite a response. 'It looks raw. How could you have enjoyed that? Then I will have your rear. I see it's freshly greased, that's something. It is not my favourite orifice on a girling, but it will serve as well for the purpose. When we are done Her Majesty will know the rendezvous has been made!'

He grasped her hips and drove his hard cock into the small round mouth of her anus, opening her ring, and then with a grunt slid the rest of his shaft all the way up her. Alice lay limply across the tree trunk as though she did not have a stranger's penis up her rear.

Sir Rubin withdrew a little and slapped the back of his hand across her still tender bottom. 'Respond to me, slut, or I swear I will have the hide off you!'

Alice sighed miserably. She could not fight it so she had to let it happen. Mechanically she began to wiggle her hips and push back against him. Gritting her teeth she squeezed her muscles about his cock and uttered a vague moan.

'That's better, girl,' he said, and went back to his metronomic thrusting.

Alice closed her eyes as she was ground against the trunk, allowing instinctive reflexes to take over within her. It would be a cold pleasure but she could make herself come. That was her only strength and now she must use it. But how she wished it was Leonus having her like this! How tender he had been with her for all his strength. Of course he was so big he might burst her if he used her anally, but she'd gladly take the risk. No, she corrected herself immediately, she would simply stretch a little wider for him, because it was meant to be. Did she really believe that? Her mind was in turmoil. How could she think of Leonus like this after having known him only a few hours? But what did time matter here? In Underland the strangest things could meld together and the impossible happened every day.

She orgasmed with Leonus's image firmly in her mind, ahead of Rubin's spoutings into her entrails.

He sank over her for a minute, gasping for breath, then slowly recovered himself. 'You're a hot one under it all,' he said.

Still coupled with her he paused as though listening. 'Yes, she knows we're here, I feel it.' He slapped Alice's bottom almost playfully. 'There, that was a real man having you! Wasn't it better than a beast?'

His words revived Alice's fear and anger. She twisted her head round so that she could look him in the eye. 'No. You're not half the man he is . . . and I mean that in every way that counts!'

He glowered at her. 'It will take Her Majesty a few hours at least to reach us,' he said levelly. 'Then we must travel the rest of the way overland because she must save her strength for the final square. There need be no great haste now, as I know the Alabastrine Queen is still waiting in Brillig for Sir Blanche to join her, and he moves slowly these days. Besides, if she believes you are now in the lion's keeping and unavailable to Her Majesty she will not hurry either. Too late she will be disabused of that false assumption.' He smiled. 'But meanwhile it allows me time to teach you who your betters are!'

Alice whimpered in pain. Sir Rubin jerked the leash again. 'If you want to save yourself further suffering you had better pay more attention!' he warned her.

She stumbled after him, keeping close to his side, alert for any change in his pace or direction. Together they marched up and down the glade, her ankle chains cross-linked into a hobble shortening her stride. A master taking his girling for a walk. But how cruelly she was leashed!

The Red Knight had found and cut a long bramble cane and curled and twisted it in his thickly gloved hands into a large loop. Then he had backed Alice against a tree and forced the loop over and around her breasts, ignoring her yelps as the thorns pricked her soft heavy globes. Only when they bulged out of their new restraints was he satisfied, gazing with approval into her agonised features as she tried not to move or even breathe too hard for fear of adding to her misery.

'Perhaps this will teach you not to insult your betters, girling pawn!' he told her with evident relish.

Taking a length of rope from his saddle pack he slipped it through her enforced cleavage and tied it about the two sides of the bramble loop, pulling them together a little more and so driving the thorns deeper into her. Alice bit her lip, eyes bright with tears. The free end of the rope he passed through her collar ring, forming a leash which when pulled transmitted the pressure to her cruelly imprisoned breasts.

'Now you'll learn to walk to heel like a proper girling should,' he said.

And so they began marching up and down, Alice fearfully following close behind the Knight, alert for any tightening of the leash that might signal a change of direction. Sir Rubin's improvised discipline harness was horribly effective, and she did not want to inflict any more torture on her breasts, which already felt as though they had been turned into pincushions. She knew it had been stupid to insult him that way, but she was still furious at him for what he had done to Leonus. An image of the lionman filled her thoughts once more. No, he was strong, he was a fighter! Even if he had been knocked out he would survive. But would she ever see him again? The intensity of her longing shocked her. Was this what true slavish love felt like?

'If Her Majesty allows, I'll train you like I would a dog,' he told her with relish. 'Eventually this streak of insolence will be driven out and you will learn your proper place, like a good little bitch. I'll have you eating out of my hand and thanking me for it.'

Alice gritted her teeth. She must let go of her pride and allow her submissive side to take over fully. It was not being disloyal to Leonus. Embrace the pain and humiliation, she told herself. You don't have to like this pompous creep to get off on what he's doing to you . . .

'Yes, Master,' she said in a small voice. 'I'm sorry for what I said, Master.'

'That's better.'

He halted by a large tree. 'Now relieve yourself like the lowborn thing that you are,' he commanded.

Alice rested a foot on the curve of the lower trunk and crouched slightly so her legs were well splayed and she could pee neatly. As the urine hissed out of her she felt Rubin's eyes upon the open pout of pubes and the stream issuing from it. How men loved to watch that act she thought once again, with a little thrill. Underneath his armour and title she suspected he was no better than the Tweedle twins. Perhaps she could trick him as she had them. How long had she got before the Red Queen arrived?

When she was finished he tied the end of her leash to an overhanging branch, pulling it taut so she had to stand almost on tiptoe to spare her breasts additional pain. He then wrapped the trailing chains round her ankles again, binding her legs together and making it harder to keep her balance. But worse was that the branch was swaying gently in the breeze, rhythmically drawing the noose about her breasts tighter, digging in the thorns then easing once again. She felt a small hot trickle of blood run out from the twist of bramble and down her chest. Rubin walked round her, admiring the taut lines of her body, the trembling firmness of her buttocks and the way she had to bow her back and lift her chest to ease the strain on the leash.

He flicked and pinched her erect nipples, then chuckled. 'So, your kind really do like being treated harshly. I should have known. Well, I can guarantee plenty more of that, girl. Just wait until we're done with this quest and –'

He broke off, twisting his head round as though he had heard something. For a moment Alice wondered what it was, then came a distant jingle of harness and the sound of approaching voices.

Alice was tethered close to the winding track that ran though the middle of the wood. Keeping low, Sir Rubin ran to its edge and peered along the trail. Whatever he saw caused him to retreat quickly back to Alice, his face grave.

'It's the White Queen!' he hissed. 'Curse her for being ahead of time. I must slow them down. Though it may mean my life, I may at least weaken them! The Queen will find you when she comes. She still has a chance.'

And he ran to his horse, the larger of the two he had brought with him, mounted up, drew a mace from its sheath, dropped the visor of his helmet and thundered past Alice and out onto the trackway. Ignoring the pain, Alice twisted round to see him go. Through the trees she saw him take up position on the track barring the way. Facing him she could just make out a group of three riders with someone on foot following behind as they came to a halt. She strained her eyes to make out the last figure. It was a girling. It must be Juliet!

'I challenge you to a knightly combat, Sir Blanche!' Sir Rubin called out loudly.

There was a pause, then came an unexpectedly weary reply: 'Stand aside, Rubin. I do not wish any more killing.'

The White Queen's sharper voice interjected. 'I do not care what you wish. Remove him from the path, Sir Blanche!'

'As Your Majesty commands,' the weary voice replied.

Through a gap in the trees Alice saw one of the riders throw off a long cape, revealing a suit of silver armour.

He drew out a mace like Sir Rubin's, lowered his visor and galloped towards his counterpart. The two Knights met in a crash and bang of metal on metal. With snorts and drumming hooves, their two mounts wheeled about each other even as their riders swung their maces and strove to stay in the saddles.

A disconcerting sense of déjà vu suddenly struck Alice. It was the battle of the Red and White Knights almost exactly as portrayed in the book – except that the vicious impacts of their blows were making her wince. No, this was no Punch and Judy combat; this was life or death! In the book the Red Knight had been chased off. She did not think Sir Rubin, for all his faults, was a coward. Which meant the contest could only end one way.

Even as the knowledge impinged upon her the White Knight caught Sir Rubin a sickening blow on the side of his helmet. As Rubin swayed back drunkenly, his opponent struck him again full on his visor. Like a falling tree, man and beast crashed to the ground in a rattle of armour . . .

And faded away as though they had never been!

Alice blinked in disbelief, but there was nothing there where knight and horse had fallen except trampled grass.

Through the fog of her confusion came an image of the strange statues ringed about the Red Queen's tent on the edge hills. A playing 'piece' had been killed in combat, or by the rules that shaped the chessmen's lives, he had been 'taken'. Is that where they went? Did the White Queen have a matching collection, somewhere beside which a statue of Sir Rubin had just materialised? And when the game was over, would they revert to being of flesh and blood again?

Alice wrenched her mind away from the eerie mystery to face more immediate concerns. One way or another Rubin was gone and the White Queen's party would surely be moving on. If she kept quiet they probably would not realise she was there, but she would have to wait for the Red Queen to arrive to be freed, however long that would take. Meanwhile, what would happen to Juliet?

'Hallo!' she shouted, wincing as she did so. 'I'm over here!'

They rode cautiously through the trees and surrounded her. She saw Juliet was being led on the end of a chain from her collar hooked to the back of Albinous's saddle. At the sight of Alice her face lit up in surprise and delight.

'Extraordinary!' said the White Knight. 'What's a girling doing out here?' His visor was open once again, revealing a mild face adorned with a white moustache.

The White Queen, now wearing her crown openly but still looking plain and dumpy, said impatiently, 'She's the one I told you of, Sir Blanche. Obviously Sir Rubin obtained her from Leonus somehow and she was left here awaiting Magenta's arrival.'

Dismounting briskly from the small horse she was riding, the Queen walked round Alice inspecting her closely. Bending over she slid a finger between Alice's buttocks and it came out wet with Rubin's sperm, which was still oozing out of her anus and down her thighs.

'Quite fresh,' the Queen pronounced. 'A signal recently sent to Magenta that her knight and pawn had, ah, "mated", I suppose.' She looked Alice in the eye and held up her sceptre, no longer disguised as an umbrella, for her to see as a warning. 'How long before she arrives?'

'Rubin didn't say exactly,' Alice said honestly. 'I guess a couple of hours. You know better than I do how fast you people can travel if you want.'

The White Queen beamed. 'Then she will be too late, for by then we shall be in the crown square.'

'Look, take me and let Juliet go,' Alice said. 'I promise I'll open the barrier for you. You don't need her.'

'Once again the noble gesture, and once again I cannot accede to it,' the Queen replied. 'You see, while I was in Brillig I learned more about the guardian of the Crown and its peculiar habits. So I will take both you and your friend with me, not only to frustrate Magenta's plans but also to serve mine. Any control Magenta may be able to exert over you now will do her little good. Cut her down and secure her with the other one,' she commanded.

As they freed Alice from her bramble bra and attached a chain to her collar, her mind raced. What was the guardian of the last square?

Alice plodded on beside Juliet, both their chain leashes now clipped to the back of Albinous's saddle. Alice's hands, like Juliet's were still fastened behind her back, but at least they were not gagged so they could converse in low tones.

'Thank you for trying to make her let me go,' Juliet said. 'It was very brave of you.'

'I'm sorry the Queen seems to have changed her plans. How have they been treating you?' Alice tried to look Juliet over. Her face was as pretty as before but she seemed subtly different. Then she caught a glimpse of her friend's bottom and saw livid purple weals. 'What happened in Brillig?' she demanded.

'Nothing much. I was locked away in a room for a few days. They were waiting for Sir Blanche to come from another square. He finally turned up last night so we set off early this morning.'

'But what did they do to you?'

'Oh . . . the Queen had Albinous cane and rape me a few times. She said she wanted me to be "responsive and malleable", at least that was the way she put it.'

Alice felt a rush of compassion for her sweet-faced companion. 'I'm so sorry. I know this isn't the right sort of life for you.'

Juliet's eyes shied away from Alice's. 'It wasn't worse than what they did to me on the train. I'll get over it.' She turned her face back smiling.

'Now you're being brave,' Alice said.

'But what about you?' Juliet asked. 'Your boobs look terribly sore. Is that blood on them?'

'Yeah, but it looks worse than it is. Anyway, you know I get off on that sort of thing.'

'How's Suzanne? Tell me what happened to you. The Queen came back last night very angry that you'd got to Brillig somehow.'

Alice related their adventures from when they were thrown from the train to Leonus and the boxing match.

'I like the sound of your lionman,' Juliet said with a grin, 'and I'm glad Suzanne's back with her master. At least one of us got back home.'

'We will, too,' Alice said firmly. 'I just wish I knew what these chesspeople were really up to. It's more complicated than picking up this golden crown and saying I won. The White Queen said on the train it changes things, but on how big a scale? And why are we suddenly more important to getting it?'

'Does it matter?' Juliet wondered. 'I mean they'll either let us go or not at the end anyway.'

'Maybe.' Alice frowned. 'Underland is shaped by stories from our world, right? Which means it's also changing as the stories get bigger and more dramatic, like blockbuster films having to outdo what they did last year. And action fantasies are really big now, which might explain why what was a chess game has got more like a fantasy quest, with a quickfix sort of ending. You know, when at the last moment the heroes find the gadget/magic ring/gem/spell-thing, whatever, that solves everybody's problems in a puff of CGI. Well, I can think of a few stories where the thing they're looking for can destroy a world. And here it would really exist.'

'Oh, I see,' Juliet said, looking more subdued.

'So that's why we must be ready to escape the first chance we get.'

'But what about getting rid of your feathers?'

'I'll just have to put up with them until I find another cure somewhere. Anyway, you see why we've got to be prepared for anything? Do you know what this guardian of the crown square is?'

'No, sorry. The Queen did go to a library while she was in Brillig and she came back looking very thoughtful. She talked to Albinous afterwards about an "it" as though he knew what she meant, but they didn't give a name. There was something about the barrier round the next square even keeping the locals out because they were so afraid of what was inside.'

'Which is why only girlings, being outsiders, can get them through I suppose.'

'I think so.' Juliet looked at Alice with a rueful smile. 'Maybe you'd have been better off waiting for your Red Queen. She certainly won't cure you if she finds out you've been helping the other side.'

'I wasn't counting on it much anyway. Tell you the truth, the more I've found out about these chesspeople the less I trust any of them, Red or White.'

'Oh, I think Sir Blanche is all right,' Juliet volunteered unexpectedly.

Alice gave her a searching look. 'How can you tell? You've only known him a few hours.'

'Sometimes you just can,' Juliet said defensively. 'He's different. He's a sort of old-fashioned gentleman.'

Alice gazed curiously at the armoured figure ahead of them. It was true that in the story the White Knight was one of the more sympathetic and often comic characters. He had become obsessed with making impractical inventions and kept falling off his horse, as she recalled. Though Alice could see some extra baggage slung about his huge war charger, Sir Blanche rode with a stiff back and she knew he could fight and kill if required. How close was he still to his fictional precursor?

She looked back at Juliet. 'So you like him, then?'

Juliet blushed. 'I'm only saying it because it's true. Listen for a bit. He keeps arguing with the Queen. Albinous does everything she says like a robot, but Sir Blanche sounds pissed off with this whole war thing, only he wouldn't say it quite like that. He's too polite.'

They passed out of the wood and onto a bleak open plain, dotted with scrubby trees and low hillocks of withered grass. It was the largest stretch of unused countryside Alice had yet seen in Underland. Did nobody want to live here? Beyond, like a vast backcloth, was the shimmering wall of the final barrier. Alice shivered. It looked ominously dark and foreboding. What else was in there apart from the Crown?

As they rode deeper into the desolate landscape, Alice heard Sir Blanche say to the Queen, 'Need we involve these poor girlings, Majesty? To fight against a worthy foe on sporting terms is one thing, but to employ such methods. There are so many better uses for such pretty things.'

The Queen's retort was sharp and unsympathetic. 'I will hear no more about it, Sir Blanche. I believe you have spent too long amongst the natives.'

'Any time I have spent down here has been at your order, Majesty. As to the natives, they are merely rebuilding their land with energy and invention. You admitted you yourself travelled on one of their trains, Majesty. Wonderful things, aren't they?' He added wistfully, 'I just wonder why everything changes around us but we do not.'

'Then you will be pleased to learn that this will be the last battle, after which there will be great changes, I assure you.'

'But at such a price, Majesty?'

She did not answer him.

* * *

They stopped in the shadow of a scrubby group of thin trees and dismounted to water the horses. After he had seen to his animal, Sir Blanche brought his canteen over to the two girls and allowed them to slake their thirst as well.

Close to, Alice saw he was not quite as old as she had at first imagined. It was the white moustache that gave the impression of age, she decided, and the weary lines about his eyes. But otherwise his face was firm and he certainly carried himself well, moving easily in his armour.

He looked her up and down admiringly as she drank but otherwise did not touch her. As it would do no harm, she said, 'Thank you, Master,' when he took the spout of the canteen from her lips, and received a slow mild smile in return. Juliet beamed at him brightly when he watered her, and received a pat on the head when she thanked him.

'Enough of that, Sir Blanche,' the Queen snapped. 'Albinous, I want both the girlings roused and sensitive. Shaft and strap each, but don't allow their pleasure to peak. They must be primed, not satiated.'

'Yes, Majesty,' Albinous said.

He pushed Alice and Juliet down to their knees and then forward onto their faces so, with their hands still bound behind them, their breasts scraped on the dry hard earth and their bottoms were raised in unwilling invitation. Albinous took up position behind Alice and methodically laid a dozen strokes across her pale buttocks with a leather strap, until a rosy blush spread across their soft curves. Alice bit her lip but willed herself not to respond. In between blows Albinous felt her pubic pouch and noted its unexpected dryness.

'Warm up, girling. Don't tell me that beast drained you.'

But Alice submitted to the strap with evident lethargy, waiting patiently.

Finally Albinous put the strap aside and knelt between her spread legs, freeing his erect penis which was already anticipating its release, and drove it into the cleft of her pudenda. Alice let herself go loose, so he had little friction as a reward. He thrust harder and faster, working hard to rouse her.

Suddenly Alice moaned as though caught up in the throes of an orgasm, clamped her internal muscles down on his jabbing penis and squeezed it tight, even as she vigorously ground her hips back and forth. Albinous panicked, trying to pull out of the warm lovemouth that now seemed to be intent on sucking the life from his member.

'Stop it, you bitch, I . . . no, no . . . ughhh!'

Helplessly he came inside her, finally pulling free of her clutches in time only to send the last of his sperm splattering in hot spurts across her reddened buttocks. Turning her face to the ground as though also spent, Alice secretly grinned in triumph.

'I told you to rouse her, not relieve her!' the White Queen said angrily as she strode over, alerted by Albinous's angry cries. Albinous looked up at her in acute embarrassment.

'Sorry, Your Majesty. I . . . er, couldn't help myself.'

'Well riddle the other one with more care.'

Albinous blushed. 'I can't, Majesty. Not for a while. This one's . . . drained me.'

'Men!' the White Queen exclaimed in exasperation. 'Tend to my horse then.' She turned to Sir Blanche. 'You see to Juliet. Strap and shaft her.'

'Me, Majesty? Must I?'

'Yes! And don't take too long about it! That is an order!' And she turned about and stomped off.

Alice was looking at Juliet as the command was given and saw a strange look in her eye.

Juliet glanced up at Sir Blanche and, with a shy smile, eased her legs wider apart and pushed out her bottom a little further. The ripe peach of her sex pouted between her thighs, a glistening dew appearing on its deep cleft. She was blatantly encouraging him to carry out his orders.

After a blink or two, understanding seemed to dawn on the knight. He picked up the belt Albinous had cast aside and swung it across Juliet's proffered buttocks. There was a smooth crack and the girl flinched as a red stripe appeared crossing the swelling fullness of her two nether hemispheres and a shiver ran through her flesh. But though the blow had been firmly delivered she held her posture of abject surrender. By the third crisp smack tears were filling her eyes, but still she held steady. Alice gazed at Juliet in surprise. She was smiling.

When Juliet's bottom was an even rosy red, Sir Blanche put down the strap and knelt between Juliet's spread knees. How is he going to manage with all that armour? Alice wondered. But a small hinged panel over his groin was raised, the knight reached inside and drew out a good-sized erection which he fed into the plump pink-lipped cleft before him.

Juliet sighed as he slid into her. As he began to shaft her with a steady rhythm her face became blissful and her eyes took on the glaze of mounting arousal. In a minute she was wriggling and moaning happily.

'Oh, yes! That's so nice. Oh ... I think ... I'm going to come. Please finish me ... please!'

'Sorry, my dear,' Sir Blanche said, pulling his now glistening cock out of her. 'Tis a consummation devoutly to be wished ... but not this time, I'm afraid. Perhaps later.' He frowned. 'We shall see.'

The Queen looked over at the helpless frustration written large on Juliet's face and nodded with approval. 'That's the state I want them in. Now to your horses.'

The party mounted up again. The girls scrambled to their feet as their leash chains grew taut and followed in their wake. As they went Alice gave Juliet's still flushed and excited features a searching glance.

'Did you know what you were doing?' she asked softly.

'I think so,' Juliet said, as though still surprised at herself.

'And how much was acting just to make Albinous look more of a fool?'

But in answer to that question Juliet only smiled.

In another hour they reached the edge of the Brillig square. Before them the edge barrier hung out of a bleak sky, with the normally pearly Underland light dimming through sticky yellow into purple grey gloom. The slight breeze had died, leaving a heavy sense of anticipation, as though for a storm that would not break.

They reached the very edge of the square bounded by the last brook that separated them from the Crown. The Queen dismounted and for a minute walked up and down a length of the narrow channel in silence, peering intently at the shimmering translucent wall that ran along it and the dark and blurred land on the further side.

Finally she nodded to herself. 'Bring them here.'

Albinous unclipped their leashes and dragged Alice and Juliet over to her. She pinched their chins in her stubby strong fingers and forced them to look into her eyes, which now shone with a new and dangerous inner light. When she spoke her voice held such an undertone of malicious glee that Alice shivered.

'Now, if you're the perverse little girlings I judge you to be, this will excite you. You will need all that masochistic longing for suffering to pass through into the last square, because in there you will face the most depraved creature in all Boardland. I found it mentioned in a little cautionary rhyme during my researches. I suspect Magenta has been attempting to discover more about the Crown itself, but what good will that do her if she cannot get past its guardian? Do you want to know its name?'

She recited:

'Beware, fair maid, the slavishing beast,
Vilely tongued and blazing eyed.
Upon girlings does it hungrily feast,
Who first have been well sodomised.

On claws that clack and wings that flap,
The tulgey wood it prowls.
In a snip and a snap a girl it will trap,
Careless of how she howls.

Clutching her tight it begins to test,
The plumpitiousness of its new find.
By sticking and pricking her titiful breast,
And prodding her bouncy behind.

But bestially worse a girl has to fear,
From its gnurlious twice-pronged cock.
Quick as a leer it will rend front and rear,
So beware the cruel Jabberwock!'

The White Queen beamed at them as the image of the
Jabberwock from the book knotted Alice's stomach. It
was the one true monster in the story. And in Underland it liked girls . . .

'A fitting guardian for the Crown of Auria, don't you
think?' the Queen said. 'It's large and vicious, preying
on any people or animals that enter its lair. However, as
the rhyme suggests, it has a special affection, call it a
weakness, for girlings. One might say it likes to play
with them. Nothing you have ever experienced before
can prepare you for what that means. There will be pain
and torment and, yes, perhaps, a few moments of the
most exquisite rapture so intense you may not survive.'

Juliet was looking deathly pale. Alice spoke, trying to
keep her voice level. 'And while it's playing with us,
you'll be sneaking round to steal the Crown, I suppose?'

'Exactly. I promise, if I achieve my goal in time, I will do all I can to save you. Think of it as another reason to keep the Jabberwock amused for as long as possible. In any case it would be unwise to let it get bored with you.' As she spoke she dropped her hands between their legs, thrusting stiff fingers up into the depths of their vulvas while grinding her thumbs down on their clitorises. 'How long do you think you can last while such a creature ravishes you?' she asked as she toyed with them. Juliet whimpered and Alice felt her body responding in the only way it knew; meeting the prospect of depravity head on with uplifted nipples and a slippery crotch.

The Queen lifted her hands to inspect the intimate dew they had deposited upon them. 'I see girlings are such slaves to your natures that you cannot help becoming aroused, even when the prospect terrifies. Good, I knew you would not let me down. Now open the way for us!'

Extra leashes were fastened to their collars and, with Albinous holding one set, they were made to climb down the bank and wade out into the middle of the brook. For the first time Alice felt some resistance as she pushed though the barrier curtain until it rippled through the middle of her body, teasing her senses and trying to insinuate itself up her cleft. Tilting her head she glimpsed tall dark trees on the other side of the divide. Juliet took up position facing Alice with a gap between them large enough for a horse to pass.

Sir Blanche guided his nervous mount between them, leaning into the barrier as it resisted his passing. Alice felt it stretching and tugging at her, but their presence must have weakened it enough, for knight and horse suddenly slipped through. She felt Sir Blanche pick up their second set of leashes on the other side and draw them tight. There would be no last-minute escape after the others had passed.

The Queen was about to ride though when Albinous suddenly pointed up at the sky in the direction they had come. 'Look, Majesty!'

At first Alice thought it was a bird he was pointing to silhouetted against the low band of bright sky, gradually flapping its way towards them and into the shadow of the perpetual overcast. Then the White Queen laughed loudly as she realised what it was.

The Red Queen was coming. Her cloak billowed behind her as her legs pumped away in their improbable distance-devouring strides that drove her through the air.

'The strength it must have cost her to travel so far and fast!' The White Queen said, with a hint of admiration. 'A last sad reminder of how we used to bestride this world, but a careless move. She found the wood empty and she must know Sir Rubin has been taken. Even if there was one to hand, she cannot carry another girling with her to breach the barrier. And, once within, you will be beyond her control. She has lost!'

She rode through the brook between Alice and Juliet with Albinous close behind her. Alice had a last glimpse of the Red Queen swooping desperately down out of the sky like a vengeful eagle, before a tug on their leashes jerked her and Juliet into the gloom of the final square.

Eleven

The wood was vast and gloomy, its trees straight and tall, their lower branches mostly lying broken and fallen to the ground. Those that remained spread into a tangled canopy high above their heads. This further muted what meagre light the sky delivered, filling the hollows with shadow. And over all this was the sense of an unseen and malicious presence.

These threatening new surroundings did not please their horses, which began to toss their heads and scrape their hooves nervously. Albinous held his mount on a tight rein while the Queen gave hers a warning tap on its head with her sceptre. Sir Blanche bent forward and patted and stroked his charger's neck, and whispered reassuringly in its ear, 'Don't take fright now, Snowdrop.'

He drew a long slim cylinder from out of the baggage pack slung behind his saddle and tucked it under his arm. There was a click and hiss of greased metal, and the cylinder expanded into a tapering pointed shaft four or five times its original length.

Even through the churning fear that was consuming Alice's mind, she recognised it as a telescopic lance. Neat trick. She glanced at Juliet, hoping she was showing a brave face. But she was staring blankly ahead of her and did not notice.

As the party made its way deeper into the woods the horses' anxiety became worse, until both the Queen's and Albinous's mounts were threatening to unseat them. Finally the Queen said, in a voice less assured than Alice had yet heard, 'Leave them here, else they will alert the beast before we are ready. We must continue on foot.'

They all dismounted. Albinous slung a pack over his shoulder and then unhitched Alice and Juliet's leashes. In his free hand he held a sword. The Queen grasped her sceptre tightly, her small chin thrust out in a show of determination. Only Sir Blanche hung back, his face pinched with worry. Suddenly he said: 'I cannot countenance what you are going to do to these girlings, Majesty. I will have no further part in it.'

'What!' The Queen spun round to face him with a look of disbelief rapidly shading to anger. Alice was sure it was only the knowledge of where they were that prevented a titanic outburst. As it was her words were hissed from between clenched jaws as her pale cheeks flushed. 'Do you know what you're saying? You would sacrifice your honour for a pair of girlings? This is treason!'

'I stand upon my honour,' Sir Blanche said resolutely. 'That is why I can continue no further.'

Alice saw Juliet watching him with an expression of sad pride, in contrast to the fuming rage of the Queen. When she found her voice again she spat out, 'Then stay here and mind the horses. When this is over I will deal with you!'

He bowed stiffly. 'As you will, Your Majesty.'

The diminished party continued onwards, Albinous dragging the girls by their leashes as he followed after the Queen.

They reached a thorny thicket that seemed to extend like a wall across their path. Albinous hacked a way through with his sword. Beyond the wood seemed even darker. Alice began to notice half-seen things in the shadows. Here was a discarded spear and there a helmet, and were those white sticks actually bones? How many had passed this way before them . . . and how few had returned?

A clearing of sorts opened before them and the Queen called a halt. 'This will do,' she said softly to Albinous. 'Have you sufficient for the both of them? They must be secure, yet the beast must also be able to carry them off easily.'

'Yes, Majesty. I bought additional materials in case of need while in Brillig.'

'Then prepare them. And be quick.'

Selecting one of the few intact overhanging branches within reach, Albinous dragged across a fallen branch so that it lay beneath it. Removing their leashes but leaving their hands bound behind them, he made Juliet and Alice climb upon it so they stood facing each other a little apart and below the upper limb. He then threw lengths of chain over the branch and gathered up the dangling ends, which were fitted with large blunt hooks. A pair of these he slipped into their collar rings, ensuring they stood straight with their heads up. Grinning into their helpless faces, he secured the next larger set of hooks into the ready made sockets of their front passages, his strong fingers parting their pudendal lips as he slid the curving metal tips inside them. They gasped and squirmed as they felt themselves plugged, though they did so with hardly a squeak for fear of what a raised voice might call out of the menacing woods. As the chains were tightened the upper shafts of the hooks pressed against their clitorises even as the buried tips stimulated those sensitive organs through the walls of their vaginal tunnels.

Albinous then secured the third and last set of hooks into their rectums, forcing their anal rings wide and giving the hooks a tug to make sure they were firmly in place. Juliet was staring at Alice in mute disbelief that they could be so humiliated, but Albinous was not finished with them yet.

209

From his pack he brought out a reel of strong thin cord and two pairs of bulldog clips. He tied the clips in pairs linked by short lengths of cord and clipped them onto their nipples, making them whimper as the metal clamps bit into their soft paps. The rest of the cord was tied about the lengths linking the clips, passed over the branch above them and run off in the cover of some straggling bushes well clear of the tree.

'Do you wish them gagged, Majesty?' Albinous asked as the Queen inspected his handiwork.

'No, the more noise they make the better. The beast is attracted to girling voices, but it does not understand speech, so they cannot warn it of our intentions.' She smiled at Alice. 'You see, it is in your best interests that we track the beast back to its lair and so find the Crown quickly. So do not stifle your feelings. Right, start them singing . . .'

Albinous heaved the fallen branch out from under their feet and then he and the Queen retreated to cover, leaving Alice and Juliet hanging like pieces of meat in a butcher's shop with their weight supported only by their collars and cruelly hooked orifices. They yelped and whimpered as their vaginas and anuses were stretched unnaturally open, feet kicking about in mid air in a reflex attempt to find some new support. But that only made their discomfort worse so they soon desisted. Even with their legs still they wobbled wildly as they tried to find some point of balance, rocking and yawing about on their chains while groaning with the tingling pain in their clamped nipples. And with each incautious move-ment the hooks twisted inside them in a way no girling could resist. Inexorably their natural lubrication began to flow about the curving prongs of metal.

Alice could see the hook buried in Juliet's cleft stretching it into a forced vertical smile, and felt her own anus similarly gaping, allowing the open air to enter her rectum, no doubt also carrying the scent of their arousal through the wood. How long before it reached the Jabberwock?

'I was lying,' Juliet said suddenly, blinking through her tears.

'What?'

'About not belonging here. I just wanted you to know that . . . whatever happens next.'

'I don't understand,' Alice said.

'What I said in Gyre about having a wonderful family and just wanting to get back to them wasn't true.'

Alice shuddered in her bittersweet torment. 'Is this the time for confessions?' she gasped.

'What else can we do?' Juliet said. 'Please listen. It may be the only chance I have. You thought I was being brave putting up with everything because I'm not a natural submissive, but it's not true. I want you to know about the real me . . . aah!'

A sharp tug on the cords lifted their breasts by their clamped nipples making them into fat pink cones before they dropped down again with a bounce and shiver, sending Alice and Juliet swaying in their chain slings afresh and forcing cries of pain from their lips. It was a reminder that they were not going to be allowed to remain still or quiet. They were the bait in a trap and had to squirm like masochistic worms on fishing hooks.

But a new light was burning in Juliet's eyes and she raised her voice defiantly. 'Please let me tell you the truth about how I got here!'

Alice sighed. Juliet was probably right. What else was there to do? 'Go on.'

'We were well off and I did live in a nice house . . . but my parents weren't in love. Maybe they had been once but that had all gone by the time I was old enough to realise what was going on. I don't know why they had me or why they stayed together. Habit, maybe. It was all horribly cold and mechanical. I spent a lot of time out with friends or on the web. Then by accident I found a site showing S&M and CP images. It was really pervy and I felt repelled and yet fascinated at the same time, you know? Of course, my parents caught me watching it and for once in their lives agreed on something – they were both disgusted with me. I got angry and said I'd rather do something like that than stay at home with them any longer. They said OK, thinking I'd back down, but I left the next day ... aaahh!'

Their nipples were wrenched upwards once again by the Queen's unseen hand and they writhed and swayed, impaling themselves deeper on their hooks. Alice felt her juices soaking through her feathers and begin to drip to the ground.

Juliet fought to keep her voice even as she grimly pressed on with her story. 'So I left home ... but there had been an address on the bondage site which was only in the next town from where I lived, and I thought I could earn some money posing to get me started living independently ... or maybe it was to test my nerve and shock my parents when I sent them a set of pics. I'm not sure now. Anyway, I found the studio and the man who interviewed me was a bit odd but friendly enough so I thought I'd risk it. In an hour I was trussed up like a turkey having a camera almost shoved up my pussy. I was scared stiff but really turned on at the same time.

'They paid me enough to stay in a cheep hotel that night and said come back the next day. This time they wanted me to do a sort of jokey set of pictures with an actor dressed up as Humpty Dumpty.'

'He's also in the Looking Glass story,' Alice said.

'Is he? Maybe that explains what happened. Anyway, Humpty blamed me flashing my pussy for making him fall off the wall, so once he got put back together I got punished. There was heavier bondage mixed with a bit of CP, which really got me going. I think I must have come under all the pain and stimulation because I fainted. I don't know it if was planned or not, but when I woke up I was down here in the square next to Ruddle's garden. I wandered in and got tricked into becoming one of his flowergirls. But I felt so stupid for what I'd got myself into and ashamed of being a masochist, or whatever I am, that I pretended I didn't belong here. I just wanted you to know the truth, that's all.'

Alice forced herself to smile through the pain and mounting arousal in her hooked and clamped and helpless body. 'If that's the truth and you're happy being what you are, don't feel any more guilt. We'll get through this by finding pleasure in pain, freedom in chains and be able to get off on whatever screws us, however gross he, she or it is. Nobody who isn't a girling at heart can ever really understand, but that's our secret strength . . .'

She faltered because she saw a light moving through the trees over Juliet's shoulder. Juliet noticed her expression change and gulped. 'Is it coming?' she asked faintly.

'Yes.' Alice grappled for some final piece of advice, even as her own stomach was tying itself in knots. 'Whatever he does to you, try to look as though you're having fun.'

Two baleful glowing eyes emerged from under the treetop canopy, set in a bulbous tendrilled head that wove about on a sinuous neck. Fluttering batwings supported a green-scaled and lumpy body with vast four-clawed hands and gangling three-clawed feet. A long tail slithered across the ground in its wake. A vast absurd pink waistcoat covered its upper torso. It should have sent Alice into a fit of giggles, for who could take any creature seriously dressed in such a garment? But the waistcoat was streaked with the rust-brown stains of dried blood.

The Jabberwock's pinched mouth opened to reveal two pairs of huge peg-like teeth and it vented a snuffling, braying siren-blast that made them jerk in their chains. Juliet's yelp of fear became a shameful curse as her bladder cut loose and she peed messily over her cunt hook.

The beast came to earth with eerie grace and padded over to them, looming higher and larger. It was a literal monster, Alice thought, trembling in unashamed terror. The great head snaked down to peer at them through its featureless glowing eyes and the contents of Alice's bladder joined that of Juliet's on the forest floor. It snorted and the tendrils about its head shivered. Were they part of its olfactory sense? Alice wondered in a fleeting moment of detached curiosity.

Two clawed hands like mechanical grabs reached out and closed about them. Juliet screamed and screwed up her eyes. Alice wished she could do the same but hers seemed frozen in a petrified stare. The Jabberwock picked them up like rag dolls, their hooks sliding from their wet sockets and the chains falling away. The long cords tied to their breast clips were loosed and trailed after them.

The beast turned the girls over curiously, examining them from every angle and ignoring their feeble struggles. Its mouth opened and a darting blood-red tongue flicked out, its slimy tip passing over Juliet's body, savouring the swelling contours of her breasts, the palpitating curve of her stomach and the complex folds of her pubic mound. It repeated the process with Alice and she had to stifle her impulse to retch. She felt she would never be clean again.

The Jabberwock gave a grunting snort, repeated in quick succession, for all the world like a snivelling malicious chuckle. It was enjoying their fear!

It tipped Alice onto her back so that it looked up between her kicking legs and its tongue flicked out again. Alice caught her breath as its tip slid into her bottom hole and forced its way in . . . and in! It was like a greased snake slithering up her arse, worming its way through her bowels, tickling and burning as it went, disgustingly exciting, utterly degrading. Then it wriggled its way back out, leaving her anus gaping dumbly. While Alice sobbed helplessly at her violation and the shocking emptiness it left behind, the Jabberwock lapped its sodomising tongue across its ghastly lips, braying happily to itself. It was savouring the taste of her rectum! How gross, Alice thought dizzily.

Juliet was shaking her head in horror. 'No . . . please, not that!'

'It's . . . not as bad . . . as it looks,' Alice choked out, trying desperately to reassure her.

Juliet shrieked and burbled as the Jabberwock tongue-raped her in turn, the glistening organ sliding up between her soft thighs into the deep cleft of her buttocks and stretching her anal mouth with its inexorable progress. Alice could only watch in pity and fascination, aware of the hardness of her nipples and the wet swollen lips of her vulva. She could not deny her own arousal at the bizarre sight, rising as it did from those strange dark depths that knew no moral sense. In fact she must not deny it! That perverted response was all that she or Juliet had to support them through the ordeal. They must turn fear and pain into excitement and pleasure.

The tongue pulled out of Juliet with a sucking glop, drawing a fresh moan from her as she twitched feebly in the taloned grasp of the great clawed hand.

'Are you all right?' Alice called to her.

Her heart lifted as she saw Juliet manage a feeble smile, and gasp out, 'And I thought . . . having one of Ruddle's bulbs . . . stuffed up me . . . was bad!'

As the Jabberwock slobbered over the unique taste of Juliet's bowels, Alice saw something bulging from between its ridiculous thighs where only moments before there had been only scales. At the sight her mouth went dry. Oh God, the rhyme had been correct. Alice felt sick with despair and the will seemed to drain out of her. Her legs were like rubber ... no, not like, they really had become useless! She could hardly move them ... nor her arms, even the slight amount her bonds and the Jabberwock's grasp allowed. What was wrong? She could still feel her body but could hardly move her limbs.

Juliet called out fearfully. 'Alice ... my legs! I can't move my legs! And my hands ... what's it done to me?'

'I feel it too. I think it's just numbed us, to make us easier to handle. That tonguing was not just to get a taste of our arses. Some relaxant in his saliva ... it's probably only temporary. We couldn't fight it anyway while it's holding us. Just let it happen. Surrender, remember?'

'I'll ... I'll try.'

The Jabberwock began to move off. Back in the shadows, Alice knew the Queen and Albinous were cold-bloodedly watching them being carried away. 'Satisfied?' she called out in desperate anger. 'Going to follow us now? Well, I hope this thing rips your guts out, do you hear?'

But they were already beyond the clearing, being carried along a twisting path through the dark trees.

Juliet, hanging limply in its other claw, said in a tremulous voice, 'Where do you think it's taking us?'

'To its den or lair or something, I suppose.'

'And ... what will it do then?'

'You know what.' Alice tried to sound offhand. 'The same thing everybody in Underland does to a girling if they've half a chance.'

'But it ... he's ... huge!'

'It'll be a challenge. Girlings don't fight, we say bring it on!'

'When he's done it ... will he eat us?'

'No, because he'll be tired out after his screwfest, and while he's sleeping it off we'll get away!'

'Do you really think so?'

'Yes, if we do what we're best at and give him a ride he'll never forget. We're hot juicy girling sluts, right? You can't blame him for wanting us. And gross as he is, he's male and we're female. He's got to work to provide the filling but we've got the holes readymade. We can do it ten times to his one.'

Juliet bit her lip. 'I'll try . . . but he's so horrible!'

'Oh, I don't know.' Alice pretended to appraise their monstrous captor. 'A little cosmetic makeover, a new suit, ten litres of deodorant . . .'

Juliet was laughing hysterically by now, then suddenly choked off. 'I think we're here.'

The ground had risen slightly and the trees opened to reveal an isolated knoll of jumbled boulders. As they were carried up to it they saw the huge slabs formed a shallow cave. On a patch of beaten earth before it was a crudely made standing frame of roughly cut and lashed timbers, and a single gnarled thorn bush. Hanging in the upper branches of the bush was a golden crown, which shimmered even in the dull light of the wood, sending splashes of colour across the grey dry ground.

'That's the Crown of Auria!' Alice breathed, impressed by its magnificence despite everything.

'It's beautiful!' Juliet said. 'Oh . . . where are the Queen and Albinous? Didn't they follow us? If they can get to it quickly enough . . .'

'They won't hurry on our account. We just do what I said we do, right?'

'I'll try.'

The Jabberwock laid Juliet down in front of the timber frame and turned its attention to Alice. One huge clawed finger picked curiously at the cord still dangling from her nipple clips. Then with a flick it pulled it them off.

Alice yelped at the pain of the metal jaws scraping over her tender flesh, then clamped her lips shut. The

217

Jabberwock might not be able to understand words, but it might sense mood. She didn't want to get anything that big angry with her.

'Thanks,' she said aloud. 'My nips were going a bit numb.'

The clawed finger was brushing across her breasts, making them sway from side to side and tormenting her ludicrously erect nipples.

Alice gulped. 'Do you like big tits? I think mine are pretty good. You can play with them if you like ... that's it ... ow ... ouch!'

The finger was flicking the sides of her breasts with the power of a slap, making them jiggle and rebound from each other. The Jabberwock gave another of its grunting chuckles. Suddenly two claws came together on her right breast, imprisoning it between them and pinching inwards. Alice winced at the exquisite agony as her plump flesh distorted. He would skewer her tit like a kebab! Then the claws opened, leaving white indentations on either side of the heavy globe. As the colour returned to them two spots of blood appeared in their centres.

Alice gasped in relief. 'Thank you,' she said in wretched gratitude. 'Great claws you've got there. Very sharp. I don't suppose you could use them to get this rope off?' She wriggled her shoulders as well as she could, trying to indicate her bound arms.

To her amazement it turned her round and began picking at the rope about her wrists. After a few moments it fell away. Her arms were free – still almost useless, but free!

The Jabberwock laid her limp body on the tilted timber frame, arranging her as one might a doll until she was spreadeagled. There were thick coarse ropes hanging from the lattice of timbers and these it carefully coiled about her neck, wrists and ankles, tying them with huge clumsy knots. As it did so a sickening realisation struck Alice. She knew what the frame was for. It would bring their groins level with his.

When it was satisfied she was secure, it picked up Juliet and began picking at her bonds. In a couple of minutes she was tied to the frame beside Alice.

The beast rumbled with pleasure, admiring its two pretty captives, pinching and prodding them to see how easily their flesh could be manipulated. Their squeals and gasps of pain seemed to amuse it. As life returned to their limbs they began to squirm helplessly under its torments, which entertained it even more. In fact its pleasure was all too plain to see.

An erection as long as Alice's arm and even greater in girth was jutting out from between the thing's legs. The last third of its heavily veined length was forked, dividing into an upper head and a slightly smaller lower one. There was no sign of any foreskin, but from slots in the twin cock tips clear fluid dripped to the ground. He was ready for them.

Juliet saw the monstrous thing and moaned, 'It'll kill us!'

'No, we only have to manage the heads,' Alice said. 'We can do that. It might even be fun.' She gritted her teeth and lifted her hips invitingly. If it had her first it might be a little easier on Juliet. 'Well here I am!' she called out. 'Think you're big enough ...?' Her voice faded to a fearful burble. It did not need any more encouragement.

The Jabberwock shuffled round to stand between her spread legs. Its clawed thumbs hooked round the inside of her knees and wrenched them outwards and apart, opening her inner thighs and her feathered lovemouth. Its forked shaft bobbed about as though questing for sheaths to suit his pleasure. The double heads like twin fists caressed her thighs, slithering upward into her groin, butting harder as they sought points of entry into her body which was being driven up against the ropes

219

that bound her to the frame that creaked under the load. Her fear-locked orifices gave way under the inexorable pressure and suddenly the massive forked cockheads slid simultaneously into her, front and rear.

Alice howled.

It was like having fence posts rammed up both orifices, filling them to bursting and round into her cervix violating her womb and her clit being squeezed so hard it was going to pop right out of her and her bladder spraying what little it still held and her cunt and bumhole stretching and stretching and she screaming and screaming at the top of her voice driven by the most raw disgusting frightening incredible sensation she had even known . . .

Then the Jabberwock pulled its penis out for half its length and did it all to her again with its second thrust.

On the tenth agonisingly slow-motion penetration Alice came, her screams of pain becoming cries of desperate release and her body arching about the twin poles that impaled her.

The Jabberwock threw back his monstrous head and let out a siren-blast of delight that echoed through the woods. Its huge penis pulsed, pumping hot sperm into Alice like a fire hose, flooding her vagina and intestines until her stomach bulged. For a moment Alice thought she would burst like a balloon. Then it squirted back around the corks of the twin shafts and out of her distended pudenda and anus in sticky gobbets and streamers over her thighs.

Alice collapsed limp, trembling and utterly spent, hovering on the edge of insensibility. She was dimly aware of the Jabberwock pulling out of her with a terrible suction that still left the mouths of her passages gaping wide and only slowly, painfully, constricting. At some point she felt the frame rocking under her as the Jabberwock began to screw Juliet. As though from a great distance she watched her lovely bound body shuddering under his onslaught, her belly swelling with each thrust of the huge double cockheads, her back arching and sweat-sheened breasts heaving, nipples hard-pointed, tear-wet eyes bulging and disbelieving, her mouth seeming not to close as she vented forth a stream of shrieks and moans. But Alice had not even the energy to open her own mouth to utter some words of comfort. What could she say anyway?

She seemed just to blink but must have passed out for a few minutes, because when she opened her eyes again Juliet was hanging limp and sperm-splattered beside her while the Jabberwock was hunched over, drawing in its breath in almost comic steam-train wheezes. That image rekindled a spark of defiance in her. They had drained it. It was shagged out! Monsters – nil, Girlings – one!

However, her legs felt useless. All the tendons in her groin had been stretched to their limits. Even if they were untied how far could they get?

'At least we got though round one,' she said to Juliet, her voice rasping in her dry throat. 'Are you all right?'

'Just . . .' Juliet replied faintly.

'But you came? You got your bit of pleasure out of him?'

'Yes . . . and it was incredible . . . but I don't think I could do it again. My insides hurt so. Next time he'll split me open!'

'Yes you can! We'll let it screw itself silly if necessary –' She stopped. The heads of the White Queen and Albinous were peeping over the boulders on the other side of the Jabberwock's lair.

'They're here,' she whispered to Juliet.

'Now? Why couldn't they have sneaked in while it was screwing us and snatched their bloody crown?'

'I don't know, but we'd better keep Big Bad's attention if they're going to do it. It's our only chance.' Loudly she called out: 'Hey, handsome. Want another go? I'm just getting warmed up!'

'Me too!' Juliet shouted desperately. 'Unless you're not up to it, of course.'

The Jabberwock slowly raised its head to stare at them. Alice realised its glowing eyes were set almost on the sides of its head, giving wide peripheral vision. That, together with its mobile neck, meant it would not be easy to sneak up on. Was that what had caused the Queen to hesitate?

'Come and take us!' she shouted.

Slowly the great beast loomed over them, flexing is claws. Behind it she saw Albinous, sword at the ready, sprint from cover towards the thorn bush. As he did so the Queen raised her sceptre.

Juliet painfully lifted her hips to offer up her ravaged orifices once again. 'Here I am all ready and waiting. Can you get it up again?'

Albinous had reached the bush and, heedless of the thorns, stretched his free arm up through its tangled branches.

'I'm gagging for it!' Alice shouted.

Albinous grasped the crown and began to withdraw his arm. As he did so a thorn twig caught on his sleeve, bent and snapped.

The Jabberwock's serpent neck twisted round and the baleful light of its ghostly eyes fell on Albinous. The chessman tore himself free from the bush and began to back away, sword raised.

'Do not try to stop me, beast, or you will suffer!' he warned.

With a trumpet cry of anger the Jabberwock lunged at Albinous. As the soldier slashed at the descending claws a brilliant blue-white bolt of fire leapt from the Queen's sceptre and struck the Jabberwock in the chest. The nightmare beast reared up and let out such a foghorn blast of pain that Alice and Juliet shrank back in their bonds and tried to bury their heads in their shoulders to shield their ears from the terrible sound.

The Jabberwock swayed, but did not fall. As Albinous turned to run the creature's great whip of a tail lashed across the ground and scythed the legs out from under him with sickening force, sending him spinning through the air, the Crown flying from his grasp. Albinous struck the ground like a discarded rag doll, rolled over twisted and broken . . . and vanished.

The Jabberwock turned about, its head weaving about as he looked for the Crown that bounced and rolled down the slope towards the trees. With a hoot of pleasure the beast bounded after it.

The White Queen rose from the rocks, her cloak billowing behind her as she flew through the air with frantic strides. A second bolt from her sceptre struck the Jabberwock on the back of its head. As it reeled about, braying in confusion, she soared over it and dropped down on the still rolling Crown and snatched it up. The Jabberwock made a swipe at her but she tumbled aside. Alice saw her stagger to her feet and, with a look of grim triumph on her face, jam the Crown over her own filigree circlet and onto her head. She jabbed a finger at the Jabberwock.

'Now, creature, I command you to die!'

Alice caught her breath. The Jabberwock snorted and raised its arm to take another swipe at the Queen. A look of puzzlement spread across her face, then she shrieked in pain, feebly clawing at the golden Crown. 'No . . . Nooooo!' she wailed, then collapsed in a heap and the Crown fell from her head.

With a puzzled grunt, the Jabberwock prodded the still figure, but she did not move. It reached for the golden crown.

Suddenly a bolt of red fire struck it in the back, sending it reeling and snorting, its tail lashing like a wounded snake.

'That's mine!' a voice cried.

To Alice's astonishment the Red Queen came racing

through the air out of the trees. As the Jabberwock rose up to meet her she blasted it again.

Juliet gave a cry of wonder. 'Look!

With a drumming of hooves Sir Blanche and Snowdrop thundered into the clearing. For a moment Snowdrop shied and bucked in fear at the sight of the Jabberwock, but Sir Blanche urged him on, lowering his lance and riding straight at the great beast. As he did so a huge figure dressed in britches and cloak sprang into view at the knight's heels. As he caught sight of Alice and Juliet bound to their rack he threw back his head and roared.

Alice's heart leaped in joy and confusion. It was Leonus!

As the Jabberwock swatted the Red Queen from the air into the trees, Sir Blanche's lance skewered it through the thigh. It howled in pain and lashed its tail at horse and rider, sending them crashing to the ground.

Juliet gasped in horror. 'No!'

Leonus bounded up onto the boulders and from there leaped onto the Jabberwock's back, where he began to pound and tear at the creature with his great clawed fists. The huge beast wheeled and writhed about, scrabbling at Leonus who clung just out of its reach.

'He's all right!' Juliet shouted.

Sir Blanche had climbed dazedly to his feet, recovered his sword and charged at the Jabberwock, hacking at its legs as it was still trying to claw Leonus from its back.

Then Alice heard a voice from behind her say, 'Hold still while we cut you free,' and she felt a knife begin to hack at the heavy ropes that bound her to the frame.

It was Suzanne!

Alice almost choked with joy and surprise. 'How did you get here? And Leonus?'

'After I told my Master your story he began making enquiries,' Suzanne said rapidly as she hacked away. 'He didn't like the idea of the chesspeople still interfering with Boardland affairs, you see. Folk in Brillig don't talk about this square much, but eventually he found out about the Jabberwock and its nasty habits. He'd been asking after the White Queen and heard early this morning she'd left with Juliet . . .' Alice felt her legs come loose and Suzanne began working on the rope about her neck. 'We went round to the hotel to see if Leonus would be interested in helping, and found him just coming round from the mugging. We guessed whoever had taken you must be mixed up with this place and so we got some horses and followed.'

The rope fell away from her neck and Suzanne began to hack at the bindings round Alice's wrists.

'And the Red Queen?' Alice asked.

'When we got here we found her trying to get through the barrier. None of us could afford to waste time fighting each other out there so I got us all through. As we followed your trail we found the White Knight having a wrestling match with his conscience. Seeing us made him decide to do the right thing . . .'

Alice's arms came free. Feebly she slid her sperm-greased body off the frame and into Suzanne's arms, receiving a passionate kiss as she did so. 'God, you're covered in the stuff!' Suzanne exclaimed. 'Is it what I think it is?'

'Yes . . . don't ask. At least . . . not now.'

As they crouched behind the frame she saw Juliet being helped down by Martes. The pine marten had swapped his fine clothes for cloak and riding boots, and had a small sword sheathed in his belt.

'Thank you, Master Martes,' Alice said with all the sincerity she could muster.

'It's been a pleasure to frustrate the plans of these chesspeople, girling,' he replied.

There was a thud that shook the ground. The Jabberwock had dropped to its knees under the combined assault of knight and lionman. Its head was weaving about in confusion, it was bleeding in a dozen places and the light in its eyes was dimming. Suddenly it looked less monstrous and more absurd and pathetic. I suppose it can't help what it is, Alice thought.

She was about to call out not to hurt it any more when a movement to one side caught her eye. The Red Queen was limping out of the trees towards the still form of the White Queen, beside which lay the Crown of Auria.

'No, she mustn't put it on!'

Alice scrambled to her feet, despite the pain in her twice-reamed groin and tottered in a bow-legged run towards the Crown. The others followed at her heels.

Just before the Queen reached it Alice snatched up the Crown and held it away from her.

To her surprise the Red Queen smiled. 'I see you got here in the end, Alice. But there was no need to be dramatic. I wasn't going to put it on. Look what it did to poor Lilian. I know it doesn't work that way.'

Alice blinked. 'Then how does it work?'

The Queen raised her sceptre and Alice saw the figurine of herself, bound by that single golden hair, mounted on its tip. 'Like this . . .'

And Alice felt her arms move of their own accord and she placed the Crown firmly on her own head.

Twelve

Alice felt the power of the Crown flow through her.

For a moment she thought she would faint under the weight of knowledge. Senses she did not know she had expanded to encompass the whole wood about her and all within it. She saw both her friends and enemies in minute detail, outside and in, and felt the texture of every cell of their bodies. Above all she saw how simple everything was. Reality was but clay to be moulded as desired, if one only knew exactly where to press and twist and stretch it into a new form. And all that knowledge was contained in the Crown. Call it magic, call it a biomorphic resequencer and matter transmutator, it would have been powerful anywhere. But in Underland, where everything was already plastic and mutable, it could work miracles. All the wearer had to do was will it.

But Alice no longer had any will of her own!

She could neither move nor initiate any conscious action for herself. She belonged to the Red Queen and the power of her mind, focused though the figurine, was gripping Alice in an invisible band of iron. So she stood straight and still and waited for her mistress's command, while a small part of her raged at her own impotence.

'Reduce that ridiculous creature to a more suitable size!' the Queen said, pointing at the kneeling Jabber-wock.

Alice reached out and squeezed.

Leonus and Sir Blanche leaped aside with oaths of surprise as the Jabberwock began to shrink, braying and snorting in confusion. In a few seconds it was the size of a farmyard chicken. It twisted about its scrawny neck anxiously and went, 'Peet, peet?'

Suzanne and Martes started forward but the Red Queen held up a warning hand. 'Do not try to help your friend or assault me, unless you want her to be the instrument of your own demise!' Leonus and Sir Blanche had run up but she stopped them with the same gesture. 'Alice is my tool under my absolute control, as in potential she always has been.'

She glanced down at the plump form of the White Queen still sprawled on the ground and with a contemptuous smile prodded her with the toe of her slipper. The White Queen groaned feebly.

'She didn't realise the Crown was never made for us, but for inferior beings who needed its power,' the Red Queen continued. 'Of course it was a trap, since their minds could not handle such forces without eventual self-destruction. Perhaps it was placed here to demonstrate the fallibility of lesser beings. It would have been a mere curio had we not fallen so low as to grasp at any means of restoring our pride and greatness. That was what I discovered during my researches. So I prepared Alice for the role. She was never intended merely as a means to breach the final barrier, but my mediatory with the Crown. And now through her I will build anew.' She raised her arms aloft. 'The great game will live on again!'

And at her will Alice filled the sky above with the bursting showers and stars of celebratory fireworks. The others stared at the Red Queen in horror.

'Your people almost laid waste to the Boardland in the past with your insane game; you cannot do it again!' Martes pleaded.

'I told my own queen there should be an end to these wars, now I tell you the same,' Sir Blanche said. 'Our day is done. Let us turn to gentler pursuits.'

'I suppose you will hunt my kind again?' Leonus snarled at her.

The Red Queen smiled. 'Why not, if we choose? You should be honoured.' Leonus's fists clenched and he bared his fangs. 'Go on,' the Red Queen taunted. 'Attack me and I will have your girling turn you into a kitten which I will feed to a pack of wolves!'

Leonus controlled himself with an obvious effort.

'That's better. What a magnificent beast you are, to be sure. I think I will take you as my special pet.'

The lionman growled but said nothing.

The White Queen groaned and slowly sat up, looking about her in confusion. When she saw the Red Queen she scrambled for her fallen sceptre. But at her mistress's command Alice lifted it high into the air out of her enemy's reach where it spun about and burnt away in a shower of sparks.

'Not my sceptre!' the White Queen wailed.

'Yes, your power is broken,' the Red Queen said.

Looking dazed, the White Queen dragged herself to her feet and faced her opposite number. Tears were running down her plump cheeks. 'I just wanted to be as beautiful as you, Magenta! That was all. Must you cheat me of that too?'

The Red Queen's face set. 'And I wish to be the only Queen in the land. And unfortunately you are the single being I could never be sure of totally controlling, even through the crown. I will find other opponents for my games in future. You are taken, Lilian. Destroy her!'

'No!' Alice shouted.

That one word of defiance had been boiling up inside Alice since she had donned the Crown, seeking some way out of the prison about her mind. And there it was:

a flaw, a tiny crack that it had forced open into a precious moment of free will.

As the Red Queen looked at Alice in astonishment, Alice reached out and the red sceptre with its gold figurine was torn from the Queen's grasp and leaped into her hand. 'Looks like you've been taken as well,' she said.

'You cannot defy me!' the Red Queen said. 'You are bound by pain, word and token!'

Alice smiled. 'Bad choice of token on your part.' She plucked at the golden hair that was twined round the figurine. 'In case you hadn't noticed, I haven't got hair any more, just feathers. This is no longer me. It just took a little while to work it out.'

And she tossed the sceptre into the air and willed it to vanish in a puff of flame. 'And now your power's gone too, Magenta,' Alice said.

Her beautiful face a mask of rage, the Red Queen leaped at Alice with her hands extended like claws. Leonus's great arm swung out and she was knocked off her feet to sprawl on her back, wheezing and clutching her middle.

'And I'm nobody's pet!' he told her.

Suzanne looked thoughtfully at the White Queen, who was standing with her mouth open as though she still could not take in what had happened, then turned to Martes. 'May I also give that woman a personal message, Master?'

'Certainly, girl,' Martes said.

Suzanne marched up to the White Queen and slapped her on the cheek so hard she fell to her knees beside the still moaning Red Queen. 'That's for throwing us off the train!'

Suzanne returned to Martes's side and knelt by him. He patted her head affectionately, took out a leash that had been tucked into his belt and clipped it back onto her collar. She looked perfectly content.

Sir Blanche was staring at Alice with desperate hope in his eyes. 'If you can really work such wonders, girl, I mean, Alice – Snowdrop, my horse, is badly injured . . .'

'Of course . . .' Alice snapped her fingers. Snowdrop's inert body twitched and then he lifted his head. Gathering his legs Snowdrop got to his feet and clopped over to his master, who stroked and patted him lovingly.

Alice looked at Juliet and waved a hand. Juliet gave a little gasp and then ran her hands over her now clean and fresh body. Cautiously she felt her pubes and sighed with relief. 'I thought I'd be sore for weeks. Thanks.'

'I've just taken away the pain and physical marks but not the memory,' Alice said. 'Never forget you survived an experience that would have had most people freaking out. It's something to be proud of because it proved how strong you are.'

Suzanne had been looking at Alice in growing wonder. 'Is that all you have to do to work miracles, just wave a hand?'

Alice looked down at herself and waved a hand as though brushing something away. The filth smeared over her disappeared, the pain in her groin vanished as her distended passages tightened again. The golden feathers on her head and pubic mound melted back into hair that she fluffed up gratefully. 'Yep, looks like it.'

'That's a pretty good trick, you know.'

Martes was frowning uncertainly. 'It seems we have won, but what do we do about them now?' He pointed to the fallen queens. 'Are they still a danger to Boardland, and should they be punished for their past crimes?'

'I know what I'd like to do with them,' Leonus growled.

The queens shrank away from him. The White Queen turned desperately to Sir Blanche. 'Would you abandon me to their mercy?' she pleaded.

'If you had listened to my council you would not be in this sorry state, Majesty,' Sir Blanche said sternly. He

231

looked at Leonus and Martes. 'I realise my opinion may count for little and I would not blame you for wishing to take revenge on them, and myself, for deeds both past and present. But I ask you to show more compassion than they would for you, were circumstances reversed. Show you are not as arrogant as my kind has been all these years.'

'We could take them back to Brillig for trial,' Martes said.

'And when the people heard who they were there would be but one verdict,' Leonus added. The queens looked horrified. Leonus frowned at Sir Blanche. 'Though we have fought side by side, I may have to leave your fate to the judgement of others.'

Sir Blanche nodded gravely.

'I think they should all have their wishes granted,' Alice said suddenly. Suzanne and Juliet gaped at her in amazement while the men frowned, still unsure how to treat a girling with her power. 'But in accord with Underland tradition,' Alice added. She looked at Sir Blanche. 'Can you prove to us that you've changed, that you're no longer playing the chessgame?'

'Willingly, but how?'

Alice nodded at the queens. 'I've seen how hard it is for those two to take off their crowns. It's as though they're part of them. Perhaps that's how you're all made, I don't know. But can you throw away your armour and give up being a knight?'

'You would not deny your heritage!' the White Queen said, aghast.

Sir Blanche took a deep breath. 'I believe I must, if things are to change for the better.'

He began unbuckling his silver breastplate. His fingers trembled slightly. Juliet quickly stepped up to him and began to help. He smiled down at her. Piece by piece the pile beside him grew until he was wearing only a simple cotton shift and leggings. Sir Blanche stretched

232

with obvious pleasure. 'Remarkable. I feel a great weight has lifted from me, more than mere metal could account for.' He looked at Alice. 'Must I surrender my sword as well?'

'Keep that. You may need it to fight for a better cause one day.'

'I swear I will only use it in good faith and honour.'

Alice snapped her fingers. The pile of armour grew hotter and burst into flames, driving the others back. In a few moments it had been reduced to ash and a few blobs of bright metal. When they looked at Sir Blanche again he was clad in boots, tunic and belt, his sword sheathed by his side.

Martes and Leonus exchanged a thoughtful glance then appeared to reach a mutual decision. 'It seems the last knight of the chessmen no longer exists,' Martes said. 'Therefore he cannot be brought before the people for judgement.'

Sir Blanche bowed solemnly to them and to Alice. At his side Juliet beamed with delight.

Alice turned to the two queens. 'Well, can you do the same? Think carefully. It might be your last chance.'

'You know I can take my crown off,' the White Queen said quickly, removing her filigree circlet. 'There, you see.'

'Coward!' the Red Queen said contemptuously.

'I don't mean keep it in a hatbox by your side, but throw it away for good, see it totally destroyed,' Alice persisted.

The White Queen's hands trembled. She made a vague gesture as though of tossing the crown aside, then jammed it back in place and bowed her head. 'No,' she said wretchedly.

'And you?' Alice asked the Red Queen.

'Never! Don't humiliate us any further. Do what you will!'

'As you like.' Alice smiled at her. 'Here, once you've said a thing that fixes it and you must take the consequences, right? That's what you told me when you used the figurine to make me your pawn. Well, now you're going to live by the same rule. Stand up, Lilian and Magenta, your wishes are going to be granted.'

Uncertainly, the pair stood.

'Keep your crown if you have to, Magenta. You wanted to be the only queen in the land, and as long as "land" means this square, your wish is granted, because this is where you'll stay until you learn better. But you won't be needing fine clothes any more.'

A blast of wind whipped up from nowhere and tore at the Red Queen's dishevelled silk dress, shredding it into fragments that blew away like confetti, leaving her naked for all to see. She moved to cover her lovely slim body, then bit her lip and stood straight and still defiant.

'And you wished to be as beautiful as Magenta, didn't you, Lilian?' Alice said to the White Queen, who nodded in mute trepidation.

The sourceless wind again sprang up and blasted the White Queen's dress into shreds. But when the shower of fabric snowflakes had settled, the body revealed beneath was not the plump form that had been there moments before. Lilian had shamefully wrapped her arms about herself as she had been stripped, but now she drew them away again with an 'Ohh . . .' of wonder.

She was still Lilian but the one beneath the pudgy features and shapeless body she had worn. Now platinum blonde hair tumbled over slim shoulders and pneumatic breasts capped by pert pink nipples. A slender waist flared out into curving hips and shapely legs, at the apex of which was a deep soft-lipped cleft thatched by a few silver curls of hair. Her astonished face still held pale keen eyes, but they were now complemented by high cheekbones, a neat nose, a small mouth and a single chin.

'There, as pretty as a princess,' Alice observed. 'Which is what you look like and why your crown's now a little smaller than Magenta's. Mustn't spoil her wish to be the only queen around here.'

After favouring Lilian with a scornful, if slightly envious glance, Magenta turned back to Alice. 'Is that it, then? We are to be marooned in this square together?'

Alice smiled. 'Oh no, nothing as easy as that. You're going to be taught a hard lesson about life. Now, where's your teacher?'

The small scrawny little creature that the Jabberwock had become had been scratching about in the dirt unnoticed. Now as Alice snapped her fingers it began to grow once again with a hoot of surprise.

'I'm not heartless,' she said to the horrified queens, 'so I won't make him quite so big as before and I'll remove his more bloodthirsty habits –' its pink waistcoat was pristine now '– but I will make him brighter and more inventive.'

The rest of the group stepped back as the nightmarish creature's head rose above them once more. But it made no move towards them and there was a new sense of purpose in its stance that kept its clawed hands neatly folded before it.

'Hallo, Jabberwock,' Alice said. 'You know what you've got to do?'

'Yes, Alice Brown,' it replied, trumpeting its words in sonorous but unexpectedly well-modulated tones. 'And thank you for giving me a new life.'

'You're welcome. Enjoy yourself.'

The Jabberwock turned its glowing eyes on Magenta and Lilian. 'Now,' it asked sternly. 'Will you be naughty or nice?'

Magenta and Lilian backed away fearfully. 'You can't leave us at the mercy of that thing!' Lilian shrieked at Alice.

'Why not?' Alice said. 'You did. And he's not a "thing", he's a "he". Can't you see?'

They could all see as the Jabberwock's great forked penis was swelling by the second. Although it reached something less than its former dimensions, it was still an awesome sight.

Suzanne sniggered. 'I think he likes you!'

'Have a taste of your own medicine!' Juliet added with feeling.

'This is not a life sentence,' Alice told the two ex-queens. 'You can leave when you learn to think like girlings. Your arrogance made these barriers. It'll take humility to get through them. It's up to you . . . and the Jabberwock.'

The two women turned and ran. The Jabberwock swooped after them on his batwings and scooped them up before they reached the trees. Clutching their struggling naked bodies tight in his huge claws, he upended them and drove his sinuous tongue into one and then the other of the two tight anuses at his disposal. Their shrieks filled the clearing as their intestines were subject to his intimate probing.

'Ahh,' the Jabberwock said, licking his lips. 'Such fine deep rich bottoms.'

'You left him that disgusting habit?' Juliet said to Alice as she watched, saucer-eyed.

'I didn't want them to miss out.'

'Good!'

As the muscular inhibitor took hold, the Jabberwock laid Magenta and Lilian's limp bodies down before his cave and began dismantling his crude frame with remarkable dexterity. In minutes he had constructed two tripod stands that supported a long pole running between them. From this he suspended Magenta and Lilian, first binding their wrists to their ankles so they dangled freely beneath it. Their deep-cleft pubic mounds pouted from between the swell of their taut thighs, one furred in red and the other in silver. Below them the dark puckers of their anuses were exposed now for all to see and, as the pair were about to discover, horribly vulnerable.

The Jabberwock broke off a thornbush branch and swished it through the air in front of his helpless victims. Their eyes widened in disbelief.

'No, please don't!' Lilian cried.

'You cannot do that!' Magenta yelled. 'I command you to . . . eeek!' The thorny lash had swished across her buttocks leaving a pattern of red and purple dots on the smooth skin.

The Jabberwock thrashed each inviting set of buttocks in turn until neither woman any longer pleaded or spoke except to moan and whimper. When their stretched bottoms were liberally pricked and bleeding, he lowered the branch.

'Do you want more pain or do you beg to please me?' he asked.

'No . . . never,' Magenta moaned faintly.

'Think on it. What about you, Lilian?'

'I beg to please you . . . Master,' she said.

'Coward!' Magenta rasped.

'It's over, Magenta,' she said wearily. 'Even we change . . .'

The Jabberwock clasped Lilian's swaying form, turned her to him and his forked penis sank into the vagina and anus of the once proud queen.

They watched until Lilian and Magenta both hung limp from the pole, their orifices beneath their scarlet buttocks red raw and distended, dripping sperm. For the moment all trace of defiance had been wiped from them. In their tear-wet eyes was only fearful expectation as they looked on their strange master and wondered what use he would find for them next.

'Everybody satisfied?' Alice asked the others quietly.

'I believe a kind of justice has been served,' Martes said.

'No less than they deserve,' Leonus growled.

'If it seems fair in your eyes, then I will say no more,' Sir Blanche added. 'In a way Her Maj– Lilian, has what she always wanted, I suppose.'

'Then I think we're done here,' Alice said. 'Let's all go home.'

Thirteen

A shimmering archway opened in the barrier and they stepped over the brook from the Jabberwock's forest back into the Brillig square. Leonus and Martes's horses were waiting patiently where they had been tethered.

Juliet was looking at Alice with a mixture of awe and concern. 'Do you know your eyes glowed when you did that?'

'And you're getting taller,' Suzanne added in alarm.

Queen Alice, ruler of the world, the Crown whispered inside Alice's mind. You can do anything, be anything you want . . . Aloud she said, 'The Crown is going to my head a little, I know.' She focused her thoughts. 'Is that better?'

'Yes, but please be careful,' Juliet said. 'It's a bit frightening.'

'Don't worry,' Alice promised. 'I won't be wearing it much longer.'

Leonus looked at her with a frown furrowing his huge brow. Juliet ran over to Sir Blanche who was adjusting Snowdrop's harness and spoke to him urgently. Alice watched them with a thoughtful smile.

'Are you going back to your home now?' Suzanne asked Alice.

'Yes, I've got something to put right. But I won't forget you.'

They hugged and kissed.

'You know where I live, if my master will allow it,' Suzanne said.

Martes said quickly, 'Of course. You may visit Suzanne anytime, Alice. You will be very welcome.'

'I'm just a girling, master Martes,' Alice assured him. 'I don't expect special treatment.'

'A most unusual girling, I would say.'

Juliet skipped over, her faced flushed with excitement.

'So, are you ready to go back home?' Alice asked her.

Juliet beamed at them. 'Well, actually, I don't think I want to. I've offered myself to Sir Blanche and he's accepted. I'm going to be his slave!'

Alice and Suzanne hugged and kissed her.

'Are you sure?' Alice asked.

'Yes, absolutely,' Juliet said. 'Now I know what I am and what I want.'

'Not many girls can say they've found themselves a genuine knight in shining armour,' Suzanne said. 'Well, ex-knight, anyway. I hope you'll be happy.'

'I will be. Sir Blanche will be staying in Brillig until he works out what he's going to do next.'

'So I might be dropping in on both of you some time,' Alice said. 'Bye . . . and good luck.'

Martes led Suzanne over to their horse. She went down on her hands and knees and he climbed onto her back and up into the front of the unusually long saddle. It allowed Suzanne enough room to climb up and sit comfortably behind her much shorter master and see over his head as they rode. She extended her arms around him and he secured her wrists to cuffs and a chain bolted to the front of the saddle and then handed her the reins. This left him free to lean back against the body of his slave and rest his head on her breasts as she guided their mount.

Juliet had run back to Sir Blanche and knelt before him, offering up her crossed wrists in the classic gesture of submission. He patted her head, lifted her to her feet, turned her round and bound her hands behind her with a strap from his pack. He did something to the pommel of his saddle that caused it to slide forward and hinge up into a phallus. With easy strength he lifted Juliet up onto the saddle and sat her down so that she was impaled on the phallus with a little squeak, then climbed up behind her, pushing her over Snowdrop's neck while he opened the front of his britches, then pulling her back into his lap. Juliet gasped in surprise and then relaxed as her master's cock slid up her rear and she was doubly penetrated. How many orgasms would she have before they reached Brillig? Alice wondered.

'That's most ingenious, Sir Blanche,' Martes called out to him.

'Thank you,' said the former knight. 'It's my own invention, you know.'

'Really? There might be a market for such a device . . .'

They rode off side by side still talking.

Alice watched them go. Two girlings who knew exactly where they belonged. But what about her?

She turned to Leonus, who had been watching the departures in silence, only to see his face was clouded.

'What's wrong, Master?'

'Magenta said the Crown was a trap. Ordinary people would destroy themselves if they used it.'

'But I'm not quite ordinary, Master. I can feel what it wants me to do, but it can't tempt me like that. It's not because I'm better than other people, but because I'm a submissive masochist. I don't want to rule but to be ruled. That's my only strength. But if you want the Crown, Master, I'd give it to you now. Maybe Underland needs a true lion king.' She made to lift it from her head but he stopped her.

'No! That would be more temptation than I could resist. I marvel you can control it, Alice. You are a much more extraordinary girling than I ever imagined.'

'No, Master, I just want to find my proper place and be happy,' Alice insisted. 'There's something I must use the Crown for, then I'll get rid of it. Please come with me. Or we can agree somewhere to meet. I know how I can get back to Underland more easily now. Just tell me where you'll be and . . .'

She trailed off as her heart sank. The look on his face told her it was too late. She had lost him. She had achieved something beyond his ability; she had braved a danger he would not face. Innocently she had wounded his pride. They could never be master and girling after that.

But you have me, the Crown seemed to whisper. She could make him want her again. She could make him forget. No! They could not base their relationship on a lie. Sometimes living the fairytale dream bore a heavy price in Underland.

Leonus brushed the tears from her eyes. 'I'm sorry, Alice. I hope we shall meet again . . . but I do not know how I could be a proper master to you after this.'

Alice bit her lip. 'I know. I'm so sorry. I won't forget you.' Was it only last night? It already seemed like a dream.

'Can I take you anywhere?' he asked.

'No, the Crown will do that. The sooner I've finished with it the better.' She reached up and kissed him. 'Goodbye.'

Alice watched Leonus ride after the others until he was out of sight. Only then did she look away. Suddenly she became very aware of the collar round her neck. But now there would be no master's leash to clip to it. Sadly she wished it gone and it was. Now she felt naked.

She wiped her eyes and pulled herself together. There was a very particular place she had to be and loose ends she had to tie up. 'All right, Crown. This is what you're going to do . . .'

* * *

Alice peered round the oak tree. There was the door as she remembered it. But was it the right time? If it had worked then any moment now . . .

Sure enough the door opened and her earlier self stepped out into Underland, looking about her uncertainly. Alice ducked back out of sight as her *doppelgänger* suddenly flinched and twisted round suspiciously. Now she knew who had been watching her. She had.

The other Alice walked away down the path. A few moments later the Red Queen flew past in her paranoid pursuit of spying insects. From round the corner came the crack of her sceptre and then the sound of voices, one of them her own. Alice slipped round the tree and through the door of her mirror room. Once inside she made her last wish.

The Crown seemed to become lighter. Cautiously Alice took it off and examined it closely. It was no longer lustrous metal but only gold-painted wood.

She hastily stuffed it into the bottom of her reversed wardrobe and, taking a deep breath, stepped back though the mirror into her own room and her own world. Now she had to get dressed. In about ten minutes her earlier self would be bringing the Queen through her mirror, and the bedroom had to be empty by then.

Just then the door opened and her mother peered in anxiously. She blinked at the unexpected sight of her daughter standing naked in her bedroom in the middle of the day, and said quickly, 'Sorry, dear. I was calling but you didn't answer. I only wanted to see if you were all right.'

All the concerns of the past weeks were written in her mother's face. Alice ran over and hugged her.

'Mum, I'm absolutely fine, and that's official.'

'I'm so glad, love. We've been worried about you.'

'Well, you don't have to be any longer. I was just . . . changing. I'll be down in a minute. And Mum . . .'

'Yes, dear?'

'I'd love a cup of coffee.'

Nexus

NEXUS BACKLIST

This information is correct at time of printing. For up-to-date information, please visit our website at www.nexus-books.co.uk

All books are priced at £6.99 unless another price is given.

------ ✂ ---------------------------

Please send me the books I have ticked above.

Name ....

Address ....

....

....

.... Post code....................

Send to: Virgin Books Cash Sales, Thames Wharf Studios, Rainville Road, London W6 9HA

US customers: for prices and details of how to order books for delivery by mail, call 1-800-343-4499.

Please enclose a cheque or postal order, made payable to **Nexus Books Ltd**, to the value of the books you have ordered plus postage and packing costs as follows:

UK and BFPO – £1.00 for the first book, 50p for each subsequent book.

Overseas (including Republic of Ireland) – £2.00 for the first book, £1.00 for each subsequent book.

If you would prefer to pay by VISA, ACCESS/MASTERCARD, AMEX, DINERS CLUB or SWITCH, please write your card number and expiry date here:

....

Please allow up to 28 days for delivery.

Signature ....

Our privacy policy

We will not disclose information you supply us to any other parties. We will not disclose any information which identifies you personally to any person without your express consent.

From time to time we may send out information about Nexus books and special offers. Please tick here if you do *not* wish to receive Nexus information. ☐

------ ✂ ---------------------------